KNOCKFANE

KNOCKFANE

A Novel

HOMAN POTTERTON

MERRION
PRESS

First published in 2019 by
Merrion Press
An imprint of Irish Academic Press
10 George's Street
Newbridge
Co. Kildare
Ireland

www.merrionpress.ie

9781785372490 (Paper)
9781785372506 (Kindle)
9781785372513 (Epub)
9781785372520 (PDF)

British Library Cataloguing in Publication Data
An entry can be found on request

Library of Congress Cataloging in Publication Data
An entry can be found on request

Typeset in Sabon LT Std 11/15 pt

Front-cover image: Adobe Stock.

Prologue

IT WAS NOT a normal time of year to go swimming – Edward knew that. But then, even in high summer, he was not supposed to bathe in the swamp in the Bracken field. It was dangerous, his father always insisted, and it was forbidden.

But that afternoon, when Dympna Canty had appeared in the yard and suggested going down to the swamp, Edward had followed her. It never occurred to him that she would think of swimming. It was, after all, only February but it was one of those clear blue-skied days which cold nights and early-morning frosts sometimes usher in and, even though there were no leaves on the trees, it looked like summer. At least, it looked like summer to Dympna Canty.

At fourteen, she was almost two years older than Edward. She was one of 'those Cantys' as people referred to them. A family of twelve with a drunken no-good of a father and a put-upon mother, they lived in a cottage about a mile from Knockfane and they were known as thieves and as trouble. But Willis Esdaile, who as a general rule looked for the best in everyone, had a soft spot for 'the poor Cantys' and tried to help them as he could. To that end he employed Mrs Canty one day a week to do the laundry and Dympna would sometimes accompany her.

'Will you be gettin' in?' Dympna said to Edward.

She had climbed up on the wooden paling that surrounded the swamp and was sitting on the top rung. Her socks were down around her ankles and Edward could see the holes in the soles of her boots.

'The water would be far too cold,' said Edward.

'How would it be cold?' said Dympna, 'and the sun burstin' out of the sky. Are ye a man at all, or what?'

'The Master,' said Edward, referring to his father, 'forbids anyone to bathe in the swamp, even in summer.'

'He couldn't be forbidin' me,' said Dympna. 'Take off your socks and shoes and just try it at the edge.'

She jumped down from the paling and, seated on the grass, began to pull off her boots. Barefooted, Edward ducked under the paling and put his foot in the water.

'It's freezing,' he shrieked.

He looked round and was stunned to see that Dympna had stripped down to her knickers. In a flash, she jumped through the paling and pushed him, fully clothed, into the water and then, hesitating for a moment to bless herself, she jumped in after him.

He screamed. And so did Dympna when she felt the cold of the water. And they continued to scream, and scream, until they had pulled themselves out.

Willis Esdaile had intended to go into Liscarrig that afternoon. It was his day for going to the bank. But hearing from Daly, the herdsman at Knockfane, that some of the ewes looked like lambing very early, he had gone down to Tubber, the field next to the Bracken. Sauntering among the ewes, none of which seemed in any danger to him, he heard the screeching from across the hedge. Rushing towards the swamp, he saw the naked figure that was Dympna running madly around and jumping up and down. Then he saw Edward, still in his clothes, but dripping wet, and covered in the mud of the swamp.

When Dympna saw Mr Esdaile coming through the gate she gathered up her tattered and grubby dress and cardigan and dashed off, like a snake, through the field towards the road. Mr Esdaile was white: it was as though the moon had suddenly replaced the sun in the sky. Coming towards Edward, he raised his arm as if to strike him. Then he stopped still, like an animal unexpectedly startled by an alien sound.

'So this is the sort of thing you get up to when you think my back is turned,' he said. 'Playing around with a little trollop like that. Who knows what it might lead to?'

'It wasn't me,' Edward pleaded, 'it was her. She just came up behind me and shoved me in.'

'That's it,' said Willis, 'always blame someone else. Well, I'll teach you.'

He had become flushed. His brow had moistened. He leant against the paling. Turning towards Edward after a moment, he said:

'Get your clothes and go back to the house and up to your room. I'll come and see you there and decide what to do about this wickedness.'

Willis Esdaile did not come up to see Edward that afternoon, or later that evening. All alone – his sisters Julia and Lydia were forbidden to go and see him – Edward was very frightened. It had not at all been his fault. Dympna Canty had brought him down to the swamp and it was she who had pushed him in.

'You and I have to have a talk,' his father said when he came into Edward's room the following day, 'and this is as good a time as any. It's overdue.'

Edward sat up in the bed.

'Put on your dressing gown and sit over there in that chair.'

Edward was puzzled. His father seemed not to be angry. He wondered if, before being accused, he should attempt to explain what happened yesterday.

'You'll be going away to boarding school next September,' Willis said. 'St Stephen's will suit you very well. You should be happy there with other boys of your own age to mix with, and games and the like ...'

Edward nodded. He wondered what going away to school had to do with Dympna Canty. He waited for an outburst about yesterday's incident, but none came. He had answers ready but his father did not mention anything.

'... and then, when you leave school in five or six years' time,' Willis continued, 'you'll be going to live with your grandparents in Derrymahon. I've never told you this before but your mother and I agreed on that almost as soon as you were born. It was what your Grandpa wanted but your mother and I didn't really mind.'

The words stung Edward. They came to him as a shock but, in spite of that, he understood them immediately. His parents had decided, when he was still only a baby, that they would give him away and they 'didn't really mind' about it. Feeling tears, he looked away to conceal them from his father.

'There are other things you have to know,' Willis said.

He got up from where he was sitting and went over to the fireplace. Leaning with an elbow on the mantelpiece, he looked into the empty grate.

'About the family, your mother ...' he continued.

Edward's thoughts swam and he felt his stomach empty.

'No, Pappy, please ...' he said.

Willis raised his palm to silence him and started to speak. When he had finished, it was almost as though Edward did not know where he was. Much of what he had heard, he had not fully understood. He did not like being reminded of his Mama – his Mama was dead, after all – and the Mama he heard about that morning from his father was not the Mama he remembered. He was at a loss.

'Dympna Canty has brought all this on,' he thought after his father had left the room.

He wanted to get back into bed and he wanted to sleep. But his father had told him to get dressed and come downstairs. He sobbed as he did so. He was relieved that he had not been punished but he did not understand.

It was only in years to come, and when he was much older, that he would appreciate the full import of his father's words to him that day. They had not been intended as a punishment and his father could not have understood how cruel they were. But cruel is how the words seemed to Edward and, although he tried to put them out of his mind and never think of them again, they were to haunt his existence for ever after.

1

The Master of Knockfane

THE YEAR WAS 1952, the month was August, the time was evening, and the Master of Knockfane was at home, alone. This was Willis Esdaile and he was not happy to be left alone. He was irritated that his two daughters, who had gone off to play tennis in the early afternoon, could be so inconsiderate as to be this late in returning.

He was fussed in himself as he got up from his tea and moved to the morning room. He liked to smoke in the evening. It was the only time of day he did so and he kept his pipe, a light maple with a serpentine amber stem, on the mantelpiece along with his tin of flake tobacco. There they bullied into disorder a black marble clock, several Staffordshire figures, a pair of china vases, calendar cards, notices from the Royal Dublin Society, the Lune Union Harriers, the county Archaeological Society, and the myriad other organisations whose activities impinged upon his existence. The resulting clutter made for an untidiness that no wife would have tolerated but, with no wife to chide him – although his daughter Julia had recently started to remark upon the 'mess' – Willis never considered leaving his pipe and tobacco anywhere else.

Settling into his chair on that particular August evening, he looked at the clock.

'Almost seven,' he said to himself, 'nearly time they were back. Mrs Cox always wants her tennis parties to go on far too late.'

He missed his two girls when they were not there, even when they were only absent for a couple of hours; and he always longed for those weeks when they were at home, Julia from university at Trinity College in Dublin and Lydia from boarding school in Westport. He found it difficult not to indulge them and he nearly always pandered to Lydia's sensitivities and succumbed to Julia's demands. He made it his excuse that, as they had no mother, it was up to him to provide them with love enough for two. He did not like to dwell on the past – there had been too much tragedy – and when he thought of the future and what might happen to Knockfane, it only made him unhappy. For that reason and for his own contentment, he chose to live in the present and the present was Julia and Lydia. His son, Edward, he thought of differently which is not to say that he thought of him very often, because he did not. There was no reason to do so. Edward no longer lived at home in Knockfane but with his Odlum grandparents at Derrymahon, and that arrangement suited his father very well.

It was pleasant at this time of day in the morning room as it caught the last of the sun. Slanting through the huge weeping ash and across the grass outside, it dispatched shafts of warmth through the open French windows, bringing the evening's pollen in its wake and filling the room with the scent of the roses which hugged the wall outside. The room, with its low ceiling and cluttered furnishings, had a cosiness that was alien to the grander drawing room and dining room to the front of the house. Its walls were papered in a busy pattern of cascading roses against a latticed background and from a picture rail hung a collection of watercolours framed in oak and mounted with gilt borders. Brightly coloured, these seemed at first glance to be quite conventional with pleasant streams and ponds, mountains, forests and animals and people engaged in daily chores. But viewed close-up, the costumes, the faces, the trees, the water and the daily chores revealed a stranger world: they were all Chinese so that what looked like a bog was really a paddy field, a peasant in a shawl was in fact wearing a shawl and tunic; and a distant view which suggested the Sugarloaf mountain in County Wicklow was inscribed *The Mountain of the Nine Lotuses.* The artist was Great Aunt Dora Esdaile who, denied the opportunity of becoming a professional artist, had devoted herself to religion instead and had spent her life as a missionary in China with the China Inland Mission.

In spite of the apparent chaos and dilapidation of the room, its armchairs and sofa lacking any semblance of being a match, it had an air of reliability that went beyond the expectations of ordinary comfort. There was a peacefulness in its lack of pretension. It was a room at ease with itself, a room with a history, and one that had adapted to change. In all these respects it reflected and complemented the character of its principal occupant, Willis Esdaile himself.

He had been born in 1897 – the year of Queen Victoria's Diamond Jubilee as his mother never tired of telling him – and, from the perspective of the mid-twentieth century, the overall impression was that he was, if not Victorian, then certainly an Edwardian. It was possibly on that account that many people thought of him as old. On the other hand, it could have been because he was a widower and had been, or so it seemed to most people, for ever. For his own part, Willis did not mind being thought of as old and he explained it to himself as the consequence, not of his widowhood, but of his having been Master of Knockfane for almost as long as anyone could remember: his father had died when he was only fourteen and that was more than four decades previous.

A handsome man, portly rather than fat, he was endowed with what might be called 'bearing' while a fastidiousness about his dress suggested a certain vanity. He was a country man and his clothes were country too. A dun-colour tweed suit, a stiff shirt collar, gold cuff links and a fob chain, also in gold, that anchored a watch in a waistcoat pocket, polished brogues. His hair, snowy and well trimmed, gave no hint that baldness might be on its way; and, as if to allay any suspicion in that respect, he sported a fulsome moustache. Also white, it highlighted the robust complexion that came from a life lived out of doors.

'Now, where have the matches gone?' he mumbled to himself before realising that he had them in his hand. He started to clean the pipe. After a moment, he got up and fetched *The Irish Times* and settled down to read but his mind soon wandered to matters on the farm. Summer would be properly over in no time. The wheat and barley were ready to be harvested and, if there was no rain in the next week, the crop promised to be very good. The hoggets were nearly at the stage when they could be sent up to the market in Dublin and sold. The sheds, where the stall feds spent their winters, had been all cleaned out and the manure drawn out to the fields ready for spreading in the winter. The hay needed to be brought in. There was so much to do and, in no time at all, there would be the threshing.

Engrossed in such thoughts, Willis thought he heard footsteps on the front gravel.

'They're home,' he said to himself.

Then the dogs shot past the window barking their heads off and after a couple of minutes the hall doorbell sounded. He heard Rose come through the kitchen and go to the door. He didn't recognise the voice, a man, and wondered who it could be at that time of day. Rose knocked and came into the morning room, shutting the door behind her.

'It's that young Mr Benson,' she said. 'I told him Miss Julia and Miss Lydia were not here but he says it's you he's come to see.'

'That's all right, Rose, show him in.'

2

Family

RATHER THAN BEING irritated that the peace of his pipe-smoking evening should unexpectedly be disturbed, Willis was charmed to welcome a visitor and, all the more so, as the visitor was someone he liked very much. Not that he knew Richard Benson well, he did not. Fresh from his ordination as a deacon, the young man had only been curate in the parish for a bare two months.

'I can see I'm disturbing you, Mr Esdaile,' Mr Benson said when Rose ushered him into the room. 'It's just that I was out for a cycle ride and passing by the end of the road and I thought I would call in for a few minutes. I don't know many of the parishioners yet and the rector is keen that I make calls, although I'm not sure he would regard my coming here, when I've already been invited several times, a proper call.'

He shuffled from one foot to the other while still remaining at the door. He looked flushed, and ill at ease in his clerical collar, his dark grey suit ill-fitting and somewhat crumpled.

'Well, I'm here on my own, a lonely old man, abandoned by his daughters, and with nothing in the world to do, so your coming in to see me is an act of great charity,' said

Willis 'and I'll tell that to Canon Shortt when I next see him. 'Take a chair. You're beginning to settle in and getting to know people, I hope?'

'Well, it's a bit of a change from divinity school and Trinity before that; and sometimes it's hard to see how the teaching we got, theology and the like, applies to life as it's lived in a country parish like this.'

He looked down. He wondered if he had been correct in coming to call. He crossed his legs and then he uncrossed them; he leaned forward, he leaned back; he put his hands on the arms of the chair and then removed them again. Ignorant of the fact that anyone familiar with Knockfane would never choose to sit in the chair he had chosen, he tried to make himself comfortable but succeeded only in looking awkward. Not that he was naturally ungainly; he was not. On the contrary, he was markedly athletic, tall with fine features and broad-shouldered. His chestnut hair was naturally wavy, well brushed and trimmed above his ears; his face, without being exceptionally handsome, was more than pleasing, with hooded eyelids and bushy eyebrows. An ample brow, an incisive nose, and a forceful chin gave him a certain authority, which, when combined with the hesitant shyness in his manner, lent him a particular appeal.

A fine young man, Willis thought, but lost around here with very few people of his own age for company. When Julia goes back after the vac, he will just have little Lydia to talk to when he comes here and that is hardly the same.

'The girls should be home soon,' Willis said, 'they'll be glad to find you've called.'

Mr Benson coloured.

'This is a fine old place, Mr Esdaile,' he said, 'it reminds me of my grandmother's house. It has the same used and untouched look.'

The broken leg of the sofa caught his eye.

'I don't mean that rudely of course,' he added. 'You've lived here forever, I suppose?'

'Yes, and my grandfather, great-grandfather, and great-great-grandfather before me.'

'And your son, Edward? Will he come into Knockfane after your time?'

It seemed to Mr Benson to be a natural thing to ask.

'That's a difficult one,' said Willis. 'It's not straightforward. You see, his mother had no brothers so that when Edward was born, my father-in-law – Edward's Odlum grandfather – decided to make him his heir. There was no one else for Derrymahon. It too is a very fine farm and has been in the Odlum family almost as long as Knockfane has been in ours. No one could have foreseen what would happen and that my wife and I would never have another son.'

There was a silence in the room. Mr Benson knew that the girls' mother had died years previously but he had not intended that, in making a general remark about Knockfane, he would have encouraged Mr Esdaile to confide in him so readily.

But now that the conversation had taken this course, it would have seemed rude to change the subject. Besides, Mr Esdaile seemed quite philosophical about the tragedy of his wife's early death.

'History can sometimes repeat itself,' Willis continued. 'The family nearly died out in the nineteenth century when my great-grandmother died young like my late wife, in childbirth. But Great-Grandad married again, his wife was a second cousin, only eighteen and thirty years his junior and next thing is they had eight children.'

He chuckled and smiled across at Mr Benson. Getting up, he replaced his pipe on the mantelpiece.

'Not that I can see that happening again,' he said when he turned around. He grinned. 'I think I'll leave it to Julia, or even Lydia, to produce an heir. Things are clearer nowadays when it comes to property descending in the female line.'

Mr Benson looked embarrassed and Willis noticed that he had blushed. 'He's only known Julia for two months, and he's already smitten,' he thought.

'I don't know what my two good daughters are up to that is making them so late,' he said. 'Mrs Cox always hates to be left alone at the end of a good day. She must have detained them.'

'Well, maybe I should be on my way,' said Mr Benson.

'I'm sorry you have only had an old man like me for company,' said Willis. 'Why don't you come for your dinner after Morning Prayer on Sunday? You'll have a chance to see the girls then.'

'That would be great,' said Mr Benson.

Willis showed him out to the hall and opened the front door. Tucking the turn-ups of his trousers into his socks, Mr Benson collected his bicycle and, with a wave as he mounted, stood on the pedals and headed off down the avenue.

'A grand lad,' thought Willis. 'Julia would be lucky to get him.'

3

Romance

LIKE MOST OF his kind at the time, Willis Esdaile was familiar with the Bible and whenever he sighed or complained affectionately at the difficulty of bringing up two daughters on his own he would shake his head and say, 'Laban's lot is not an easy one.' He was referring to the story, told in the Book of Genesis, of Laban and his two daughters, Leah the elder and Rachel the younger. 'Leah was tender eyed; but Rachel was beautiful and well favoured' and when Willis Esdaile looked at Julia and Lydia he was in no doubt but that Lydia was his 'tender-eyed' Leah, Julia his 'beautiful and well-favoured' Rachel. Neither of the girls was exactly like their mother and, unlike Edward, who was an Odlum through and through, neither of them took after their mother's side of the family, although Julia could be fairly sharp and determined. Annette's mother was a gentlewoman: beautiful, educated, refined, talented in a myriad ways, but long suffering and, 'if the truth be told', as people used to say 'far too good for T.E. Odlum'. He had married her for her money, or rather for Derrymahon, which was her family home; but her parents always despised him as 'an upstart from the west of the Shannon and not a proper Odlum at all'. In the end, after he had persuaded them to sign over Derrymahon to him and when he immediately evicted them, they were proved right.

Whatever his faults, however, T.E. Odlum knew how to farm and was singularly astute when it came to business affairs. He pulled Derrymahon, which had been in decline for decades, together and even though it was not the most propitious time for a Protestant in Ireland to acquire more land, T.E. bought up several of the neighbouring farms and ended up owning well over a thousand acres. Many people saw it as some sort of justice when he had no son of his own to inherit all that he had accumulated but T.E., once he came up with a plan to 'adopt' his Esdaile grandson, did not mind unduly; and, in actual fact, he took pleasure in a perverse way in depriving Willis Esdaile (whom he disliked) of his own son.

Not that Willis was particularly dismayed by this turn of events as he had rarely seen eye to eye with Edward and, even when his son was a little boy, he had not actually cared for him all that much. When, therefore, Edward left school at sixteen and went to live at Derrymahon, his father was not very bereft. It was entirely fitting that Edward had inherited the Odlum genes, and his father often thought (but never said), that Edward and T.E. were made for each other. Besides, Edward's departure left Willis to enjoy the company of his two daughters without any of the aggravation that is occasioned in bringing up a son.

Annette had died in giving birth to Lydia and within a year of her death, and in that awful September of 1939, war broke out in Europe and what was known as 'the Emergency' was declared in neutral Ireland. At Knockfane, it was Julia who, although only five at the time, took charge. At least that was how it seemed. She became mother to 7-year-old

Edward, nurse to the baby Lydia, and she became wife to her father.

In the early years of his widowhood, Willis often considered marrying again but he never considered it with any great intent. He felt a strong loyalty to the memory of his dear Annette and he was sure that he could never love another as he had adored her. The difference in their ages of fourteen years had never made any difference to them as Annette had adored Willis too; and when her father, T.E. Odlum, opposed their marrying, which he did with firm resolve, his intransigence only served to make the bond between the two of them all that stronger. When, eventually, they did marry they had been supremely happy together; and Knockfane, which had been such a lonely house for as long as Willis could remember, had sprung to life as a result of Annette's effervescence and gaiety.

Willis Esdaile was one of two, his younger brother, Todd, being just eighteen months his junior. Neither of their parents had loved the boys very much and nor had the parents loved each other very much either. Yet when his father died, his mother, ignoring the reality of what her marriage had been and filled with remorse for the wasted years, went into a deep mourning and cut off almost all contact with the outside world. She became distant from the affairs of Knockfane and distant too from her elder son; but that was as nothing to her treatment of Todd. While she had always disliked the younger boy, she now came to loathe him. Old Mr Holt the solicitor eventually intervened when Todd was scarcely seventeen. In return for the boy's agreement that he would leave Ireland – even though the world was in turmoil with the First World War – and emigrate to New Zealand, his mother paid him £500. At the same time Granny Esdaile took to her bed and there she spent her remaining years, willing herself to die. Eventually, on the eve of Willis attaining his majority and coming into Knockfane, her wish was fulfilled so that, instead of a celebration, Willis's twenty-first birthday, in the severe winter of 1916–17, took the form of a wake.

As he struggled with the farm, taking over its management from the series of incompetent farm managers who had allowed it to deteriorate in the years since his father died, Willis had little time to think of sweethearts or marriage and, when he did think of either, it was only to come to the conclusion that his options were fairly limited.

Turning thirty, he held out little hope of romance although, at the same time, he did not give way to despair. Then in September of that year, on a beautiful Indian summer afternoon, he strolled into the household produce tent at the annual Liscarrig Agricultural and Fatstock Show and at that very moment his eyes were opened to love. On the far side of tables laden with fruit cakes and seed cakes, simnel cakes and sandwich cakes, Madeira cakes and Victoria sponges, a laughing girl dressed in peach was pencilling notes on the catalogue of the show. More than any of the confectionery, even that which had already been awarded a highly commended badge, the girl was – in Willis's view – utterly and indescribably delectable.

Forgetting himself entirely, he moved across the tent to where she was standing.

'We don't often see a stranger in these parts,' he said.

She peeped out at him from under her straw hat and beamed.

'I'm Annette Odlum,' she said.

Willis just stared.

'T.E.'s daughter ...'

The name was vaguely familiar to him.

'You know ... Derrymahon Herefords ... we came all the way from Waterford this morning. Papa is here to judge the cattle and the ladies' committee has asked me to help assess the cakes.'

'That's a dangerous task,' said Willis 'Of course I know the Odlum name ...'

He looked down at the dress she was wearing. It wasn't silk but was in a fabric somewhat similar, plain and, as it was the late 1920s, in a sack-like style with no waist: just a ribbon of satin at thigh level and the suggestion of a flared skirt below.

'By the way, I'm Willis Esdaile,' he said, holding out his hand.

'How do you do?' said Annette.

She smiled. Her eyes were a delicious brown and liquid like a raindrop left behind on a petal after an early morning shower.

And that was that as far as Willis and Annette were concerned. Like others before them, they 'no sooner met but they looked; no sooner looked but they loved'.

It would be almost three years before they would marry but, as they always admitted to each other afterwards, both of them decided at that first moment that marry each other they would.

Throughout his life, Willis often thought about that day and he often told his daughters about it too; but when they pressed him with 'What happened next?' he was always less forthcoming.

'Why was it three years before you got married?' they would ask. 'It can't just have been because Mama was only seventeen that Grandpa was against it. You were old enough to have sense enough for the two of you. And you were already in charge at Knockfane.'

But, however pressed, their father would never go into any more detail.

'We married when we did,' he would say, 'and didn't the pair of you arrive into the world in time enough?'

4

Knockfane

KNOCKFANE WAS SITED, not on the hill that was Knock Fane itself, but at some distance from it and almost in a hollow. It was as though it was on its hunkers, crouching there, unruffled, like a hen on her nest. The name derived from the Irish, 'Cnoc Finn' or 'Fionn', meaning the white or fair hill and there were several theories as to why the gentle incline to the east of the house, which was hardly even a hill, should ever have been thought of as white or fair. Possibly it was because the sun at the solstice would have illuminated its cap in a particular way or perhaps it was because it had, of yore, been planted with the white of the May, the hawthorn that was sacred to the ancient Irish. Such suggestions were variously stated as absolute facts but Old Esdaile was never exercised by such conjecture. To him Knockfane was Knockfane was Knockfane. It was where he and the Esdailes belonged and it was where they had belonged for a very long time. More to the point, Knockfane was where the Esdailes – if Willis Esdaile had his way – would remain.

An Esdaile, a younger son of a family who were not even of the yeomanry in their native Leicestershire, first came into the area in the late seventeenth century. Seeking adventure as one of a militia dispatched to subdue the native Irish, this Esdaile stayed on, as others did too, when his company returned to England. He found himself in the townland of Knockfane and in 1710 he took a lease on 600 acres 'for three lives' – as was the custom of the time – from the Earl of Mulhussey at a yearly rent of £165, 12 shillings. The name was spelled 'Esdayle' in the lease and Robert was described as 'of Knockfane' but the house was not built until 1721. That was the date carved on a stone set into the wall above the back door. Beneath it were two sets of entwined initials, 'RE' and 'MS'. There was no mystery about this inscription: it recorded that Robert Esdaile was the builder of the house and that Mary Sale was his wife.

That stone, being at the rear rather than positioned prominently on the façade, served to alert the unwary that there was much about Knockfane that was not entirely as it seemed. Unusually for an Irish country house, it faced south. This was because the place was back to front, or rather front to back; and lest there be any doubt about the matter, another stone above the hall door was inscribed with a different date and different pairs of initials. The year was 1818 and the knotted letters were 'HE' and 'FW'. What had happened was that 'HE' and 'FW' had, in 1818, built an entirely new house and tacked it on to the back of the old one. The Knockfane which emerged from this rebuilding was long and low, two storeys high with gracious rooms and an impressive staircase hall; and, even though further building took place some decades later, the appearance of the house remained largely unchanged down to Willis and Annette's time.

Even to a casual observer it would have been clear that 'HE' and 'FW' must have thought of themselves as persons of some consequence. 'HE' was Hugh Esdaile, the great-great-grandson of Robert; and, not unnaturally, 'FW' was his wife. She was always referred to as 'Forty-Thousand-Pound-Flora' in the family as that was the extent of the dowry she brought to the marriage; and it was some of that money that was spent on the rebuilding of Knockfane. Flora Willis was her name and, when Hugh married her in 1815, it was the nearest any Esdaile ever came to bringing an heiress into the family. Flora also brought her name with her and, from that time on, until the birth of Edward, the eldest Esdaile son at Knockfane was always christened, Willis.

The countryside around Knockfane was flat as far as the eye could see. Athcloon, 12 miles away, was officially the county town but it was an ugly place and made uglier by the cement works which spewed dust and smoke from a huge chimney six days a week. The local town, Liscarrig, with the remnants of the Norman tower house of the De Poers on the main street (where it now housed Skelly's butcher's shop) was, by comparison, an enchantment. It was there that the Esdailes went to church and it was there that, as little children, they first went to school. There in Liscarrig, they guarded their secrets: their money in the Ulster Bank; their wills and deeds in the strongboxes of generations of Holts the solicitors; and their health and well-being in the care of Dr Knox, first the father, then the son.

Knockfane was 4 miles east of Liscarrig, out past the new cemetery, then right at O'Hara's Cross, and down there a couple of miles. The house itself was not visible from the road and the avenue, which ran through a lower field before reaching the Lawn field in front of the house, was long.

A white-painted iron paling, sufficiently spaced as to leave a generous sweep of gravel and grass enough for a croquet lawn, fenced the house and protected it from the attentions of the cattle which always grazed the Lawn Field.

Near the house, a conglomeration of cypresses, the Monterey cypress that is called, in Ireland 'Donard Gold', faced down the avenue. As high as the house, they caused the driveway to swerve and blocked all sight of the farmyard which lay beyond.

An area to the left of the house, facing south and west and, therefore, very sheltered, was in mown grass with a sundial in the centre of a square and a high stone wall at the rear: a wicket gate in an arched opening provided a glimpse of the flower garden – always referred to as the pleasure garden – which bloomed beyond. A giant magnolia grandiflora, planted for its protection close to the house, now concealed most of the east wall. It was matched by a huge weeping ash, spaced further away from the house to the west. On the facade of the house, a climbing rose – *Albertine* – held sway: Annette had planted it her first winter at Knockfane. Almost wanton in its wafery profusion, it scented the drawing room and tumbled up almost to the roof, threatening the bedroom windows as it did so.

As to the house, Flora's £40,000, or the portion of it that was spent on the building of Knockfane, did not stretch to anything unnecessarily fancy. The Esdailes, in spite of Hugh's ambition in marrying Flora, were plain people and a plain house is all that they required. No cut-stone façade, no niches or balustrades, no pediment or any other finery was imposed upon the structure. The windows to the drawing room and the dining room, on either side of the hall door, were lofty and, in reaching almost to the ground, were undeniably elegant; but that had not been the intention. The builder, as could be deduced from an examination of the stonework, had made a mistake. Even the hall door, normally a feature of Irish houses, was undistinguished, although its fanlight could be said to be remarkable. A cumbersome pattern of wrought-iron flowers – the species was indeterminable – had been fashioned into a large semi-circle as a fulsome tribute to Flora.

The isolation of the house, at the end of a very long avenue, caused some visitors to fear the possibility that in Knockfane there might be something sinister; but the easy-going graciousness of the place soon allayed any anxieties in that respect; and if the ghosts of centuries past walked there, it was generally agreed that they did so with a friendly benevolence. Willis's father, when he married Granny, had added an annex, a jumble of rooms as offices for grooms and bedrooms for maids in the area where the old house joined the new and if Knockfane had any secrets, that was where they lurked.

Knockfane's most salient feature, and the one which always caused speculation and debate, was its staircase.

'It's a flying staircase', Willis would say, as his father and grandfather before him had also done. If a visitor protested that, as all staircases had flights of steps, they might all be said to fly, Willis ignored them. Arising out of the fact that the earlier hall door at Knockfane and Flora's new one were aligned, Knockfane had a single wide hall which extended from the front of the house to the rear. The staircase marked the halfway point and, like the hall it was made up of a combination of the earlier staircase and the new one. Sets of steps, two sets to the front, two sets to the rear, rose to meet at a small half-landing from where they sprung, or rather flew, up to two top landings (one front, one rear), off which opened the bedrooms.

'There's not another house in Ireland with a staircase like it,' Willis would say. When he was a child, the wood of the handrail and balusters was stained and grained as oak with an effect so ponderous as to make flight seem very unlikely. But when Annette came to Knockfane she had the hall wallpapered and the stairs painted a cream colour, creating a much lighter effect.

Willis slept at the front of the house in the big bedroom above the drawing room. It had the luxury of a dressing room attached, and it was here that the children, Edward and Julia, had their cots when they were babies, in order to be near their mother. There had in generations past, been times when Knockfane's six bedrooms had scarcely been sufficient – Hugh and Flora had nine children, although only six of them survived. Then there were other periods when most of the rooms had not been used at all. Willis's father had been an only child and during his time, Knockfane had been an empty lonely place, but with Edward and Julia and Lydia there, this was no longer the case. They each had a bedroom off the half landing and in the years following Annette's death, when there was a housekeeper who was also expected to be a nanny, she occupied the fourth room there. It was the least attractive, with a small window that looked out north across the dormer roofs of the annex. The window to Edward's room was almost obscured by the magnolia tree and on more than one occasion when he was still quite small, he climbed out the window and down the tree in order to terrify and alarm the housekeeper. When the last housekeeper left and was replaced by a local woman, Mrs Rooney, who came on a daily basis and did not live in, Edward moved to the housekeeper's room, saying he could no longer sleep with the noise of the starlings in the tree. Thereafter, even after he moved to Derrymahon, that remained his room and he always slept there on visits home.

The house retained the memory of Annette but, just as her life had been cut short, so too had the improvements she had intended to make to the place so that there was a poignancy about the cheerfulness of the hall and staircase, the master bedroom, and the drawing room which had all been decorated in her style. The other rooms, in stark contrast, retained the atmosphere of half-a-century earlier and the dark memory of Granny Esdaile.

'Mama had this room painted before I was born,' Willis would say and, even though the room in question – be it the morning room or the dining room – was so old-fashioned that it seemed almost modern and the memory of his mother was hardly pleasant, there would be a note of pride in his voice.

5

The Sale Sisters

WHEN ROBERT THE first Esdaile married Mary Sale of neighbouring Coolowen in 1715 he set a precedent whereby the two families would often intermarry down through the centuries. In one generation, the Sales might have come to the rescue by providing a bride when a suitable union had eluded a reprobate Esdaile son, and in another period a Sale who seemed destined for a life as a bachelor might have been saved from such a fate by an Esdaile daughter, who for long had been lodged firmly on the proverbial shelf. It was a scheme of things which had worked very well and although paying little heed to the demands of marital happiness, it had ensured the survival of both families down through the centuries.

But such an arrangement had never been an option for Willis as the three Coolowen sisters, Honor, Eleanor and Martha, were almost twenty years his senior. Honor, the eldest, married a British army captain and, when the couple had a daughter, it was assumed that – with time and a little more effort – they would later produce a son: the son who would succeed to Coolowen. But 'there can be many a slip twixt cup and lip', and Captain Dick's death at the Somme in 1916 was just such a slip, so that Eileen, his 10-year-old daughter, was left as the solitary hope for a future generation of Sales. To compound the calamity, Eileen eloped at the age of eighteen and – becoming a Catholic in the process – married an Irish navvy whom she had met on the boat to Liverpool. Honor, feeling disgraced, cut off all contact with her daughter and ignored the birth of her grandson nine months after the elopement. When her son-in-law, Liam, met his death in an accident two years thereafter, Honor made it known that she regarded the tragedy as 'just retribution' for Eileen's waywardness and iniquity. As to her grandson, Fergal, she never met him.

Meanwhile the other sisters, Eileen's aunts Eleanor and Martha, embarked upon the familiar voyage that was a life of permanent spinsterhood. 'They never married' is what people used to say of Eleanor and Martha, as though it had been their choice entirely. Their father, in making his will, had bequeathed Coolowen to Eleanor but Martha continued to live there. It was Eleanor who always took charge and Martha – who insisted that she was always in pain and 'never strong' – always gave way; and that was the pattern of their existence, an existence in which companionship and affection was constantly challenged by aggravation and discord. Their celibate state was unsatisfactory – and a source of disappointment – to both of them; but, more to the point, it meant that, as sure as leaves fall from a tree, they would be the last of the Sales of Coolowen.

When Honor died unexpectedly, in the summer before war broke out in 1939, it came as a great shock to her two sisters. They had thought of Honor, as they thought of themselves, as young, and her sudden death brought a discordant note to the pleasant melody that had for long been life at Coolowen. The outbreak of war in Europe, and the consequent privations in Ireland, as well as the loss of Honor, made Eleanor and Martha fearful for the future. Although they did not voice it much to each other, they felt – for the first time in their lives – vulnerable. They recalled Honor's persistent urgings that they must think of what was to become of Coolowen and their resulting irritation when she, no more than they, could not come up with a plan; and, while they had been content to drop the subject then, they felt the need to take it up again after her death. But no matter how often they discussed it, a solution always eluded them.

It was Martha who, without mentioning it to Eleanor, wrote to Eileen a few months after Honor died.

'Your Aunt Eleanor does not know that I am writing this...' her letter began and then she said how much they missed Eileen and having news 'about her little boy who, I suppose, must be fourteen by now'. She mentioned how they had always tried to get Honor to put the rift behind her and make contact with Eileen but that Honor never would. In the letter, Martha suggested that Eileen should write to them – 'without mentioning this letter' – as she knew that Aunt Eleanor would be open to reconciliation if the approach came from Eileen herself. She hoped that Eileen did not feel angry 'as she had every right to be' at the family's treatment of her and that 'the means might be found for her and her son, Fergal, to be made welcome at Coolowen'.

When Eileen's letter arrived a few weeks later, it was Eleanor who opened it.

'It's from Eileen, of all people,' she said when she took the letter out of the envelope. 'I wonder what she has to say for herself.'

The letter was very friendly with hardly any reference to the years of estrangement between Eileen and the family. She hoped the sisters were well and that with all the shortages – 'I know you have rationing in Ireland too although I suppose it's easier being on a farm' – times were not too difficult for them.

'Well,' said Eleanor as she took off her glasses, 'it's friendly enough. What do you think she means by writing to us?'

Martha knew that, underneath, Eleanor was very pleased to get the letter. She also knew that, if she herself expressed too much enthusiasm, Eleanor would not respond to it or pursue the possibility of a reconciliation. Over the next few weeks they talked the letter over.

'Honor made her last years very miserable by taking the attitude she did,' Eleanor would remark to Martha. 'It's what killed her in the end.'

'God never intended that a mother would cut a child out of her life the way Honor cut out Eileen,' said Martha. 'And no amount of religion could be sufficient excuse.'

'It wasn't just that Liam "dug with the wrong foot",' said Eleanor, 'it was the insult, as Honor saw it, of Eileen having to become a Catholic when she married him not to mention the fact that the little boy had to be brought up as a Catholic too. She resented being dictated to by the Catholic Church and she wasn't alone in that.'

'No,' said Martha. 'Although, if anything, Honor didn't give a fig about religion. After she married Dick and went to live in England, the Catholic–Protestant thing meant nothing at all to her. Do you remember how she used to chide us by telling us how bigoted we all were in Ireland?'

'Do I, indeed?' said Eleanor. 'She did mind, though, that Liam was only a labourer and "no class", as she used to put it, and she was mortified that Eileen had to marry him, as it were. Said she would never be able to live it down.'

'And I suppose, in a way, she never did,' said Martha.

Eventually Eleanor replied to Eileen. She invited her to come over and stay at Coolowen, bringing Fergal with her.

'It's an odd sort of name to have given the boy,' she remarked to Martha, 'I suppose it's something Irish.'

'I think it's a lovely name,' said Martha.

Although travel between Ireland and England had already become restricted, Eileen and Fergal came to Coolowen during the Christmas holidays that year and, as the visit was a success, they came again for longer in the summer. The sisters were delighted with Eileen, who seemed to harbour no resentment that she had for so many years been banished. They came to see her almost as their own daughter and they were enchanted by the 14-year-old Fergal.

'A proper little gentleman,' Eleanor said to Martha. 'Honor did the right thing in providing for his education. Ampleforth is a very good school, I've always heard that. It's already given him a lot of polish and he has beautiful manners.'

'Very, very handsome too,' said Martha.

She looked straight across at Eleanor.

'And he didn't get that from our side of the family,' she said.

Within a year or so, Eleanor had decided – and Martha had given her wholehearted approval – that they should make Fergal their heir. And, the sooner the better, as far as they were concerned. Eileen had no objection to the plan. Having been brought up in England, she had never known Ireland but in the period since the reconciliation, she had grown to love Coolowen and she was very fond of her aunts. Before the war she had had a good job as matron in a school near Birmingham and now she did what she called 'war work' without elaborating as to what that work actually was. She could not leave England but was happy that her son would make his life in Ireland.

But if the general sense of satisfaction which accompanied the sisters' decision, Eileen's consent, and Fergal's obliging willingness seemed like the arrival of spring after the cold winter that was the sisters' years of worry, there lingered an annoying wind which blighted the promise of early growth. This had hardly been referred to in all the sisters' deliberations even though it was uppermost in the minds of both. The decision that Fergal should one day inherit Coolowen had been relatively simple. He was, after all, their great nephew, their own flesh and blood, and – although slightly indirect – their only descendant. Much more difficult to accommodate was the fact that Fergal was a Catholic. It was of little significance that, being to all intents and purposes an English Catholic, and privileged by a Benedictine education, Fergal did not seem like a Catholic at all. He still was one and for a Catholic to come into Coolowen after centuries of the place being Protestant, was something that Eleanor and Martha could hardly bear to contemplate.

'I never thought I would see the day...' Eleanor would say without being more specific.

'He's not properly so,' Martha would reason. 'He is, after all, half a Protestant just as he is half a Sale.'

'No,' Eleanor would interrupt, 'only a quarter Sale. Eileen is half a Sale.'

By deflecting their conversation to a discussion of such genealogical fractions, the sisters managed to relieve their minds of more uncomfortable thoughts and, a few years later, when Fergal Conroy was seventeen, he came to live at Coolowen.

6

Fergal

FERGAL WAS ONLY seventeen when he first saw Julia.

She was just nine at the time but that made no difference: he fell in love with her on the spot. It was within weeks of his having come to live in Ireland and his great-aunts had asked the Esdailes over to tea. Lydia was only just five and Edward a tough 11-year-old; but Julia, in spite of still being a child, had the poise and allure of a debutante.

'She's such an old-fashioned wee girl,' Aunt Martha said, amused, when she overheard Julia asking Fergal why he was called Fergal.

'I'm called Julia because I was born in July: on the fifteenth. If I'd been a boy, I would have been christened Swithin.'

When tea was finished, Aunt Eleanor, who always decided such things, told the children that they might get down from the table and go out and play.

'Fergal will show you the goslings,' she said, 'and, if you're very good, he might take you into the walled garden and let you pick some strawberries.'

They went out through the greenhouse.

'This vine is hundreds, maybe thousands, of years old,' said Julia.

'Are you sure about that?' said Fergal.

'Of course,' said Julia. 'It's the true vine. It says so in Liscarrig Church. "I am the True Vine" is painted around the arch above the Communion table. That's why every year Miss Martha arranges baskets of the grapes there for the Harvest Festival.'

Their feet crunched on the gravel as they walked along the path through the trees towards the yard.

'She's still only a baby,' Julia said when she saw Lydia picking out the white stones. 'Leave her where she is. She's always dragging out of me.'

Edward had already disappeared.

'I'll show you the goslings,' said Fergal. 'Come on Lydia, I want to see if you can count them.'

'I don't like ducks,' said Julia. 'They're dirty.'

She stood where she was. She looked down at the ground and then, closing her mouth firmly so that her lips became almost white, she stared at Fergal. He chuckled to himself and smiled. Julia was used to defying her elders and betters, even on the smallest of issues, and she knew she was always successful: in the case of Edward and Lydia, she always just told them what to do.

As the years progressed Fergal became like an older brother to the three Esdailes. But with Julia there was always an additional edge. She soon discovered that she could make him do her bidding and, with the élan of someone a great deal older and more experienced, she sulked, flattered, teased, ignored, and made demands so that Fergal never quite knew where he stood. That was the way Julia liked it, and when all else failed, she would tell him she was going to marry him.

'Pappy may not allow it, so you'll have to secretly take me away in the night,' she would say.

'I'll wait till you're twenty-one,' Fergal would tease.

'No, before that,' Julia would demand.

In appearance, Fergal was striking. He was very tall and he had his father's thick black hair and blue eyes. But instead of the very pale skin that is normally found with those looks, he had a robust complexion; and, in place of the sad eyes of the native Irish, Fergal's shone with laughter. In manner too he was a mixture. He had an easy, natural, friendliness and courtesy but, at the same time, an assurance that singled him out as a cut above the ordinary.

If Julia was smitten by Fergal, she was not the only one and, if his great-aunts had been anxious that he would have difficulty fitting in with their way of life, their fears in that respect were soon allayed. He did not seem to find life in a house with two middle-aged spinsters lonely or exactly dull. On the contrary, he enjoyed everything. He chatted to them as though they were friends of his own age; he ran errands for them, accepted their advice as to how things should be done on the farm, and even teased them on occasion by poking fun when Eleanor was laying down the law. He was anxious to please, anxious to learn, and within a couple of months his aunts were devoted to him

'The only thing that makes me sad,' Martha said, 'is that Honor never knew what a pleasure he could be.'

One aspect of his new life in Ireland, however, left Fergal confounded. When he first came to Coolowen he went to the Catholic chapel on Sundays while his aunts went to the Protestant church. But after a while he did not bother to go every Sunday and on occasion he accompanied the sisters to Morning Prayer: he did not make a choice between the two options – he did not think he needed to – as the fact of the matter was that he had hardly any feeling for religion of any persuasion. Furthermore, his education under the Benedictines in England had done little to prepare him for the form of priest-fearing Catholicism that he encountered in Ireland. If he was confused as to which church he should attend and how much it mattered, he was so with some justification. It did not help that the convention in Ireland at the time was that Catholic churches, which were generally enormous, were referred to as chapels whereas Protestant churches, which as a rule were tiny, were called churches.

The spire of St Malachy's in Liscarrig soared up above the little town as a landmark that could be seen on a clear day from as far away as the Hill of Mullach, twelve miles distant to the south. The spire and the enormous structure to which it was attached – a huge building in an elaborate architectural style that might loosely be described as French Gothic – was quite out of proportion to the scale of Liscarrig itself and, as a result, it seemed to look down upon all the other buildings in the town with an air of condescension. This condescension was particularly striking when St Malachy's was confronted by another structure at the opposite end of Church Street. Tucked in behind an aged and crumbling stone wall was a building which seemed almost ashamed of its low-key understatement and lack of architectural style. A square tower which looked old and might have housed a bell was its only claim to distinction and even the tower was no higher than the aged beech trees planted nearby. This was St John's. On Sunday mornings, the tiny trickle of Protestants, the Esdailes among them, who dribbled into St John's for Morning Prayer were dignified by being members of the Church of Ireland even though they were representative of only a tiny minority among the population of Ireland as a whole. By way of contrast, the devout shoals of Catholics who thronged into St Malachy's at the same time represented the majority population; but they, nevertheless had to be content with being merely Church of Rome.

Fergal's indifference as to which church he attended was understandable in a stranger new to Ireland; but if he thought that his careless and carefree attitude could continue indefinitely in a country where religion mattered so very much, he was mistaken; and his aunts, if they had thought about it at all, were greatly mistaken too. But they had not thought about it and, accordingly, they were jolted all the more when, almost a year after Fergal's coming to Coolowen, they received a visit, as exceptional as it was unexpected, from Father Costelloe, the parish priest of Athcloon.

'This is a rare occasion, Father,' Eleanor said to him when she came through to the hall. 'The last time we saw you was when you were good enough to call when our dear sister passed away and that's nearly four years ago now. How time flies! May we offer you tea?'

Father Costelloe said no.

'Miss Martha is in the sitting room,' said Eleanor. 'I'm sure she'll be pleased to see you too.'

She gestured to the priest to follow her as she led the way out to the back hall and towards the sitting room.

'We've a surprise visitor, Martha,' she said when she came into the room.

Martha was seated by the window doing needlework. Father Costelloe shook her hand as Eleanor beckoned to him to take a seat.

He was a small man and he looked even smaller on account of being far too fat. As a result he had no neck to speak of so that it was hard to be certain if his clerical collar, with just a thumbnail of white at the front, was anchored to his chin or his chest. It was obvious that he cared little about his appearance and if he seemed rough and ready – which is how he did seem – he was clearly proud to be so. Father Costelloe was conscious that he was 'a man of the people' but he ruled the people with the proverbial rod of iron. Making it his business to be familiar with the private affairs of every one of his parishioners, he regarded it as his calling to meddle in those affairs as he deemed appropriate; and 'appropriate' to Father Costelloe meant with unbridled impunity. His parishioners claimed to have a respect for him but it was a respect born out of necessity and tempered by fear.

On this sunny June afternoon, in the sitting room at Coolowen, it did not take him long to address the purpose of his visit and, clearing his throat in a manner which caused Martha to fear that he might be about to spit, he began.

'You have your nephew living with you now,' he said, 'a grand lad by all accounts.'

He grinned rather than smiled as he said it. Martha noticed the yellowed teeth.

'Yes,' said Eleanor, 'it's such a help having him here for the farm.'

'And company for us too,' said Martha.

'That's just what I wanted to have a word with you about,' said Father Costelloe. 'Father Flynn in Liscarrig didn't like to call himself, him being just the curate, thought it would come better from myself.'

'What's that, Father?' said Eleanor.

'Well now, your nephew – Fergus is it?'

'Fergal,' said Eleanor.

'Fergal,' said Father Costelloe. 'He's been seen coming out of the Protestant church on a Sunday morning when he should have been to Mass.'

'Should have been to Mass, Father?' said Eleanor.

'Yes,' said Father Costelloe, 'he's a Catholic, isn't he?'

'Well, yes,' said Eleanor, 'but his mother is never too much bothered about which church he goes to, and nor is Fergal himself for that matter.'

'That's all right in England, Miss Sale. But here in Ireland, by the good grace of the bishops, when a man is a Catholic, the chapel is where he belongs: and every Sunday too.'

Eleanor did not immediately grasp the topic which Father Costelloe was addressing or the seriousness of his intent; but she was taken aback by the novelty of someone speaking to her so firmly.

'I'm sure we can't force Fergal to go to Mass, Father, or even to our own church for that matter. He's old enough to know his own mind,' she said.

She moved in her chair as though she was about to get up.

'Are you sure you won't have tea, Father?'

'No one is talking about force, Miss Sale,' said Father Costelloe. 'It's just that the local people don't like it.'

'Don't like what, Father? Our nephew seems to be very well regarded by everyone.'

'They don't like seeing a Catholic going into the Protestant church when everyone knows it is forbidden. And they don't like that he doesn't go to Mass every Sunday when it's the rule that he must.'

The atmosphere in the room suddenly changed with Eleanor's desire to be hospitable and friendly severely challenged.

'As I mentioned, Father,' said Eleanor, 'we can't oblige our nephew to do anything ...'

Father Costelloe interrupted her. He had not yet finished.

'People could become "uncooperative" like,' he said, 'and none of us would want an upset like that in the neighbourhood. Your Reverend West is a sound man. He and I often have a chat.'

As Martha had not been taking part in the conversation, she had been able to listen more intently to what Father

Costelloe had been saying and when she heard the words 'uncooperative, like' – she detested the vulgar expression – she rested her needle in the pincushion on the arm of her chair. She readily determined that, although the priest had stated that he was not talking about 'force', that was precisely what he was talking about; and when he spoke of the local people being possibly 'uncooperative', she was confident that she understood what he meant by that too. She was reminded of reading a year or two previously of events down south where a Catholic mother, with a Protestant husband, had sent their children to the Protestant school. The local priest denounced the couple from the pulpit and that led to some Protestants becoming virtual outcasts; and, hard though it was to imagine – the Sales had been in Coolowen for so very long – she thought what such a situation could mean to her and Eleanor. She became suddenly frightened.

'Uncooperative?' she heard Eleanor say. 'I'm not sure what you mean, Father.'

'Father Costelloe is just speaking on behalf of Father Flynn, Eleanor,' said Martha.

She turned towards their visitor.

'We'll have a word with Fergal,' she said, 'won't that do, Father?'

'I'm speaking on behalf of the bishop himself, Miss Martha, and the rule of the bishop is Mass every Sunday.'

He was flushed but he was not agitated and, as he stood up, the anger in his attitude was all the more obvious. But it was an anger which went beyond any of Fergal's transgressions. Father Costelloe was not intimidated at finding himself in the sitting room at Coolowen and he was not intimidated by the graciousness of the Misses Sale. But he was angered by them and angered, according to his view, by everything they stood for; and it was an anger which went beyond religious differences to probe the wider realm of Ireland's history as it stretched back over the centuries.

'It's been very nice of you to call, Father,' said Eleanor.

She stood up and pushed the bell by the fireplace.

'They say there will be more rain next week. It's been such a wet month: no growth at all. Everything is behind in the garden.'

Their maid, Doris, came to the door.

'Well, I'll be off then,' said Father Costelloe. 'Good day to you now, ladies.'

He hardly waited to shake their hands before following Doris out of the room.

After he had gone, neither Martha nor Eleanor spoke. Martha returned to her stitching and Eleanor took up *The Leader*. The sisters wanted to be silent and it was several days before either of them referred to the conversation that had taken place.

'It could develop into a shocking business,' said Martha. 'It would mean none of the shops would supply us, not even with the Emergency rations to which we are entitled. And if it went on, others in the parish ... Dr Knox ... the Holts ... they would suffer too.'

'And all because of dear Fergal,' said Eleanor.

The aunts did not say anything immediately to Fergal but when it came to Sunday, they suggested that he should go to Mass.

'It'll stand you in good stead to be seen by the local people,' they told him. 'It's a country thing. Playing one's part in the community, and all that.'

Fergal did not demur and, after he dropped Martha and Eleanor off at church, he drove on up to the chapel. With one excuse or another, the sisters saw to it that the same happened on subsequent Sundays as well, so that after a while it became a habit.

A habit is all it was as far as Fergal and his aunts were concerned but it was habit enough to satisfy Father Costelloe.

7

Julia

FERGAL HAD BEEN in Ireland almost four years when Julia went away to school. He had been twenty-one that summer and his aunts had given him a party at Coolowen. The Second World War had ended the previous year, rationing was still in place and there were great shortages of everything, but that did not deter the sisters in wanting to celebrate for 'their dear Fergal'. It was at the party that Julia told him that she was leaving him.

'I'm going away,' she said, as though she were an heiress jilting her betrothed.

'Really,' said Fergal who did not at all believe her.

'Yes,' said Julia, 'to boarding school. In Dublin.'

As with everything which concerned his elder daughter, her father had formed the view that, when it came to her education, only the best would do and, as a result, he had enrolled Julia in the smartest – and the most expensive – Protestant secondary school in Ireland: Adelaide College in Dublin.

'Pappy is sending me to Adelady to learn to be a lady,' she told Fergal. 'That's what the school does. It's not for exams and books.'

Fergal was somewhat discouraged by this piece of information as he thought that Julia, although only thirteen, was already quite lady enough. That did not, however, serve to diminish his interest in her and, during the years she was at school, he remained fascinated. In those years Julia passed briskly through adolescence and marched briskly towards becoming an alluring young woman. Six years later, when she went up to university at Trinity College, she cut a striking and sophisticated figure. Long russet hair, very tall and a figure that was sensuous rather than slim she dressed more formally than other undergraduates – cashmere twinsets, tailored costumes and, always, her mother's pearls. Sharing with a pair of Roedean girls a spacious top-floor flat in a Fitzwilliam Square house where doctors' consulting rooms took up the lower floors, she settled on reading 'Mod Lang'. Not that it was her intention to 'read' very much: 'having a good time', as she explained to Lydia, was more on her mind.

'College is not about getting a degree,' she said. 'Everyone gets a degree. Going to Trinity is more like "coming out" used to be. You are there to meet people and be seen.'

By this time Julia had put her childhood crush on Fergal behind her – in fact she was rather embarrassed by the memory of it – and, although she was very fond of him, it was as a brother rather than as a beau. For his part, Fergal had never declared himself to Julia. He felt that his constancy and devotedness was enough to make her understand that he wanted her and that he would wait for her.

Julia was to be twenty-one in the summer prior to her final year at Trinity and, without much persuading on her part, her father consented to give her a dance. They discussed it months in advance when Julia was home for Christmas.

'It's a proud moment my eldest's coming-of-age,' her father said.

'My actual birthday would be no use as a date for the dance,' Julia said. 'By July everyone has disappeared for the summer. It'll have to be earlier, before the vac.'

'Is that tempting fate?' said Willis. 'After Mama, I'm always terrified of the unexpected.'

'Otherwise it's the autumn or winter when it would be much too difficult for people to get down here,' said Julia. 'I'll be inviting mostly Trinity friends.'

It had already been decided that the dance would take place at Knockfane.

Thereafter, Julia made all the plans, although she discussed her decisions with her father. The carpet would be lifted in the drawing room and the dancing would take place there. The sofas and chairs would be moved into the hall. The supper would be laid out in the dining room. All the old paraffin lamps would be brought into service as, with every room in the house having to be lit, the generator could not be relied upon. At the end of the evening hot soup would be served.

'We'll have it outside, on the gravel,' Julia announced.

She had copious other ideas, most of them wildly extravagant, for the success of the evening although, in many cases, she was persuaded by her father to drop them; but in spite of such constrictions, by the time she went back to Trinity after the Christmas vac, there was very little in her head except plans for her dance.

When, therefore – unusually – she telephoned towards the end of February to say she was coming down to Knockfane for the weekend, her father and Lydia – who was home from her school in Westport for half-term – assumed it was because she had come up with some other fanciful notion and that she wanted to sound their opinions. They were looking forward to hearing what it might be but on the drive out to Knockfane – they had both gone in to Liscarrig to meet her from the bus – Julia did not mention a thing. It was the same over tea: nothing. As they sat by the fire that night, she was very quiet and not herself at all. Assuming that she was tired after the trip from Dublin, Pappy turned on the wireless and they listened to a play, but when it was half over Julia announced that she was going up to bed.

'I'll get you a hot jar,' Lydia said, 'the bed might be a bit damp although Rose had the windows open all afternoon to air the room.'

'I'll manage,' said Julia.

She kissed her father.

'Goodnight Pappy dear,' she said.

'She seems out of sorts,' he said to Lydia when Julia had left the room.

'She's probably just tired,' said Lydia, 'she has quite a hectic life, from what we hear.'

They returned to the play and listened in silence. When it was over, they turned off the wireless.

'Time for bed,' said Willis.

They climbed the stairs together. Lydia had a book with her. Under the influence of the other girls at school, she had lately developed a taste for novels of light romance and it was in just such a volume that she was engrossed that weekend. She was still reading when, at quite a late hour, Julia knocked at her door and came into her bedroom.

'Darling Lydia,' she said.

She threw herself into Lydia's bed. Then she broke down sobbing, clasping Lydia to her, and shivering. She remained like that for several minutes. Lydia's book fell to the floor.

'Julia,' said Lydia, 'what on earth ...?'

She was unaccustomed to such effusiveness from her sister and did not know what to say. Julia continued crying.

'Is it about the dance?' said Lydia. 'Has Pappy refused you something?'

'There'll be no dance ...' said Julia.

She wailed.

'... no party, no twenty-first. None. Ever.'

8

The Law Society Ball

JULIA KNEW THAT Lydia had always admired her. It suited Julia that Lydia did so and it suited her even more to know that Lydia also depended upon her. What Julia did not know was that she also depended on Lydia and at no time did she depend on Lydia quite so much as on the night she came into her sister's bedroom and announced, amid howling and sobbing, that there would be 'no dance, no party, no twenty-first. None. Ever.'

Lydia was astonished by the statement. She had been caught up in all the arrangements for the dance and, as she had none of her father's worries that Julia's plans were too extravagant and few of Julia's anxieties that her Pappy's concerns were too restrictive, she had been borne along on a cloud of enthusiastic impartiality as all the details were decided. Even if it had been her own coming of age that was being planned, Lydia could not have been more excited and so Julia's news that all was to evaporate and everything be abandoned came as an unwelcome shock and, for a moment, the thought entered her head that Julia was being slightly selfish. It was obvious that Julia was very upset but Lydia had no notion what she could be so upset about and nor was it easy to see what could possibly have occurred to make her jettison her plans so precipitously. With her sister's tears drenching the bodice of her nightdress, Lydia searched for some answers and, in allowing the scope of her reasoning fairly wide boundaries, it crossed her mind that Julia's sudden decision might have been influenced by precedent.

'Is it something to do with Mama?' she said.

She remembered it often being told that their mother had never had a twenty-first. Without lifting her head from where it was burrowed into Lydia's chest, Julia shook it vigorously.

'How could it have anything to do with Mama?' she whimpered.

Lydia remained lost.

'... Edward then?' she said.

Julia shook again.

After a while she sat up. Her face, without her mascara and as a result of her tears, was but a relic of its normal mien, and white and sunken as a cadaver. She gaped at Lydia.

'I've done something very foolish ...' she said.

Lydia, unaccustomed to such a frank declaration from her sister, awaited further elucidation.

'... although I'm not in any way to blame.'

This was more like Julia, thought Lydia.

'But I'm going to have to pay the price,' said Julia, 'and it's so unfair.'

She started to snivel again.

'The price of what?' said Lydia.

She imagined that Julia must have broken or lost something belonging to one of her friends. Julia leant forward and hugged Lydia again.

'Someone has got me into trouble,' she sobbed. The words were almost inaudible.

Like everything else about the scene that was taking place, Lydia found this statement very unexpected. Nor did she immediately grasp what it signified. But before she had a chance to enquire, Julia continued.

'He took advantage of me and now ...'

'Julia dearest, do you mean ...?' said Lydia.

'Yes,' said Julia, 'a baby ...'

'Oh! Julia,' said Lydia, 'I had no inkling that you had met someone wonderful and that you were in love and doing a line. You never mentioned him. Who is he and what's he like?'

'I'm not in love, Lydia, and I'm not doing a line and the rat whose child I am now going to have is not going to stand by me. He denies he has anything to do with it and I'm so, so frightened.'

The two stayed talking for hours as Julia went over and over what had happened and Lydia tried to provide comfort and offer advice. The father, as Lydia – to Julia's annoyance – inadvertently referred to him, was a law student, English, and only in his second year, and Julia had met him when some of her friends had asked her to make up a table for the Law Society Ball in the Shelbourne Hotel.

'He hadn't even paid for my ticket,' said Julia, 'but that didn't stop him insisting on leaving me home. I thought he was dashing, very dashing in fact, and then before I knew what, it was all over.'

'He had his way with you?' asked Lydia.

It was a phrase she had picked up from her recent reading.

'But how did you bring him back to your flat without the other girls knowing?'

'I didn't,' said Julia. 'We did it on the floor of the doctor's waiting room downstairs.'

When she first discovered her predicament Julia, by her own account, was very ashamed at what she had done but then, as she thought about it and without telling a soul, she became almost proud that she had such a secret and that she had been so modern and naughty. Although she had not cared for the experience very much, she thought she might like it more if she tried it again. She had hoped to see more of Tarquin but, to her astonishment, when she ran into him in Front Square, he barely acknowledged her. When she noticed the first sign that something might be amiss, she gave it little thought and it was only the following month that she became alarmed. She went to a doctor in Harold's Cross. When the doctor explained her condition, she became very scared and did not know where to turn but after a few days decided that she had better tell Tarquin. She dropped him a note asking him to meet her in Slattery's pub.

By the time he arrived, she had already had two gin and tonics and then she just told him straight out.

'What's that to do with me?' he said. 'From what I know, it's not here that you should be drinking gin, but in a hot bath.'

At that he walked out and there was the end of it.

'It's a love child,' said Lydia. 'That's what it is.'

'I want to sleep now,' said Julia. 'I'm very, very weary. Can I stay here for tonight?'

Lydia tucked her up, climbed into bed beside her, and turned out the light.

'I'm going to be an aunt,' she thought. '"Aunt Lydia" or will it be "Auntie Lydia"? Both sound nice.'

9

Silence to the Grave

'JULIA SAYS IT happens with girls,' Lydia said to her father in the hope that he would not probe further into the cause of his elder daughter's indisposition.

It was after all true, Lydia reasoned with herself, it did only happen to girls although that was not what she meant when she said it. Wise beyond her sixteen years, she recognised that the episode was an occasion which called for her to dissemble.

'She's just exhausted,' she added when she saw the look of concern on her Pappy's face. 'Exhausted,' she repeated, 'a good rest is all that she needs.'

Willis decided to be satisfied.

'Some "women's business",' he thought, and he did not enquire any further. Nor did he insist that Dr Knox should be called. He went up and sat beside Julia during the morning and tried to chat to her about the plans for the dance; but when she did not respond much and appeared to be drowsy, he left the room.

'It's just some "fly in the ointment",' he said to himself, 'she'll soon be back on form.' But 'the ointment' in which Julia found herself was considerably more unguent than such preparations normally are and, as for extracting herself from it, that was to demand a delicacy of effort and degree of ingenuity that went well beyond the ordinary.

Julia knew, she told Lydia, from rumours in Trinity that there were some places even in Dublin where girls in her condition might go and have things cleared up; but the rumours left no doubt that this option was very dangerous. Some students, finding themselves in a similar predicament, had been known to brazen it out and mortify their parents by getting married in the Registry Office in Kildare Street; but even if this had been a possibility for Julia, and owing to Tarquin's attitude it was not, she would never have been courageous enough to pursue it. The possibility of going to England and, unknown to anyone, sitting it out until the baby was born in some care home for what Lydia carelessly referred to as 'fallen women' until the baby was born and then having the infant adopted, was another alternative. As the sisters circled the various choices hour after hour, day after day, until Lydia was thoroughly worn out, both girls always came back to a consensus that this was the best solution and all that remained in question was how the news would be broken to their father, if at all.

Lydia felt that the shame of what had befallen his daughter would greatly affect and upset their father and she did not want him to be told but Julia was insistent that there was no alternative.

'I'll need money,' she said, 'Pappy will have to know.'

But, as it transpired, Pappy did not 'have to know'.

Julia, without sharing her thoughts with Lydia or even consulting her sister about her idea, came up with a scheme – as dramatic and brazen as anything even she had ever contrived – which would alleviate her situation, satisfy her self-esteem, and solve her quandary conclusively.

It was dinnertime on the Thursday following her woebegone arrival at Knockfane the previous Saturday when Julia came downstairs for the first time. Lydia and her father were already seated in the dining room and, when Julia walked in, they were astounded. Not only did she appear quite well, but she was also fully restored. That is to say, her makeup was all in place and she was dressed in what she called her 'country informals': riding breeches (although she did not ride), a shirt and tie, and a well-cut tweed jacket. She looked quite splendid.

'It's great to have you back among us, Miss Julia,' Rose said when she came in with a shepherd's pie. 'But Lord knows you've been a proper little soldier all week and God in his mercy was at your side. It's Him we have to thank.'

'That'll do, Rose,' Willis said, 'just leave the tray on the sideboard. Miss Lydia will dish up.'

Over dinner, Julia did not refer to having been out of sorts but chatted as though there was nothing amiss. She thought she might take the car, she said, if Pappy did not need it, and go over to Coolowen in the afternoon. As Old Esdaile was so pleased to have her well again, he did not demur. When she arrived home after six and appeared to be exceedingly cheerful, her father was reassured.

That night, after they had all gone to bed and Lydia was settled under the blankets and at last catching up with her book, Julia burst into her room.

'Lydia darling ...' she cooed, shutting the door behind her.

Lydia had heard these very same words from her sister less than a week previously when Julia had bounded into her bedroom in similar circumstances and she was not sure that she was at all happy at hearing them again now: she feared yet more of the exhausting discussions which she had been obliged to suffer since Julia's arrival home. But before she had a chance to speak, Julia had moved to the end of her bed and grasped the rail.

'I'm so, so happy, Lydia dearest,' she said, 'so, so happy. And I want you to be the first to know.'

Lydia was now perplexed. She had been the first to know that Julia was in trouble and very miserable and now, in less than a week, she was to be the first to know that her sister was deliriously happy. She did not understand. It crossed her mind that, by some stroke of good fortune, Julia may have had a little accident during the afternoon and, if that was the case, she hoped that Julia had done nothing to bring it upon herself.

'How can you be, Julia?' she said, 'what has happened? I hope ...'

Julia stopped her with a hug and then getting up from the bed, she twirled around the room like a dervish. Coming to a stop and again clasping the bed end, she announced:

'I'm engaged, Lydia. Isn't it wonderful?'

'Engaged?' said Lydia. 'But how ...? Have you been in touch with Tarquin? And the baby? I don't understand, Julia.'

'Fergal is coming over tomorrow morning to ask Pappy's consent.'

'Fergal?' said Lydia, 'but what about Tarquin?'

Julia ignored the interruption.

'Fergal says he will always love the baby as though it were his own. He doesn't mind in the least that it's not. We'll get married before it arrives.'

'Julia! ...' said Lydia.

The room suddenly seemed chilly to her and she felt goose pimples forming on her arms. In the absence of knowing what to feel, she became frightened within herself.

She stared at Julia, standing there at the end of the bed in her nightgown, looking flushed and even proud. It was a very different Julia to the one who had trembled there, like a waif off the streets, less than a week previously.

'Are you sure, Julia? I mean ... are you doing the right thing?' said Lydia.

She thought of Fergal, how gentle and kind he was, and how much like an older brother he had always been to them.

'I mean ... there are other people to consider.'

'Like who?' said Julia. 'Fergal thinks I have always loved him, he said so. And Pappy is bound to be pleased.'

When Fergal came over the following morning and asked her Pappy if he might marry Julia, Willis was as astonished by the development as Lydia had been. And then he thought to himself, 'It all makes sense. They have been sweethearts all along, under my very nose and I never realised. There must have been a tiff which is why Julia was out of sorts and took to her bed, but now all is fine.'

Later that day Lydia asked Julia if she was going to tell their father about her condition and the circumstances of Fergal's proposal.

'Don't be a goose, Lydia,' Julia said, 'of course not. Pappy doesn't need to know and why should I worry him by telling him?'

'But ...' said Lydia.

'Fergal is happy that we get married straight away and that we both go to England for maybe a year. Our baby will be born over there ...'

Lydia blinked. And then she blinked again.

'Had Julia no conscience?' she thought, 'was there no limit to her effrontery? Talking about "our baby" in this way.'

'... and no one will ever be any the wiser', continued Julia.

'But Pappy ...' said Lydia, 'he, at least, will have to be told the truth.'

'No, he won't, Lydia,' said Julia. 'Only you and I and Fergal need ever know and it is a secret we will guard to the grave.'

As Lydia was only sixteen, the sentence of 'silence to the grave' which Julia thought fit to hand down seemed to her to be inordinately severe but Lydia accepted it, as she had always accepted everything from her sister, without further ado.

10

An Heir for Coolowen

WHILE 'NECESSITY HAD been the mother of invention' as far as Julia was concerned – motherhood in all its forms was very much on her mind – her father was not slow in coming to understand the exact nature of what had taken place. When, therefore, Julia announced – soon after announcing her engagement – that she and Fergal would be marrying straight way, he was scarcely surprised. But while Willis could recognise necessity when confronted by it, he was on less sure ground when it came to invention and, when the invention involved his daughter Julia, he was generally at sea altogether. He could, therefore, be excused for not appreciating the full extent of the embarrassment in which she had found herself and nor could he be blamed for failing to recognise how inventive she had been in finding a solution to her predicament.

He prided himself on being a man of the world so that when Julia first broached the notion that, following her hasty engagement and her even hastier marriage, she and Fergal would hasten away on an extended honeymoon, he was not fooled. He did wonder, however, how he could have been so blind as not to see that the two were in love, and obviously passionately so, or the need for an extended honeymoon would never have arisen.

'Fergal needs to get away and see something of the world,' was how Julia put it to her father. 'He's been stuck at Coolowen since he was seventeen. It's been no life for a young man like him. He's seen nothing and been nowhere. This is his last chance.'

'A last chance for Fergal' was not at all how Willis viewed the situation but, nevertheless, he refrained from questioning Julia too closely and thus made it easy for her to continue her plotting. He did, however, enquire about the extended honeymoon that she was proposing and asked her just how extended she meant it to be.

'About a year or so,' Julia said.

'I see,' he said. 'Then Fergal will have to make some arrangements about who is to look after Coolowen while he's away. I can't think his aunts will be very happy though. But, if all comes to all, I would keep an eye on things for them.'

He desisted from making many more enquiries or putting any impediment in his daughter's way. He remembered his own darling Annette and the torments her father had made them suffer by making them wait before marrying and how they had vowed that they would never inflict a similar embargo on any of their own children and so he kept his counsel. As to the other anxieties which he had – and he had a great many – he nursed those to himself. He sought solace in Lydia's company and let Julia carry on with her schemes.

The Sale sisters were, initially, quite startled when Fergal told them that he was to marry Julia but Eleanor soon pronounced that she had known all along that such an eventuality was very likely.

'It makes good sense,' she said.

But when Martha pointed out that 'good sense' had never been a reason why anyone married, Eleanor ignored her. By 'good sense' she had meant that, in marrying someone they had known since she was born, Fergal had exonerated them from the tiresome task of having to get to know someone new; and that, in Eleanor's mind, was sensible. If she or Martha suspected the reason behind Fergal's sudden decision, they did not show it and they made no objection to the plan for him to be away from Coolowen for a year.

While all these things, as well as other details, were agreed to in a spirit of ready accord it was perhaps because everyone knew that there loomed over any plans for Julia's and Fergal's marriage a singular and unwelcome impediment.

In the first weeks after her announcement that she and Fergal were to marry, and to marry very soon, all mention of this stumbling block was assiduously skirted and steadfastly ignored but it could not, as everyone knew, be skirted and ignored forever.

Eventually it was Martha who raised the subject with Willis.

'Eleanor won't even discuss it,' she said, 'but it has to be discussed.'

'I dread the very notion,' said Willis, 'but I don't think there is any way round it. I did ask Canon Shortt if it could be avoided if they married in England, but evidently not. The rule applies there too.'

'Has that despicable Father Costelloe spoken to Fergal do you know?' said Martha. 'He's bound to insist they both sign the agreement that the children will be baptised and raised as Catholics.'

'It's quite iniquitous,' said Willis. 'And the notion that my daughter is obliged to be married in a Catholic chapel while her husband is forbidden by his priest to even set foot in a Protestant church makes my blood boil.'

'Iniquitous or not,' said Martha, 'it's their rules and it's for us as much as Catholics to obey them.'

'I know,' said Willis.

'It was only invented by the pope about fifty years ago,' said Martha. 'Our great-granny was a Catholic and she remained one after she married Great Grandpa. The girls from the marriage were all Catholics, the boys Protestant. It caused no division in the family, none whatsoever.'

'Whereas this *Ne Temere*, as it's called, causes a great deal of division in families,' said Willis, 'and division and suspicion among neighbours too.'

It was understood from the start that the wedding could not be in the little church in Liscarrig but, nevertheless, Willis decided that Canon Shortt should be consulted; and it was with Canon Shortt and Fergal that Willis went to see Father Costelloe.

'I'll be giving your daughter instruction,' was the priest's first pronouncement.

'Instruction?' said Willis.

'Yes,' said Father Costelloe, 'if she is to become a Catholic, she has to have instruction and it's my duty to give it to her.'

'I don't think my daughter has any intention of becoming a Catholic, Father,' said Willis.

'She still has to have instruction and then make up her own mind,' said the priest.

Willis was all too aware that Julia was more than capable of making up her own mind, indeed she had been doing so from the time she was in the cradle; and, as far as instruction was concerned, he had never known her to accept instruction from anyone about anything. He was confident, therefore, that – even for Father Costelloe – she was unlikely to change. He did not, however, share this intelligence with the priest, choosing to move the discussion forward instead.

'Perhaps you would let Mr Holt have a draft of the agreement which my daughter will be obliged to sign,' Willis said.

'It's not really a matter for solicitors and the like,' said Father Costelloe, 'it's for the couple themselves.'

'That's all very well Father,' said Willis, 'but I would like Mr Holt to see it and, if he's in agreement, he will have Miss Julia and Mr Conroy sign it.'

'It's usually done at the Parochial House,' said Father Costelloe.

'Now about the marriage ceremony itself …' said Willis

'It has to be in the chapel and at a side altar or in the sacristy and before nine o'clock in the morning,' said Father Costelloe.

The mention of an altar, side or otherwise, sent a shiver down Willis Esdaile's spine. There was no such thing as far as he was concerned. There was a chancel at the east end of a church and in the chancel there was a Communion table, unadorned. There was never even a cross, either on this table or anywhere else. The idea, therefore, that his daughter was to be married in front of an altar – even a side one and before nine in the morning – was to Willis an absolute affront.

'The wedding will be in Dublin,' he said. 'In that big chapel along from Guinness's Brewery. Canon Shortt has spoken to Father Deasy there.'

'I'm not sure that that can be allowed, Mr Esdaile,' said Father Costelloe, 'you see, it's my duty, as Mr Conroy's parish priest, to see that everything is correctly observed.'

'Indeed,' interrupted Canon Shortt, 'but it is not an obligation for the marriage to take place in the Catholic partner's parish and Mr Esdaile – and the Misses Sale, I should say – would prefer the ceremony to be in Dublin.'

'I'll see what can be done,' said Father Costelloe.

Willis did not go to the wedding: nor did the Sale sisters. Fergal and Julia did not want them to come as both understood how insulting it was to people of their generation that they had no choice but to observe the rules of a Church that was not their own. Lydia went, and Fergal's mother, Eileen; but not Edward nor Julia's Odlum grandparents. When Fergal said that he would like some 'male support', Lydia suggested asking Mr Benson as her father was adamant that he 'would not dignify the proceedings' by having Canon Shortt. It was Father Deasy who conducted the marriage. Julia only mumbled the responses inaudibly and, in a display that was most unlike her and in spite of Fergal's efforts to console her, sobbed and sniffed throughout. The entire proceedings were all over quite quickly, and before nine in the morning.

Later in the day, the little party met with Willis, Eleanor and Martha and had dinner in the Russell Hotel and, in the evening, Fergal and Julia caught the mailboat for Holyhead and on from there to London. They stayed in a hotel for a few weeks and then found a flat in Fulham. The baby was born towards the end of September and, when Fergal's aunts heard it was a son, they insisted that he would be called Samuel.

'There has always been a Sam Sale at Coolowen,' they said, 'ever since the family first came to the place more than two hundred years ago.'

Fergal and Julia were happy to comply with the sisters' wishes and have the infant christened Samuel and it was only they – and Lydia – who knew that, while the little fellow might indeed be a Sale in name, in blood he certainly was not.

But this was not spoken about, not even between Julia and Fergal. What was done was done and all was now in the past.

11

Mr and Mrs Sale

ON THE EARLY morning of that chilly April day when Julia, before the altar of St Rita in John's Lane Chapel, married Fergal, she became Mrs Conroy. But Miss Esdaile, as she had been, although relieved that 'the horrid little charade' – as she would always refer to her wedding – was over, was not pleased.

She was pleased enough to be standing beside Fergal and she was even more pleased that he had relieved her of her predicament; but, as she faced out on to the grimy Dublin street and the stench of the River Liffey wafted particularly potent, Julia had the very distinct feeling that she had come down in the world.

The marriage had solved her immediate problem, that was true; but, in doing so, it had created other problems and not all of these were entirely related to the ceremony she had just endured. First and foremost was her concern over her new name. She would not, she resolved, go through life as Mrs Conroy when she was correctly, in her view, Mrs Sale. It did not matter if Fergal could not appreciate fully the difference between Conroy and Sale, he would understand in time. Fortunately for Julia, her father and her husband's great aunts had the same sensitivities as herself and they were equally determined that the newly married couple would be Mr and Mrs Sale

The sisters had discussed it between themselves.

'The notion of a Conroy in Coolowen when the place has been Sale for centuries ...' Eleanor said.

Julia's father registered his distaste in the matter by continuing to refer to his daughter as 'Miss Julia' and never mentioning the name Conroy at all; and it did not take him long to decide that he would do something about the situation. As soon as things had settled down, and Julia and Fergal were installed in London, he went to see old Mr Holt the solicitor.

'The Sale girls have got themselves very worked up,' he said to him after one or two preliminaries. 'It doesn't matter all that much to me ...' he lied, '... but they can't abide the idea of Coolowen being lived in by Conroys, even if they are not really proper Conroys at all.'

Willis Esdaile was not bigoted, at least he did not consider himself so, and as for snobbery, it was – by his own estimation – entirely unknown to him. It never occurred to him to discriminate between rich and poor, and as to any other social boundaries, he ignored those too. He was, it has to be said, an entirely reasonable man but, no more than anyone else of his time in Ireland, he was not reasonable when it came to matters which delved into the abyss of suspicion – and aversion – that existed, on both sides, between Catholics and Protestants. And so his daughter's marriage, forcibly, in a Catholic chapel and her subsequent obligation to go through life bearing a Catholic name tested his tolerance to breaking point and it revealed in him a resolution and determination that in most other respects he was prepared to set aside. It was that resolution and determination which had brought him on this particular morning to the familiar offices of Mr Francis A Holt, Solicitor and Commissioner for Oaths.

'So, what are you proposing?' said Mr Holt.

'They'll have to ... you'll have to ... change Miss Julia's name to Sale: Fergal's as well, of course.'

'I see,' said Mr Holt.

'It's been done in centuries gone by so it must be possible to do it now,' said Willis. 'When my great-great uncle or whatever he was, Hubert, married Abigail Sale when there was no Sale son for Coolowen, Hubert took the Sale name. It's a similar situation, somewhat.'

'Things were often very much simpler in the past,' said Mr Holt. 'I'll take soundings from one or two people and see what I can do.'

'I would be grateful,' said Willis.

He got up, moved towards the hatstand, then looked again at Mr Holt.

'I'd like to push things along as soon as possible,' he said, 'while Miss Julia and my son-in-law are still in London so that everything would be clear by the time they come home.'

And so it was that when Julia and Fergal returned to Liscarrig they were welcomed as Mr and Mrs Sale and the son who accompanied them, as heir to Coolowen, was Master Sam Sale.

12

Marion

WILLIS ESDAILE WOULD always refer to 1954 as 'that year of all the marriages'. First there was Julia's, 'a strange affair', and then another, later in the year, in Cork. As to Julia's, it had crossed Willis's mind and caused him some discomfort that *The Book of Common Prayer* decreed that marriage was 'commended in Holy Scripture as not to be taken in hand unadvisedly, lightly, or wantonly'. The precipitousness of his daughter's actions, it seemed to him, might be deemed ill-advised if not exactly wanton; but on the other hand her choice of husband had lessened his anxieties in this respect.

At the Cork wedding it was other words from the marriage service – 'the causes for which Matrimony was ordained' – which occasioned Willis to reflect and, as he looked at his son Edward standing at the steps of the chancel with a pillar – like Lot's wife – of white beside him, he became subdued. The words which followed, 'First, for the increase of mankind, according to the will of God, and for the due ordering of families and households', penetrated to the very core of his being. He had no desire whatever for Edward to 'increase mankind' and, as to his son's 'ordering of the Esdaile family and their households', that promise too was equally unwelcome to him. He was not to know – although he was later to learn – that his resolve in this respect was more than matched by the determination of Marion, as Lot's wife was called, to pursue such objectives with ardour.

Edward was just twenty-four at the time of his wedding and his bride, who came from Cork, was twenty-two. Before any announcement of their engagement appeared in *The Irish Times*, Edward had come up to Knockfane to tell his father of his intentions.

'What are her people?' was his father's initial response.

'Mr Roycroft is in the bank ...' said Edward.

Willis said nothing. They were up in the Twenty Acres field where Edward had found his father as he was examining the growth of the barley. They were walking along the headland making their way back towards the house and, much to Edward's irritation, his father kept stopping to look at one thing or another and seemed very little interested in what his son had to say.

'... the Munster and Leinster, in Kanturk,' Edward continued.

'I see,' said Willis, 'and does Miss Roycroft have an employment?'

'Marion,' said Edward, 'it's Marion, Pappy. She's an air hostess with Aer Lingus but, of course, she'll have to leave that when we get married as they don't employ ... married women.'

He beamed when he said the words.

'It's a terrific job. She's in London or Paris or Rome every other day of the week.'

His father moved ahead towards the gate.

'And is she likely to be contented settled on a farm in the depths of the country when she has been leading such a very ... industrious ... life?' he said.

'Marion is very ... capable,' said Edward.

'She'll need to be,' said his father. 'And this wedding, is it to be ... where did you say ... Kanturk ?' said Willis

'No, in Cork city,' said Edward. 'Marion's grandparents live there but the reception will be in the Metropole.'

'A hotel?' said his father. 'And what has your grandfather got to say about the affair? Has he met Miss Roycroft?'

'Oh! yes,' said Edward. 'Grandad, and Grandma too, they like Marion very much and they have met Mr and Mrs Roycroft as well.'

'I see,' said his father, 'well then everything is in order.'

Willis only met his prospective daughter-in-law the day before the wedding when he and Lydia went down to Cork. Before the encounter he was resolved not to like his son's choice of wife any more than he liked his son and it was a source of some satisfaction to him to discover that Marion in person gave him little cause to change his mind.

'Busy' was how he described her to Lydia but it was the way he said it that implied much more.

'She'll certainly keep Master Edward on his toes,' he elaborated, 'she's the organising sort, you can see that. Although I'm not sure that Edward has seen it yet.'

It was only in years to come that Willis would be more specific and, in talking with Julia and Lydia, make plain that he thought his son's marriage was unworthy of him.

'But there's nothing new about that as far as Derrymahon is concerned,' he would say. 'In taking on T.E., your grandmother married beneath herself too. Everyone was shocked when she did it and, all the more so, as it was obvious that T.E. was only marrying her for Derrymahon.'

In light of his distaste for Marion and compounded by his dislike of Edward, it was a source of great irritation and annoyance to their father that, in what seemed like a very few years, the couple produced four sons.

'I told you she would organise Edward,' Willis would say to Lydia.

In later years he would be more specific.

'Edward will have his work cut out having to provide, in time, for four boys. Derrymahon is a big farm, but it's not that big. He'll certainly need her push when it comes to setting them all up, that's for certain.'

He would grate his teeth when he said it. Then he would smile.

13

Life for Lydia

AS JULIA HAD married, in such haste, wantonly as it were and then, together with her husband had departed hastily for a year, no consideration had been given to where she and Fergal would live on their return. Coolowen seemed like a big house because it was high – three storeys above a basement but it was made up entirely of low small rooms on either side of a central staircase, with the four bedrooms squeezed into the two upper floors. There was, therefore, little scope for dividing the accommodation to provide separate quarters for the young couple and the old sisters, Eleanor and Martha. Nor were there even the remnants of a dower house anywhere on the farm; and so it came as a godsend when Colonel Tarrant died unexpectedly and Raheen, which he had rented for years from the Mulhussey estate, became available.

Situated midway between Knockfane and Coolowen, the little house was altogether befitting a young married couple as, in contrast to Knockfane or Coolowen, Raheen seemed quite young itself. Neatly arranged in the landscape at the end of a short avenue, it was like a lady's powder box set down on a dressing table. In appearance it was the sort of house a child would draw; and as such it suited Julia and Fergal and the young Master Sam Sale to perfection.

With all the fuss over Julia's marriage and then her absence altogether, and with Lydia away at school in Westport, things were very quiet at Knockfane: too quiet as far as Willis was concerned. Even though he was only fifty-eight in 'the year of all the marriages' and did not feel his years at all, the 'old age' he had sometimes thought about – and dreaded – seemed to come upon him without warning. He had always known that Julia would 'fly the nest', although he had not expected her to do it quite so soon. By the same token, having always planned that Lydia, 'his little Leah', would be the companion of his later years, he had not envisaged that the need for her companionship would arrive so very punctually. With very little thought, therefore, he made a decision.

'A year or two at home,' he said to Lydia, in proposing that she should leave school, 'when you are so good with all the animals and things about the farm, will give you more real education than all that study and hockey could ever do.'

'And then what'll I do?' Lydia asked.

'We'll see,' said her Pappy, 'maybe a course in shorthand and typing, or perhaps domestic economy someplace. There are always openings like that.'

But it was not with the intention of giving Lydia any real education, or providing her with any opening, that her father brought her home to Knockfane.

He did not consider that, with her element of seriousness and application, she might actually have been more suited to going to Trinity College and studying for a qualification than Julia had ever been; and, notwithstanding the succession of other girls whom she always invited to stay during the holidays, he failed to recognise that, outside of the family circle, Lydia was outgoing and had an aptitude for friendship that would be starved by the isolation of Knockfane. Equally, although he loved her so much himself, it never dawned upon him that some other man might find her very loveable too.

Initially Lydia relished being at home and, during that first summer, she had several of her friends to stay. As this was well before her hasty marriage, Julia was still at Trinity and, that year, taking advantage of the long aummer vac, had gone to France as au pair to a French family near Limoges and was abroad for most of July and August. The weather was beautiful at Knockfane and local friends had tennis parties almost every week. There was a parish outing to Lough Fraine when everyone got very sunburned and there was the annual excursion of the Athcloon Archaeological Society that went as far as Iniskeevin and on to the Abbey of Derryconnell. Encouraged by her father, Lydia got the idea of having a big picnic down by the river one afternoon and invited about thirty guests. Eleanor and Martha Sale remembered that Granny Esdaile, before she was widowed, used to have picnics there every June once the hay was saved and all the workmen from Knockfane would come with their families as well as neighbours. Lydia asked guests to bring rugs for sitting on and most people arrived with cakes, but much of the preparation fell to Lydia herself, although helped by Rose, and she spent much of the previous week baking and, on the morning of the picnic, making sandwiches. Her father had the labourers set up makeshift tables and seats by the river bank and construct a sort of hearth where kettles could be boiled. Having been such a dry summer, the river itself had retreated to being little more than a trickle but the yellow flag irises were all in bloom and the weeping willows on the opposite bank, one of which Granny Esdaile had ceremoniously planted every year at her picnics rustled in the summer breeze.

The bullocks, displaced from their usual grazing to make way for the picnic, stood knee-deep in the mud of the river bed and stared discontentedly at the party throughout the afternoon. Lydia loved it all and that summer, away from Julia's shadow and alone with her Pappy, she felt happy and fulfilled. But when October came, and the long winter evenings began to set in, the futility of having little to do but read and listen to the wireless began to dawn on her.

With time, she took on daily chores around the farmyard, which meant that, in a way, she was tied to the place and could not easily be absent. She had the dogs to think about and then, more as an amusement than anything else, she got a couple of settings of goose eggs from Mrs Carney and hatched them out using the broody hens. Well fattened on the windfall apples in the orchard where the geese were allowed free range, she sold them, mainly to friends round about, at Christmas. The following year, people said they hoped she would have the geese again so Lydia felt obliged to hatch more that year and so it went on from year to year.

Julia often lectured her, advising her to make some plans that would involve getting away from Knockfane.

'You could go to Paris for a year, and see some life,' she would say.

But this suggestion seemed quite impractical to Lydia and typical of Julia to suggest something so ridiculous. Besides, even the idea of such an escapade was terrifying. Julia did have a point, however, Lydia could see that.

One year she went to Scotland on holiday with some friends from school when they hiked in the Cairngorms and she came back reinvigorated and the following year they went to Wales. But the next year, when they were making plans to walk the Way of St James along the north of Spain and Lydia tried to explain it to her Pappy, he was aghast.

'How do you mean it's a pilgrimage route?' he said to Lydia.

'Since medieval times,' she said. 'People – pilgrims – walk from all over Europe to the shrine of St James in Compostela, right out on the tip of Spain.'

'Shrine?' said her father. 'What sort of shrine? Is it for Catholics?'

'I don't know,' said Lydia. 'We haven't thought about it. I suppose it, sort of, must be as Spain is such a Catholic country. I can't imagine that the relics of the saint would be in a Protestant church.'

'Relics?' said her Pappy. 'Did you say relics?'

'That's what they're called, Pappy. That's what people go to see. But it's really the walk that's the thing. It can be three weeks or more and there are refuges – hostel places – along the way where you stay.'

'Have Heather and Joan discussed this with their parents, Lydia?' asked Willis. 'I'm not sure I like the sound of it at all and I'm certain that they can have no idea what's involved. It has to be entirely a Roman thing. You might as well tell me that you're going to climb Croagh Patrick.'

'It's not like that at all, Pappy. It's just the walk.'

'It's exactly that,' said her father. 'What else is a pilgrimage for, tell me, except to trap people into becoming Catholics? There's no question of me allowing you to do such a thing, no question at all.'

Lydia wrote to Heather and Joan and said she couldn't go with them that summer. Making some excuse, she did not explain why and, although she remained friends with them, they never asked her on holiday again. Years later, when Heather contracted a mixed marriage, and Lydia told her Pappy, he felt vindicated.

'There you are,' he said to Lydia, 'what did I tell you? That's what comes of walking in Spain.'

But to Lydia, for whom the prospect of any marriage at all seemed, at that stage, very distant, Heather's choice of a Catholic husband and the walk on the Way of St James seemed only very tenuously connected.

When it came to romance, Lydia's closeness to her father, and her isolation at Knockfane, curtailed her possibilities considerably. Julia had been lucky and had found Fergal, on her doorstep as it were, but the likelihood of the same good fortune befalling Lydia seemed very remote. Among the regular parishioners in Liscarrig, there was no one of interest and it was only exceptionally that some vaguely eligible young man would come to work in the bank or as a locum for Dr Knox. Giles Roleston was one. He was in the Ulster Bank in Athcloon and was very obviously appealing. Lydia mistook his attentions for more than they were, was attracted by his handsome good looks, and within quite a short time could think of nothing, or no one, else. Unable to declare her interest to Giles, she wrote to him almost every night expressing her longings and creating a picture for him of the life they would have together as Master and Mistress of Knockfane. She never posted those letters, of course, but kept them locked away and she never mentioned her feelings to Julia either. The love affair remained her secret. When, after about two years, Giles was moved to the branch of the bank in Roscrea, he became just a memory and it was a long time before she could see that as far as he was concerned she had been just a friend.

At other times she thought about Richard Benson and asked herself why she had never thought about him much before. She was very young when he was in Liscarrig and so it was unlikely that he could have been interested in her but, when she turned it over in her mind – and she began to turn it over quite often – she remembered times when they were together and she convinced herself in retrospect that he might have been near to declaring himself. When Lydia was almost twenty, he left Liscarrig to take up a curacy in Cloyne, almost the other end of Ireland from Knockfane, and it was then she realised how much she missed him. And more and more, as the years passed and her life became ever more solitary, she came to blame herself for not encouraging him.

It was about seven years after Mr Benson had left Liscarrig that her father saw the announcement of his engagement to be married in the newspaper. He mentioned it to Lydia.

'I see in today's paper that Mr Benson is still down in Cork,' he said.

Lydia looked across at her father but she said nothing.

'Evidently, he's the Rector of Crosshaven, so he has done well for himself. But then, he always had a very good manner with the parishioners and everyone liked him.'

'Why is he mentioned in the paper?' Lydia said. 'Has he done something?'

'It's in the "Social and Personal" column,' said her father. 'He's got himself engaged. I suppose he must be about thirty-three or four by now.'

Lydia showed no reaction. She suddenly felt hot inside her head but she did not blush. She put down her teacup and looked at the slice of bread with butter and raspberry jam that was on the plate before her. She did not feel like eating any more.

'Can I pour you some more tea, Pappy?' she said. 'There's still some left in the pot.'

She did not immediately seek out the newspaper after tea. Instead she went out to the yard. The labourers had gone home by then and so she was alone. She sat down uncomfortably on an old oil drum at the entrance to the hay barn and she looked around her. Everything was in order, everything was as it had been for as long as she could remember, everything that she had always loved. But at that moment, and for the first time in her life, she had an overwhelming sensation of hating Knockfane. She said it to herself and then she said it out loud.

'I hate, I hate, I hate this place Knockfane.'

She remained there for a while. She did not think of Mr Benson, she did not think of her father, nor Julia, nor Edward and Marion; but she thought about herself. She felt empty and, although it was a warm evening and she was wearing a cardigan over her summer frock, she felt cold. The dogs came and lay down beside her. Eventually she roused herself and went back into the house by way of the garden. She buried herself in her book when she got back to the morning room and it was only after her father had gone to bed that she picked up *The Irish Times* and read the announcement.

She was called Carol, 'the only daughter of Mr & Mrs K.W.E. Cotter of Craigduff, Crosshaven'.

'So he's to marry within his own parish after all,' thought Lydia.

She tore the page from the paper and threw it into the hearth. It was a few minutes before it burst into flames. Lydia watched it until it was curled up and grey and parts of it floated up the chimney.

A line came into her head, from where she did not know. 'I would that my tongue could utter the thoughts that arise in me.'

She sat on for some time and then, turning off the lights, she climbed the stairs to bed.

14

Descendants

SOME FEW YEARS after her marriage, Julia took to rearing purebred Aberdeen Angus cattle. Her father gave her some heifers and, by allowing her to graze them at Knockfane, encouraged her to breed with them. She exhibited these at agricultural shows throughout Ireland and at the Royal Dublin Society's annual Bull Show and she won many awards. Her father was proud of his daughter's achievement and would boast of her success. When it came to breeding children of her own, however, Julia was altogether less active and this was a source of disappointment to her father. It was four years after their return from London before she and Fergal had a daughter – given the name Honor – and then another daughter, Netta, was born eighteen months later. But Willis wanted Julia to have another son – an heir for Knockfane – and her failure to oblige caused him a degree of annoyance. His irritation in this respect was compounded by the success of Edward and Marion in producing four sons, all of them Esdaile in name, and all of them appropriate to succeed him as Master of Knockfane. But the trouble was that Willis, for reasons best known to himself, did not deem them appropriate. Had he done so, the worries which came to dominate his existence, as he edged into his seventies, would have been assuaged and the succession to Knockfane satisfactorily arranged.

His friends Eleanor and Martha Sale had no such concerns. Comforted by Fergal's steady presence and delighted with Julia, they were even more gratified that, in Sam, Honor and Netta, they now had 'descendants' all of whom Julia, ignoring Father Costelloe's rules, was bringing up as Protestants.

'Sam's every inch a Sale,' Eleanor would say with pride in her voice, 'it's quite uncanny.'

But neither Eleanor nor Martha knew quite how uncanny Sam being 'every inch a Sale' really was and nor were they ever to know. It didn't matter. They had an heir whom they believed to be their own flesh and blood and the future of Coolowen was secure. They had none of the anxieties which Willis Esdaile had created for himself by his resolute refusal to accord Edward what they – and most other people as well – deemed to be his only son's rightful due.

'Edward is his own son,' Eleanor would say, 'it doesn't make sense to deny him. And even if he did want to do so, he could pass Edward over and leave Knockfane to one of the boys. They are his grandsons, after all, and the second boy is even called Willis. Nothing could be more appropriate.'

The sisters would become quite agitated whenever they discussed the topic as it seemed to them to be so unreasonable on Willis's part and it was not like him to be so stubborn. They would recall the one occasion when he had properly discussed his opposition to Edward with them and how they had been puzzled that any father would feel the way he did.

'Is it because you don't care for Marion?' Eleanor had asked when Willis had remarked that Edward would never inherit Knockfane.

'She doesn't help, I admit,' he said. 'But Edward himself, he seems to think he has a right to Knockfane and he doesn't, in spite of what he thinks. His mother would never ever have wanted it, I'm confident of that.'

'Do you mean Annette?' said Martha.

She was astonished, and so was Eleanor, at Willis bringing Annette into the discussion.

'But Edward was only a small boy when his mother died, he can't have been more than eight or nine,' said Martha. 'Annette couldn't possibly have had strong views about him, the poor wee chap.'

'Well, she did,' said Willis. 'She could never take to him. She was even more averse than me.'

'That's a shocking thing to suggest, Willis,' said Eleanor, 'and I'm sure you must be wrong. Sure of it.'

'I'm not wrong,' he said, 'and out of respect for the memory of my dearest Annette, I'll see to it that Edward never comes into Knockfane.'

Then he stiffened in his chair. He saw that he had stunned the two sisters by such an outburst and he immediately regretted what he had said.

'I've gone too far,' he said. 'I'm sorry. It's not a good subject to ever discuss. It brings back too many bad memories.'

But he did not specify what the many bad memories were and Eleanor and Martha were obliged to assume that they were thoughts of Annette. They talked about it later.

'It's quite ridiculous,' Eleanor said, 'it must be about twenty-five years since Annette died and he still holds on to her memory as something sacred. It's not healthy, if you ask me.'

'It's almost as though he feels guilty in some way,' said Martha, 'and that Edward must pay the price.'

'But the price for what, might I ask?' said Eleanor. 'And guilty about what? Annette died of natural causes. Well, maybe not natural causes, but lots of women used to die in childbirth. It's not as though he deliberately let her die.'

'Or that Edward caused her death in some way,' said Martha.

There was silence for a moment. Both women were shocked at the turn their conversation had taken. They had frightened themselves.

'Let's not think any more about it,' Martha said after a while. 'We must just be content to remain in the dark and leave it at that. But it's all a mystery.'

'It's more than a mystery,' said Eleanor. 'And what is more it makes me cross.'

She got up from her chair to prod the fire and, standing on the hearthrug with the poker in her hand, she looked at Martha:

'Very, very cross,' she said.

The 'mystery' of why Willis Esdaile looked upon his son with such disfavour remained a mystery as far as Eleanor and Martha were concerned and even Julia remained forever puzzled. 'I know that Pappy worries more and more about what is to happen to Knockfane after his time,' she said, 'but he won't even hear of Edward or one of the boys taking the place on. He's adamant.'

It was a Sunday morning and, as Fergal had gone to an early Mass, Julia was driving Eleanor and Martha home from church. Eleanor was seated in the front. Mindful of the fact that she had just taken Communion, Martha was in a religious frame of mind.

'It's unchristian,' she said from the back seat, 'that's what it is.'

'It may well end up that being a Christian won't even come into it,' said Julia, 'or family feeling for that matter.'

She slowed the car and turned down the road towards Coolowen.

'What on earth do you mean?' said Eleanor.

'Knockfane could be taken over,' said Julia, 'by the Land Commission. They have already made an approach. A few years ago, in fact. But Pappy doesn't like to even talk about it.'

The 'approach' which Julia referred to was a letter from the Commission which her father had received. It informed him cheerfully, but in a form of words that was almost incomprehensible in its formality, that they had decided to take over some, if not all, of the farm at Knockfane. They were charged under several Government Acts they stated, with the task of dividing up larger landholdings and distributing them, in smaller farms, to the disadvantaged; and, as part of that general plan, Knockfane would be required. Without actually declaring that Mr Esdaile – and the other landowners who were favoured with similar communications – had no say in the matter, the wording made it seem as though the letter was merely a courtesy and the implication was that the recipient should make plans to vacate the specified lands in the fairly immediate future.

Willis was much shaken when the demand arrived. He knew that there had been land agitation locally and he had expected that, sooner or later, the Land Commission would act; but he had hoped that it would be later rather than sooner, and perhaps never at all. The threat posed by the letter made all his previous anxieties over how – in making plans for the future of Knockfane – he might sidestep Edward seem trivial and he was not sure what to do.

Old Mr Holt the solicitor was already dead by the time the Commission's interest in Knockfane first manifested itself but his son, who had taken over his office, seemed to Willis to be a go-ahead and practical young man and, feeling comfortable in consulting him, he showed him the Land Commission letter.

'My late father always advised, "when in doubt, do nothing",' young Mr Holt said after he had perused the contents. 'That's probably the best course of action, Mr Esdaile.'

Gratefully accepting the suggestion and putting the letter back in his pocket, Willis went home and did his best to put the menace of the Land Commission out of his mind. When nothing happened for a year or so, proving the wisdom of the late Mr Holt's counsel, he felt relieved.

15

Edward and Marion
Come to Knockfane

NOT TALKING ABOUT the Land Commission was Willis's
means of coping with the unwelcome threat to Knockfane
that it represented; and even when the Commission identified
130 desirable acres on the other side of the Liscarrig road
and took them over, he still did not want to talk about it.
That did not, however, prevent Lydia insisting on discussing
it with him when she saw how distressed her father was
by the loss and when in time he received another similar
unsettling missive.

Willis was never in two minds but that the Commission's
benevolence in making such plans for his property should be
taken seriously and, even if he had any doubt, he would be
made aware of the realities by learning of other landholdings,
similar to Knockfane, which had been appropriated, divided
up and re-distributed.

There would often be reports of such happenings in
The Irish Times. On one occasion there was a photograph
on the front page of a road painted with the words, 'Brits
Out' and 'Irish land for Irish people', and the accompanying
article reported the sale, or attempted sale, of a large farm

in the midlands. The slogans painted on the road were a protest by the local people who wanted the lands to be divided among them.

'What does it mean, "Brits out" and "Irish land for Irish people"?' Lydia asked her father.

'The Waldrons have had that place for generations,' he replied, 'and have always given employment in the area.'

'Then they're not British, they're Irish,' said Lydia.

'The local people don't think so. The Waldrons are Protestants, that's what matters. And, as far as a lot of people in Ireland are concerned, that's the same as being British.'

'Do you mean that people would think of us as British?' Lydia asked.

'Some people would,' said her father 'quite a few, if the truth were known. But it's always beneath the surface, as it were.'

'It says in the article that there is agitation locally for the Waldrons' place to be taken over by the Land Commission and divided up,' said Lydia. 'Could that happen even if the Waldrons didn't want it?'

'Of course,' said her father.

'But the Commission couldn't just take the land, they'd have to pay for it.'

'The Land Commission doesn't pay,' said her father, 'they give compensation, that's what it's called. But it's not fair compensation. The Waldrons would be given useless land bonds that pay less than 3 per cent, and they'd be beggared as a result. They'd be left with nothing and that's what the Land Commission is about. It's about driving people like us out of Ireland.'

'But where do they think we should go?' said Lydia.

'"Back to England" is what they would say,' said Willis. 'They don't concede that we belong here, right here in Ireland.'

'I don't think I've ever met an English person in all my life,' said Lydia, 'except the time that you took Julia and me to London when we were little.'

'It makes no difference, Lydia. The Esdailes came here from England some 250 years ago. That's yesterday as far as a lot of Irish people are concerned and, in their view, it's time we headed home again.'

The lands at Knockfane were among the best in Ireland. Almost all the 622 acres were a heavy clay and rich in lime, providing a lush pasture that was best suited to grazing cattle. In a survey of the farm that dated from the time of Hugh and Flora's marriage in 1815, most of the fields were described as 'upland' with only about 23 acres of 'course bottom' and very little bog. A mere 20 acres or so were wasted on woodland.

By Lydia's father's time very little had changed, except that the woods had been increased by a long belt of hardwoods stretching along the western boundary of the farm: these had been planted by Lydia's grandfather at about the time he inherited Knockfane. All the fields were well watered as the River Scarva, a tributary of the Trevet, flowed through towards the east and, in places where its waters were not accessible, ponds had long ago been created so that, even in the driest summers, there was always drinking water for the cattle. The hedges, mainly of hawthorn – but with some blackthorn too – growing on banks with ditches to either side, provided shelter; and it was obvious from their logical layout that the hedges had been deliberately sited to provide fields of the optimum size, that is to say between 15 and 40 acres.

Four such fields were situated on the opposite side of the Liscarrig road to the rest of the farm and it was these fields that were identified first as suitable to the Land Commission's requirements and they took them over. The centuries-old hedges were uprooted and four ugly little houses were constructed to house contented families transplanted from the west of the country.

Edward and Marion were incensed by what had taken place. Edward did not accept that there was nothing his father could have done to prevent the confiscation and he cited the case of Derrymahon, which was still fully intact. Grandpa Odlum was dead by this time and Edward was master of the estate; and the fact that he and Marion had four sons – he boasted – was a protection against the onslaughts of the Commission. As one year gave way to another, the loss of the Liscarrig road fields became an obsession with him and, on the rare occasions when he came to Knockfane, he would talk of little else. 'Iniquitous' was how he described the activities of the Land Commission.

On the pretext that they had not been to Knockfane for so long, he and Marion announced on one occasion that they would come up and visit on a Sunday. They would stay the night. They had never done this before, but as they wanted to do it now, neither Lydia nor her Pappy objected. Lydia saw to it that the bed was made up in the spare room and she ordered a larger sirloin joint from Skelly's than usual.

'It would be nice,' Lydia thought, 'for Edward to be closer to his father now that Pappy is getting on in years and Marion may have fewer edges than she had when they were first married.'

All went well on the Sunday and, after chatting round the fire in the drawing room in the evening, Lydia went to bed early so as to give Edward and Pappy the chance to talk. She was sure that Marion would follow her but, in the event, her sister-in-law sat on and it was nearly one o'clock when Lydia heard all three coming upstairs. In the morning, Pappy had gone out to see the workmen in the yard by the time Edward and Marion came down to breakfast and Lydia was surprised to hear from them that they would be going home that morning.

'Pappy will be sorry if you leave,' she said. 'He was looking forward to your coming. Stay on, at least until after dinner. I'll make rissoles with the leftover beef.'

'We have to get back,' Marion said. 'Besides, I couldn't sleep a wink in that room with the noise of the jackdaws in the chimney.'

They said their goodbyes when Pappy came in from the yard and off they went.

'They might have stayed a little longer,' Lydia said, 'having come all this way.'

'It was long enough,' said Pappy, 'Edward hasn't changed, and as for her ...'

'All the same ...' said Lydia.

'What right do they think they have ? ...' said Pappy.

But he said no more and Lydia was left in the dark; and it was only later, after Pappy had confided in Julia, that she heard what had passed between them.

'Edward is not all bad, you know,' Julia had said.

Lydia had gone over to Coolowen to collect some damsons: the tree was coming down with them, Julia had told her, and it would be too late to bottle them if Lydia left it much longer. They were having tea in the big sitting room and Julia's maid Attracta had made a Sally Lunn.

'He and Pappy have never seen eye to eye,' said Lydia.

'Evidently Marion started by saying what a fine young man Willis – that's the second boy – was growing up to be. That annoyed Pappy to start with. You know how he has always disapproved that they called the boy Willis.'

'I remember him fussing at the christening,' said Lydia, 'but I was never sure what it was about.'

'Pappy said he wasn't fooled at the time, he knew exactly what they were after by giving the boy that name, and now he knows he wasn't mistaken.'

'What does that mean?' said Lydia.

'It means that they hope that Pappy will leave Knockfane to Willis. In fact, they more than hope, they expect it. That's why they came up to see Pappy,' said Julia.

'But how?' said Lydia. 'Knockfane is our home, it's not theirs. I live there.'

'That's neither here nor there to them,' said Julia. 'They want Pappy to make the place over to Willis, in trust, now. They said it was the only way to protect it from the Land Commission. It would be more difficult for the farm to be taken if it was held in trust for an Esdaile boy.'

'And to think,' said Lydia, 'that I left them there to talk to Pappy and went up to bed. And all they wanted to do was plot behind my back.'

'It was more than plotting,' said Julia. 'They had actually gone so far as to have a deed of trust drawn up. They wanted Pappy to sign it, there and then. They became quite angry with him when he wouldn't sign. Edward was even abusive, Pappy said.'

Lydia helped herself to more butter and spread it on her Sally Lunn.

'It's her,' she said. 'Edward wouldn't do such a thing.'

'Edward would,' said Julia, 'and furthermore he has a point.'

'Do you mean in wanting Pappy to make Knockfane over to them?'

'Yes,' said Julia. 'What good would it be leaving it to you? You'll never have anyone for the place and what's to become of it after Pappy's gone? You can't farm it.'

'That's hardly a nice way to talk,' said Lydia. 'Pappy will be with us for a long time yet.'

'Not for ever, Lydia. Be realistic ... but then you never were. It would be much the best thing to have Knockfane settled on young Willis, in fact it's the only sensible thing to do and I said as much to Pappy when he told me what had happened.'

Lydia was troubled when she went home that afternoon. She loved Knockfane, she loved every field, every tree, she loved the garden, she loved the house itself, and she did not like to think of it as just being a commodity to be battled over between father and son, between Julia and her. It was 'home' to her and she had thought that it would have meant the same to Edward and Julia but now she saw that it did not. In making plans for the future of Knockfane, Edward and Marion had not considered her at all and Julia, it seemed, was already on their side. It had never occurred to Lydia to imagine that she had any right to Knockfane any more than anyone else, such as the young Willis, had; and, as she had never contemplated what would become of the place after her Pappy's time, she did not expect that Edward, Marion or Julia would have done so either. Julia's words had come as a shock to her and she knew they would have come as a shock to their Pappy too.

As to Edward and Marion, contact with them was almost severed altogether thereafter, and it was only very occasionally that Lydia, but never her father, would have any word from them. They had taken to having what Marion called 'a Continental holiday' every year and postcards would arrive at Knockfane from places like Lloret de Mar, Rimini and even Tenerife. Willis would hardly look at the cards.

'The extravagance of it,' he would say. 'What's wrong with Tramore, might I ask?'

16

Death at Knockfane

WHEN WILLIS TURNED seventy in the December of 1966, Julia and Lydia talked of having a party at Knockfane but their father would not hear of such a thing.

'We'll just have a quiet day,' he said, 'and besides, I don't want the whole neighbourhood knowing that I am old. I don't feel it. Apart from anything else, June is a busy time on the farm with the haymaking and everything. Maybe at Christmas we'll have a small do and ask a few people in for a fork supper.'

But, by the time Christmas came, he had changed his mind. Martha Sale had died in the autumn and he made that his excuse.

'It wouldn't be right,' he said, 'when we are all in mourning for poor dear Martha, to have any form of celebration. When Eleanor died two years ago, I felt the same.'

'But you'll never be seventy again,' Julia and Lydia said.

'Maybe when I am seventy-five,' their father responded.

Willis had perhaps good reason to be circumspect when it came to making plans for birthdays. He never forgot the time of Julia's twenty-first, all the discussions there had been and all the plans that had been made, and then the drama when the whole thing was called off.

Thinking about Julia brought to mind the time of his own twenty-first birthday and his mother's unexpected death two days beforehand. That had been a shock, and a trauma.

'It's hard to believe that was all fifty years ago now ...' he thought to himself, ' .... well before Annette.'

Whenever he reminisced, either to himself or to the girls or to anyone else, he always came back to Annette, her early death, and his bereavement and sense of loss and he always hated and dreaded any death as a result. And so he felt the passing of Eleanor and Martha very keenly even though they were both well into their eighties when they died. He missed them both, they had been like older sisters to him throughout his life, and Coolowen was his second home. It remained that when Julia and Fergal and his grandchildren moved there after Martha's death, but it was different without Eleanor and Martha. He thought sometimes about his own death but he did so with the confidence that it was still some years in the future. He enjoyed life and, furthermore, he intended to enjoy it for a number of years more.

It was all to the good, therefore, that he never became an invalid and that his death, thirty-three years after that of his beloved Annette, was so sudden. He was only seventy-five.

It was October and there had been torrential rain for days and the ground was very wet with the River Field flooded almost out to the road. One morning, Daly – the herdsman at Knockfane – came in to the house to report that a bullock was caught in a drain down in The Clump. Standing in the scullery with his hat in his hand, he was unusually agitated, and wet, sodden from the rain with a drip on the end of his nose.

'It's unlike Daly to be so put out,' Willis thought when he came through from the kitchen.

'All right, Daly,' he said, 'it's not the first time it has happened. Get the rest of the men to go down with you and ease the bullock out. An animal like that can get frightened in such a situation and panic but, when he knows there is human help, he'll more or less pull himself out.'

'I wouldn't be sure, and beggin' your pardon Sir, that it's ever going to be as aisy as that,' Daly said. 'With the woeful downpour, and them ditches burstin' with the flood, the bank has collapsed. And that auld ash, which has been hangin' on for years, has fallen. Its roots stuck above in the air and the bullock trapped beneath the trunk.'

'I see,' said Willis, 'so it's a bit more serious than I thought. I'll come down myself. We'll probably have to saw the tree, I expect. Have Duffy come down with the tractor and get all the ropes you can find. It might be possible to pull the tree aside.'

Daly backed out of the scullery and headed down the passage to the back door. There was a trail of drips on the cement floor from when he had come in and Rose, grumbling to herself, was making a show of mopping them up.

'You're not going out in that rain surely,' Lydia said to her father when she saw him heading for the boot room. 'You'll catch your death of cold.'

'I have to,' said her father, 'there's a bullock in trouble. I won't be long.'

But in the event he, as well as all the men, spent most of the day down in the field. The tree would not budge no matter what way they tried to ease it and there had been nothing for it except to saw it through. The bullock was stuck in the drain. He had broken his leg and it was folded back under him.

'The poor animal is in agony,' Willis said when he realised this. 'He'll have to be put down. Run up to the house one of you and ask Miss Lydia to ring the vet.'

'I could do it with the shotgun,' Daly said. 'It wouldn't be a problem.'

'Are you sure?' Willis asked, 'I wouldn't want him to suffer any more than he already has.'

Daly went back up to the house to fetch the gun. It was kept in the locked press in the boot room. Only Lydia and her father had access to the key.

'Are you certain that a shot will kill him instantly?' Lydia said as she handed the gun and cartridges to Daly. 'I wouldn't want him to endure further misery.'

'It's been done before, Miss Lydia,' said Daly, 'it'll be very quick.'

When he went back down to the field, nothing had changed.

'Be careful now,' Willis said, 'we don't want any more accidents.'

Daly took close aim and shot the bullock in the forehead. The blood spewed out, spattering the bank, and causing the muddy water in the drain to turn a rusty green. The men turned away. Young Corrigan ran over to the hedge and vomited.

It was several hours before they were able to get the ropes around the bullock in such a way that they could pull him out of the ditch with the tractor and then the dead animal had to be brought up from the field. Willis was soaked through when he eventually got back to the house around dusk. He was also shaken by the experience of witnessing the bullock suffer so much and the sight of him being shot.

'Would you ring Brigadier Seymour?' he said to Lydia as soon as he came in. 'The people from the hunt kennels will be glad to get the carcass for the hounds. Seymour can arrange it.'

Lydia was horrified when she saw her father.

'I've stoked up the boiler well, so the water is hot,' she said. 'Go up and take a bath. But have this cup of beef tea before you do.'

'I'll just change out of these wet clothes,' Willis said.

'No,' said Lydia. 'I want you to take a bath and then lie down for a while. I've put a hot jar in your bed.'

As it was only ever very rarely that Lydia was so firm with her father, he was taken aback and when he had drunk the beef tea he did what she said. He went up and had a bath and then he went to bed.

It was to be the last time that he would ever climb the stairs at Knockfane.

By nine o'clock that night he was in a fever and Lydia persuaded him to take some brandy which she mixed with hot milk, honey and lemon. He slept well through the night: in fact, he slept too well and then continued to sleep for much of the next day. When Julia came over in the afternoon, she was alarmed at how irregular her father's breathing was and startled at his high temperature. But she waited until the following morning before telephoning Dr Bell, who had taken over Dr Knox's practice and asked him to come up to Knockfane straight away.

Dr Bell was calm in his diagnosis.

'I'd be a bit nervous about his heart,' he said to Lydia as he folded away his stethoscope. 'You'll remember that he had that murmur a few years back. I'd quite like to get him to the hospital. I think it would be wiser.'

'Do you mean in Dublin?' said Lydia.

'Yes, the Alexandra,' said Dr Bell. 'I'll go down if I may and ring and see if I can get him a bed.'

He went downstairs to the telephone. Lydia stayed with her father who seemed to her to be in a sort of delirium. He tried to move in the bed. And then he was still.

Dr Bell came back into the room.

'That's fine,' he said. 'They can take him this afternoon.'

'It may be too late, doctor,' said Lydia. 'I think he's gone.'

She moved from where she was standing beside the bed and went over and drew down the blinds. The rain had stopped in the night and the sky was clear with the light of the milky October sun shining directly on the windows. Warmed in tone as it passed through the cream-coloured holland of the blinds, it illuminated the room with a quiet ochre hue.

17

Getting Down to Business

EDWARD AND MARION arrived at Knockfane the afternoon
after their father died. As they stepped out of their Rover, it
was clear that they were both in a practical frame of mind
and everything about Marion's stance indicated that she felt
it was going to be up to them 'to cope'. It came as something
of a disappointment to them, therefore, when they discovered
that Fergal and Julia had already 'coped' very well and that
most of the necessary plans for their father's funeral had
already been put in place.

That the funeral would be in Liscarrig Church, and the
burial in the little graveyard on the edge of the Knockfane
lands, required no discussion as the funeral would follow
the very same pattern as the funerals of earlier generations
of Esdailes before him. The burial ground was little used
now and it had become overgrown, a wilderness of ivy and
brambles: only the grave of Annette was saved from the
general entanglement. Willis always had it cared for and
it was there, in the same grave, that he would be buried.
His mother, Granny Esdaile, and his father, were further
away; Great Aunt Dora was mislaid somewhere near a
quartet of yews; and sundry other Esdailes were adrift in the

undergrowth. Only Hugh and Flora, interred underneath a huge limestone table-tomb, could be easily located.

In centuries past, the coffin of the Master of Knockfane was always carried down the avenue – as he left Knockfane for the last time – by the farmhands and so it was with Willis. Edward and Marion, Julia and Fergal and Lydia followed, the grandchildren after that. The church was crowded, but only with Protestants: Catholics, forbidden by their bishops to enter a Protestant church, congregated outside. By the time the funeral was over, it was late in the afternoon and almost dark as people made their way back to Knockfane.

Edward, Marion and their boys stayed at Knockfane that night. Fergal and Julia were also there during the evening but Sam, Honor and Netta had gone home to Coolowen. It had been a long and very sad day for Lydia, with no one to lean upon. Perhaps she felt the loss more keenly than the others did, but as she went about preparing a supper of macaroni cheese for them all, she hid the extent of her distress. Leaving Rose to bring in the meal, she went into the drawing room.

'The supper's ready now,' she said.

When the meal was almost over, and the Derrymahon boys had excused themselves by asking if they could go and watch television in the morning room, Edward, at a glance from Marion, brought up the subject that was uppermost in his mind.

'I had a chat with Mr Holt after the service,' he said.

Julia looked up. Fergal was helping Lydia by clearing the plates to the sideboard. Marion remained seated and made a show of brushing some imaginary crumbs from the tablecloth.

'That fellow is not half the solicitor his father was,' Edward continued. 'The old man was very astute. This fellow strikes me as a bit of a fool. He's all affectation and dressed up like a gentleman when everyone knows he could be no such thing.'

'I never liked the father,' Julia said. 'He dealt with the business over us changing our name from Conroy to Sale and, to tell the truth, I've never been certain as to what exactly he did or whether it's legal at all or not.'

'You call yourself Sale, don't you?' said Edward.

He was anxious not to be delayed or deflected from what was on his mind. Like a gelding at the start for a steeplechase, knowing that there were difficult hurdles ahead, he was ready for the off.

'... and that's what you sign yourselves, isn't it? So what does it matter?'

'I'd like it to be more precise,' said Julia.

'Precise,' said Edward. 'That's the word. This fellow, he is all precise and that's what I can't stand about him.'

'Pappy liked him,' said Lydia.

'He tells me the will is in his safe,' said Edward.

Lydia felt herself shudder. Julia looked at Fergal.

'Evidently, Pappy made it about five years ago and it's all in order. The previous will, he said, had been very out of date.'

'I expect Mr Holt will let us all know in due course what your father wanted us to do,' said Fergal.

'We can't hang about like that,' said Edward. 'There are things to be dealt with in circumstances such as these. I've arranged that we all go and see Holt in the morning. He says he'll read us the will, as if that was necessary. That's what I mean about him: full of old-fashioned notions. Mind you, it's him and not his father who drew up the will, so who knows what sort of a fist he'll have made of it.'

The following morning they all met at Mr Holt's office. Miss Jessup, who had been the secretary for as long as anyone could remember, showed them into the waiting room. This was furnished as a dining room and, indeed, it had once been a dining room as the house that 'Francis A. Holt & Co., Solicitors and Commissioners for Oaths' occupied on Castle Street in Liscarrig had previously been the Holt family home.

After about ten minutes, during which all five – Lydia, Edward and Marion, Julia and Fergal – remained in a silence interrupted only by the ticking of the clock on the mantelpiece, Miss Jessup came in again.

'Mr Frank will see you now,' she said.

In Miss Jessup's mind there was only one Mr Holt and the fact that he was dead more than ten years since made no difference: his son would only ever be Mr Frank to her.

They moved across the hall to the old family drawing room where Mr Holt awaited them. His desk was in front of the fireplace so that his dapper form was framed by the brown marble columns of the chimney piece and the clients who sat before him could see themselves reflected in the gilt overmantel affixed to the chimney breast above. He ushered the party to the leather-seated mahogany dining chairs in a supposed Chippendale style that he had placed in a row before him and they sat down.

'Yesterday was a very sad occasion, a very sad occasion for you all,' Mr Holt said. 'Indeed, the whole community is still shocked by your father's death.'

'Thank you,' Julia and Lydia murmured.

'But the funeral went off very well, I thought,' he said. 'That is if such occasions can ever be said to go off well. Nevertheless, very dignified: everyone said so.'

'Now, I think you said you'd read our father's will to us,' Edward said. 'That's why we're here.'

Mr Holt stiffened.

'Yes, yes,' he said. 'I have it here.'

18

Testamentary Dispositions

ALTHOUGH 'MOURNING' HAD almost gone out of fashion by the early 1970s, seated in Mr Holt's office Fergal and Edward wore black ties and Julia, Lydia and Marion were dressed entirely in black. Lydia in a skirt and twinset and Julia wearing the wool dress that she had worn to the funeral the day before. Black stockings, black shoes, black gloves, even black hats, bereavement became the two women in a way that they would not have wished. Only their fur coats alleviated the forlorn note to their appearance. Lydia weighted down in her mother's musquash, and looking much older than her thirty-three years, and Julia in the dark Canadian squirrel that Fergal had given her a year or two previously.

Marion's aspect was quite different. It was obvious that she was dressed for an occasion although it was questionable if the occasion for which she was appropriately dressed was one and the same as the occasion in which she was actually participating. She wore a fashionable costume which, as Mr Holt observed to himself, was very well cut: indeed it was so well cut that Miss Jessup had taken an instant dislike to its wearer. Her hat – in Miss Jessup's opinion – was equally objectionable. It had a plume to the fore and foliage to the rear, all of which shimmered when Marion moved, and it was perched at an angle that was clearly intended to take some years off the age of the well-powdered face below. As a gesture to the cold of the November day, she wore a fur muffler. This was modest in its proportions but, as Marion was given to boasting, it was mink. As such, it was intended to eclipse in its luxury the musquash and squirrel of her sisters-in-law. To the untutored eye, it may well have done so but to Julia and Lydia it seemed merely ostentatious and, in their view, typical of the vulgarity of the woman who wore it.

They both looked at each other when they saw their sister-in-law and they both had similar thoughts.

'Does she think she's going to a wedding or what?'

Mr Holt took up the will and cleared his throat. Edward observed that the document, rather than being typed, was handwritten in his father's hand.

"'I, Willis Edward Esdaile of Knockfane, Manor of Ballinacor and Barony of Kilmolyon, Ireland, being of perfect mind and memory, calling to mind that it is appointed for all men to die, do make and ordain this my last will and testament that is to say principally and first of all wills or other testamentary dispositions at any time heretofore made by me .'"

Mr Holt paused and glanced over his spectacles as if to check that the quintet before him were seated comfortably. Then he continued.

"'I appoint as executors my dear daughters Julia Rebecca Sale and Lydia Annette Esdaile, and Mr Francis Holt, Solicitor of Liscarrig. I desire my executors to ...'"

'Just a moment, Mr Holt, before you go on,' said Edward. 'Did I hear correctly that my late father has left only the two girls as executors? What sort of a provision is that?'

'It's what is in the will, Mr Edward,' said Mr Holt.

And then he corrected himself.

'Mr Esdaile,' he said. 'And myself of course. I am the third executor.'

Marion shifted on her seat, adjusting her mink as she did so.

'Shall I continue?' said Mr Holt.

Edward nodded. Julia and Lydia were both looking down as they fiddled with their gloves.

'"I desire my executors to give the following sums within one year after my death if cash is available out of my deposits – two hundred pounds to the Royal Hospital for Incurables at Donnybrook asking the Governors to appoint my two daughters life governors of the hospital; such sum of money to the Royal Victoria Eye and Ear Hospital, Dublin as will endow a bed to be called the Willis & Annette Esdaile bed; two hundred and seventy-five pounds to the Alexandra Hospital, Dublin for the purpose of medical equipment; one hundred pounds to the China Inland Missions in memory of my great-aunt Dora Esdaile; one hundred and twenty-five pounds to the Hibernian Bible Society; two hundred pounds to Mrs Smyly's Homes and School for Necessitous Children; seventy-five pounds to the Representative Church Body; one hundred and seventy-five pounds to the Incorporated Association for the Relief of Distressed Protestants …"'

'Are there many more of these bequests, Mr Holt?' Edward interrupted. 'They all seem so trivial. I think my sisters and I would like to know how my late father has disposed of his real property.'

'I'll come to that, Mr Esdaile,' said Mr Holt. 'It's beholden on me to read the will in its entirety.'

'How many pages are there?' said Edward.

Mr Holt ignored the question. 'I'll continue,' he said, 'these are the further ...'

He looked at Edward.

'... trivial ... bequests.'

Willis had been generous and wide ranging in bestowing his charity and the list of benefactions which Mr Holt proceeded to recount was testimony to a man who had a love of doing good, albeit in a modest way, and within relatively limited parameters. No sums of money were mentioned that were sufficiently large as to attract undue attention once the content of the will would be known and the beneficiaries were all drawn from some few Catholic charities, the GAA sports club in Athcloon, St Malachy's Community Hall in Liscarrig and, of course, several Knockfane employees.

Lydia and Julia listened attentively as all these provisions were read out, nodding in agreement at some of them and smiling at each other, registering their approval of their father's thoughtfulness at others. Edward and Marion did not seem to be similarly moved but, instead, demonstrated a growing exasperation by fidgeting and shifting on their chairs in a manner that caused some discomfort to Mr Holt.

'Now, there are some family bequests,' said Mr Holt.

Edward and Marion looked at each other.

'"To my four grandsons, sons of my son Edward, the sum of one thousand pounds each."'

'You would think he could have named them,' Marion said to Edward in an audible whisper. 'They have names, after all.'

Edward signalled to her to desist.

'"To my granddaughters Netta and Honor Sale the sum of five thousand pounds each and to my grandson Samuel Sale the sum of five thousand pounds."'

Lydia leant over and touched Julia on the arm.

'"To my daughter Julia and her husband Fergal Sale I give, devise and bequeath for and during their lifetime grazing rights at Knockfane for their herd of Aberdeen Angus cattle free of all charges."'

'What?' interrupted Edward. 'Grazing rights? And for their lifetime? And no mention of how many head of cattle. How could a bequest like that be put into effect, Mr Holt? It's far too ... too ... unspecific.'

'I think your father would have believed that, as it is within family, there would never be any dispute,' said Mr Holt.

'Of course there could be a dispute,' said Edward. 'How could I be expected to farm Knockfane when my sister and her husband might just claim rights to as many fields as they wanted?'

'It's your father's will, Mr Esdaile. And I think you'll find that he has been fair to all of you.'

'It seems extraordinary,' said Edward.

He glared across the desk as Mr Holt turned over to the next page.

'"To my son Edward my Land Bonds at three per cent from the Irish Land Commission in respect of the Commission's purchase of part of the lands at Knockfane."'

'You see what I mean, Mr Esdaile,' said Mr Holt.

Edward said nothing. But he saw that Mr Holt was nearing the end of his reading.

'And now,' said Mr Holt, 'we come to what may be supposed to be the main provision of the will: Knockfane itself.'

19

Speculation

SUBSEQUENT TO THE occasion when Edward and Marion had come to Knockfane with the express intention of having their father settle the place in trust on their son Willis, and when the discussion had proved so disastrous, Edward had never again been able to raise the subject of Knockfane's future with his father.

Once they recovered from their anger at Willis's refusal to sign the deed that they had had prepared, Edward and Marion had persuaded themselves to be content to let their father and Lydia – and even Julia – 'stew in their own juice' as they put it. It did not matter to them, they convinced themselves, if Knockfane 'went to the wall' and if Lydia found herself 'on the side of the road' or worse still 'at the mercy of Julia'. Their father was a contrary old man, they reasoned, and they wanted nothing more to do with him, much less Knockfane. But, in time, this exceptional reasonableness on the part of Marion and Edward dissipated, and was replaced by a growing frustration. It irked them that Knockfane might be wasted for a generation – they knew it had to come to one of their sons eventually as there were no other Esdailes in existence – when having the place assigned immediately would give their second son the chance to be prepared and made ready to take over when he came of age. But however much they discussed their frustration, and for a time they discussed very little else, they could not see how they could put their designs into effect. It was hopeless to try and enlist Lydia's support in their efforts to have their father change his mind or at least make known his intentions with regard to the future of Knockfane and the same applied to Julia. Although she was as much convinced as they were that the proper thing was for her father to make Knockfane over to Willis and have him come and live at Knockfane, she was not prepared to say as much to her father. Nothing, therefore, took place to disturb the status quo and Edward and Marion, and Julia and Lydia, were left in the dark as to what would happen to Knockfane after their father's death. That remained the situation for a number of years and it was still the situation when Willis died.

As Mr Holt droned through the lengthy list of bequests which Edward deemed to be trivial, it did not properly dawn on Julia and Fergal or on Edward and Marion that, in all that they had heard so far, there had been no mention of Lydia except for the fact that she had been appointed an executor of the will. Nor had it impinged on Lydia's mind. She was desolate that her father had just died – and so suddenly as well – and she hated his death being treated as an excuse to, as it were, share out his spoils when all she could think of was how much she had loved him and how much she was going to miss him. She was uncomfortable at Edward's obvious agitation and, although she knew that Marion had every right to be present at what Lydia regarded as a very sad and private family occasion, she wished that Marion was not there. At the same time, she was grateful for Fergal's presence and took comfort from the support he provided.

The reading of the will had gone on for much longer than she had expected and she was tired. She was also too hot and she wanted a cup of tea. Although she had a high regard for Mr Holt and knew that her father always had as much confidence in him as he did in the elder Mr Holt, she found herself irritated by him on this occasion as he enunciated all the legal wording with such particular emphasis on delicacy and refinement. It seemed unnecessary to her.

'Your father was very particular about the wording of this very important clause of his will,' said Mr Holt as he flattened the document on the desk before him. 'We discussed it many times before he was satisfied and even then he insisted that I take an opinion from a Senior Counsel in the Four Courts.'

'Pappy liked nothing better than a bit of a legal conundrum,' said Julia. 'He always said that, had he not been born to Knockfane, he would have made a splendid lawyer.'

'Did he say that?' said Lydia. 'I never remember him bringing that up.'

'He was always saying it, Lydia,' said Julia, 'how could you forget?'

'Well, I just don't remember him being so emphatic about it,' said Lydia. 'I remember how he thrived on challenging the Land Commission and his gratification when he defeated them over their original demands. But that was hardly a legal issue.'

'Of course it was a legal issue,' said Julia, 'well, as near as makes no difference. He fought them point by point. And don't you remember his tussles with the bishop over the closing of churches?'

'How could I not remember that?' said Lydia. 'It went on for years. Pappy insisted that just because there were many fewer Protestants today didn't mean that there would not be many more in the future. And that was his reasoning when Bishop Salmon wanted to deconsecrate so many of the churches in the diocese.'

'He defeated Salmon in the long run,' said Julia.

She chuckled.

'And then ...' said Lydia.

Mr Holt drummed his fingers gently on the desk. He glanced across at Edward and Marion.

'Girls!' said Edward. 'Do you think you could have this discussion at some other time? We're here for Pappy's will. Mr Holt would like to get on with the reading.'

Lydia and Julia composed themselves as Mr Holt took up his spectacles.

20

Knockfane Decided

MR HOLT APPRECIATED to the full the apprehension which must have been uppermost in the minds of the family who sat in his office that particular morning; and, cognisant of the possibilities for drama which the legal profession afforded, and knowing for long the contents of Willis Esdaile's will, he savoured to the full the position in which he then found himself.

'As I have mentioned,' he said, 'your father was greatly exercised as to how he would leave matters regarding Knockfane and he took enormous pains over the disposition which follows.'

At this point the sun shining through the windows, which up to then had given the room a mellow glow, went behind a cloud and Mr Holt's office became altogether more sombre. He switched on the lamp on his desk. The light coming through the green glass shade altered his complexion to a particular pallor that contrasted with the brightly lit pages on his desk.

He began reading.

'"As to my freehold interest in the farm and dwelling known as Knockfane situate in the Manor of Ballinacor and

Barony of Kilmolyon I give, devise and bequeath the same together with all the stock and crops thereon to my beloved daughter Lydia Annette Esdaile to have and enjoy during her lifetime under the following condition viz that she assign the said freehold interest either during her life or upon her death to a male Esdaile except in the event of the birth at Knockfane of an infant, male or female, either by name or blood an Esdaile during the said Lydia Annette's tenure in which circumstances full tenure and possession of the house and lands of Knockfane shall pass immediately to the said infant to have and to hold unto his or her heirs and assigns forever."'

Mr Holt looked up and surveyed in turn the faces of those who sat before him. But if he had hoped to perceive a reaction to the words he had just read, he was to be disappointed. Fergal and Julia, Edward and Marion, and Lydia all remained still. No one spoke. Mr Holt noticed the look of puzzlement and incomprehension which enveloped them all and, as a result, he found himself, unusually, at a loss for words. He was not certain if he should continue reading. There was still, he was aware, the final clause of the will, introduced by the familiar phrase 'as to the rest residue and remainder of my estate'. He wondered if the immediate revelation of the details of that disposal would satisfactorily defer the explanation – which he knew would be demanded of him – of the exact meaning of Willis Esdaile's disposition of Knockfane.

He glanced first at Lydia to see if her expression would provide a clue as to whether or not he should proceed but found her face devoid of all encouragement. The same was true of Julia and Fergal. They had not even looked at each other and, while they continued to face him, they did so blankly as though he was no longer there. Sensing that Edward and Marion could be relied upon for a reaction one way or another, Mr Holt grasped his courage and looked towards them. They seemed not to see him either and continued sitting as though they had been frozen to their chairs.

As Edward had left St Stephen's College at sixteen, he was largely uneducated in the subtleties of words and language and nor was he over familiar with the uses to which irony and understatement might be applied. In spite of these handicaps, however, he was capable of being exceedingly deft in expressing himself in certain situations and the situation in which he now found himself – as he sat across from Mr Holt – was one of those situations.

'Perhaps, Mr Holt ...' he began.

Mr Holt looked down at his papers.

'Perhaps, Mr Holt you might be so kind, for the benefit of my sisters and my wife, to elucidate ...'

And then he remembered that Fergal was also present.

'... and my brother-in-law of course ... elucidate exactly what my father meant by the clause you have just read. Or should I say what you mean. It is you after all, if I am not incorrect, who drafted the will. I am at a loss, you see, to understand what precisely the words mean and I feel sure that the others are equally in the dark. In fact, it crosses my mind that my late father may not have understood them properly himself.'

Mr Holt hesitated.

'Believe me, Mr Esdaile, your father was, as we say in the legal profession, "of sound mind and memory" when he made his will. He knew distinctly what he intended. I had very little say. Indeed, as I already mentioned to you, he did not entirely trust me to draft his wishes explicitly, within a proper legal framework that is, and as a result had me seek expert counsel.'

'Well then ...' said Edward. '... what did he have in mind? We are listening.'

'Your father wanted Knockfane to go to your sister Lydia for her lifetime,' said Mr Holt.

'I think we can all understand that part, Mr Holt,' said Edward. 'Absurd though it may be. It is the babies, male or female, and "by name or blood an Esdaile" which leaves me confounded and I think I speak for my sisters as well. Does my late father give any indication as to where such babies might be found?'

'Surely Pappy meant that if Lydia got married and had a baby, Knockfane would descend to the infant immediately at birth,' said Julia. 'It's obvious that he had Mama in mind and the tragedy that occurred when Lydia was born. He wanted to leave nothing to chance.'

Mr Holt beamed at Julia.

'There we have it in a nutshell, Mr Esdaile,' said Mr Holt. 'Your sister has got it in one.'

'Then why couldn't he simply say that Knockfane was to go to any child, or should I say "any issue", Lydia might have, unlikely though that is?'

Mr Holt was about to speak when he was interrupted by Marion.

'In my opinion it's all stupid and absurd,' she said. 'Lydia is never going to get married and she was never likely to get married even when my father-in-law made the will. It was ridiculous to take that into account. And as for having a baby, that was always about as improbable – and still is – as the man in the moon coming to live at Knockfane.'

Edward, Julia and Fergal all looked at Lydia. As she sat there, tears welling in her eyes, she felt embarrassed at the frankness of Marion's outburst. She did not look at her sister-in-law and when Julia put her hand to her lap, she sobbed audibly. Reaching to the floor for her handbag, she took out a handkerchief and blew her nose.

'I never ever wanted Knockfane,' she said. 'Never ever. And I don't want it now either. Anyone who likes can take it as far as I'm concerned.'

'Lydia,' said Fergal, 'this is an emotional time for everyone. We are all upset at your Pappy's death. It's too soon for any of us to know anything of what we really think.'

'It's not too soon for us,' said Marion. 'I know precisely what we think. Your father has made a will that is as twisted and contorted as his behaviour always was during his lifetime. Forever pushing us away and ignoring our Willis. It's obvious that Willis, his grandson, is his proper heir – that's why he is called Willis for goodness sake – and it is Willis, and Willis alone, who is entitled to Knockfane. Am I not right, Edward?'

Edward was by no means a meek man. His sisters could endorse that view and nor had his father ever witnessed any sign of timidity in the make-up of his son. Mr Holt did not know him well but over the past few days he had come to appreciate that dealing with Edward in the course of obtaining a Grant of Probate in the Esdaile will – even though Edward was not an executor – might not be easy. However, in coming to this conclusion, Mr Holt had hitherto not taken Mrs Edward into consideration. But now he saw that, within the purlieu of his marriage, Edward was a mouse while his wife, Marion, was at best a greedy harridan and, at worst, a villainous shrew. In an instant, therefore, Mr Holt was confirmed in his view that, when Willis Esdaile had decided to disinherit – to all intents and purposes – his only son, he perhaps had good reason to do so. In spite of that, Mr Holt, who was a fair-minded man, was able to sympathise with Edward's position. For the father of four sons, Willis Esdaile's grandsons, to be denied an inheritance which tradition, custom and common sense dictated as rightfully his, was unjust; and all the more so as the terms of the will – and Mr Holt had to admit this to himself – were so deliberately obtuse.

Shedding the condescension with which he had addressed Mr Holt throughout the morning, Edward adopted a more taciturn tone as he looked at his wife.

'Please, Marion,' he said, 'it's not the moment. Now Mr Holt, it's probably best if you finish reading the will. There's the residue to be dealt with, I think you said.'

'Yes, yes,' said Mr Holt. 'The residue. Indeed.'

In leaving the residue of his estate to be divided equally between Julia and Lydia, Old Esdaile delivered a final blow to his son and daughter-in-law. Marion was quick to make a mental tally. 'Just £1,000 to each of the four boys and some useless Land Bonds for Edward, and that's it,' she said to herself. 'Meanwhile that pair,' she eyed Lydia and Julia, 'going off with everything. I always knew he was a rotten old skinflint but I hadn't counted on just how despicable and unscrupulous he could be.'

She stood up and signalled to Edward to do the same.

'We'll fight it all the way,' she thought. 'They'll soon see who Knockfane properly belongs to.'

The reading of the will, therefore, came to a rather abrupt close as Mr Holt ushered the family out into the hall. There had been a prior arrangement that the five of them would go to the Mulhussey Arms for their dinner but Marion soon scotched that.

'This has all taken much longer than we expected,' she said. 'Edward and I need to get back to Derrymahon before dark so, if you don't mind, I think we'll be on our way without delay.'

She bustled out the hall door leaving Edward to say goodbye to Mr Holt and the others.

After the warmth of Mr Holt's office and the comfort of the coal fire in the waiting room, the hall was cold and Julia, Fergal and Lydia were not of a mind to linger too long in thanking Mr Holt for his kindness. Nor was Mr Holt anxious to prolong the engagement: Mrs Holt expected him home for his dinner and he was already later than usual.

He had, unusually, been unnerved by the morning's proceedings. The Esdaile will was, most likely, the most important – and the most interesting – will he would ever have the privilege to draft and he had looked forward for several years to the day he would be required to read it. He always knew it would give rise to discord but the lawyer in him – rather than the man – was excited by that probability as well as the hours of deliberation and exposition that would be demanded of him in order to tease out the full implications of the bequest. He could expect to have to advise Lydia as she came under pressure to make Knockfane over to her nephew Willis and he could foresee the disputes that might arise over Julia grazing her Aberdeen Angus at Knockfane. His experience told him that there would certainly be family rifts and feuds which were likely to endure for many years and it was well within the bounds of possibility that matters might go to court. Up to this, Mr Holt had had very little opportunity to demonstrate his legal brilliance in the High Court in Dublin but defending the challenge to the will that Edward and Marion were almost certain to pursue would provide him with just such an occasion and he had long since decided the stance he would take and the demeanour of his defence.

Meanwhile, as he stood in his hall, he was overcome with sympathy for Fergal, Julia and, more particularly, Lydia, and he felt the need to say something, anything. He gestured towards the set of engravings in black frames which lined the walls of the hall.

'My mother never cared for these,' he said, 'so when my father built the house on the Athcloon road and we moved there, she said she was leaving them where they were.'

Fergal moved to peer at the prints. He read out the inscription on one of them.

Wellington and Blücher at Belle-Alliance.

'Yes,' said Mr Holt. 'The eve of Waterloo. They are all Waterloo. This is *Quatre Bras* ...'

He moved along the wall towards the hall door.

'I suppose they don't make a lot of sense in a solicitor's office,' said Mr Holt.

'I don't know, Mr Holt,' said Julia who often surprised herself by how much she had learned at Trinity, 'Napoleon had planned for all contingencies; isn't that what the law is all about? He was not to know that, in spite of his planning, he would be defeated in the end.'

They all said their goodbyes and went out the door.

21

Miss Esdaile

WHEN IT EMERGED that Willis Esdaile had passed over Edward and bequeathed Knockfane to his younger daughter, people in the neighbourhood were taken aback; and the news, deemed to be very unexpected, became the talk of Liscarrig and Athcloon in the months that followed the death. The specific details of the will remained irritatingly elusive to the wider world but that did nothing to curtail gossip and, within a very short time, copious minutiae of conjecture and surmise were being stated as solid fact. It was accepted that the bequest to Lydia would be for her lifetime only and it was conceded that there must be further conditions too, although what those conditions were remained unclear. Some people averred that it had been stipulated that Lydia was to marry within a year, others were confident that it specified that she was not to marry at all. Somehow it leaked out – although how that might have happened remained a mystery – that a baby, or even several babies, had been referred to by Mr Esdaile but the whereabouts of such infants – or indeed their origin or purpose – was clouded in ambivalence. Some were happy that Lydia had, as they saw it, been 'rewarded' for the years of her life that she had given to her father but others had quite a different reaction.

'A shocking thing to do,' they said. 'Saddling a woman, and she is still young, with a responsibility like that for her lifetime. It's a noose round her neck but then he always was a selfish old man. An income for life out of the place would have given her freedom and allowed Edward take it over.'

In the weeks and months following Old Esdaile's death, Lydia inevitably felt his absence and she felt it a great deal. She was not alone at Knockfane as Rose lived in her room above the kitchen wing; but, although the two chatted during the day as they went about chores in the kitchen, it would have been unheard of for them to sit together in the evenings. Some few evenings, Lydia might have visitors – Reverend and Mrs West, the Coxes, even the Seymours – calling to express their condolences but scarcely bothering to disguise their pity for Lydia 'all alone in that enormous house'. After expressing pity, the callers would generally demand of Lydia what 'she was going to do' and then offer advice as to what they felt would be best for her. Lydia did not think she needed 'to do' anything. Knockfane was her home, she had never known another, and being alone there did not seem to her to be any undue hardship. Furthermore, the house did not seem enormous to her.

Julia set out to be supportive. Initially, she insisted that Lydia come over to Coolowen every Sunday for her dinner but after a while Lydia would make an excuse and not go. She did not care to be under any obligation to her sister and Julia barely disguised the fact that the invitations were issued in a spirit of her 'being kind' and with a sense of family duty.

Julia was of the view that her father's decision to leave Knockfane to his unmarried daughter had been foolish, and although initially she was considerate enough not to say this to Lydia, she did carp on about it to Fergal.

'Everyone knows how difficult it is for a woman on her own to farm,' she would say. 'People take advantage, no matter how much she is respected.'

In his heart, Fergal knew that to be true but he did not voice such an opinion to his wife.

On the Derrymahon front, all was silent for some time and Julia, Fergal and Lydia could not help wondering if this was a bad omen.

'No news is good news,' Lydia thought to herself.

Prompted by Julia's constant carping, she had become anxious in case Edward – at Marion's insistence, of course – would go to law and attempt to have the will overturned. Lydia dreaded the prospect of this happening, the rancour it would cause, the years of litigation it would entail, and for what? She would willingly give up Knockfane to avoid any such development.

But as the months passed, and life at Knockfane continued, nothing was heard from Edward and Marion; and, as to Julia's anxieties about it being difficult for a woman to farm, Lydia's adept management of cattle and crops, labourers and land, budgeting and balances, cash and cheques caused those to eventually dissipate as one farming season gave way to another.

Eventually, after about a year, Edward rang Julia one day out of the blue.

22

Plans

WITH VERY FEW preliminaries, Edward said to Julia on the phone that he would be in Dublin the following week for the Bull Show and, on the assumption that she and Fergal would also be there, he wondered if they might meet up. It was his way of stating that he wanted to see them.

Julia, although surprised by the call, consented and they arranged to meet for dinner at one o'clock in the Gresham. Julia and Fergal were relieved when they went into the lobby and saw Edward at the reception desk: Marion was not with him. There was a slight unease among them as they ordered: all three had the roast beef. Edward suggested a bottle of claret and, although Fergal and Julia only rarely took wine, they agreed. By the time the soup came, Edward had dispensed with such small talk as he was prepared to make and asked straight out:

'And so, how is her ladyship managing on the family estate? Or perhaps she's been too busy sifting her various proposals of marriage to think about much else? No sign of a baby yet, I suppose?'

'Really Edward, that's unnecessary,' said Julia.

But Edward ignored her.

'We've taken legal advice,' he said. 'And it seems as though we would have a very good case.'

'A very good case for what?' said Julia.

'For taking Knockfane over, of course,' said Edward.

The waiter wheeled the silver trolley over to the table and rolled up the lid. All three said they would have their beef well done and they watched in silence as the man carved. When he was gone, Edward returned to his theme.

'We've discussed it in full,' said Edward. 'Marion thinks we should go ahead but I have a few reservations. A court case over Knockfane might open up further land agitation locally. It wouldn't be good for the family to be seen to be fighting among ourselves over the farm. It could perhaps create a lot of bad feeling in the neighbourhood.'

'But Edward, Pappy made his will,' said Julia. 'It's legal and it's valid and it expresses what Pappy wanted. It's not for any of us to try and alter things. It's not Lydia's fault she's been left Knockfane.'

Edward seemed not to hear her.

'There is a way out of the situation without recourse to the law,' he said, 'and I think I could talk Marion round to it.'

As Edward proceeded to lay out the plans which he had hatched in respect of Knockfane, Julia – and Fergal as well – gradually lost sight of the fact that legally the place belonged to Lydia. Knockfane was Lydia's for her lifetime and Lydia, and Lydia alone, was entitled to live there. There was no question about that. And as there was no question, it might be concluded there was no need for an answer either. Yet Edward presented his case as though there was a problem for which a solution must be found and, without fully realising it, Julia and Fergal gradually fell in with him. When he proposed, therefore, that much the best thing would be for Willis – who would be seventeen next birthday – to go and live with Lydia at Knockfane – as Edward, at a similar age, had gone to Derrymahon – and gradually take over the management of the farm, they brightened at the idea. In fact they wondered why they had not thought of such a thing themselves. And when Edward said that there would be no need for Lydia to sign the place over to Willis 'just yet' and that such a step could be taken in a year or two when Lydia knew and appreciated what a help Willis was, Julia and Fergal both reflected on how very reasonable Edward seemed to have become. As the discussion went further and they talked about how greatly relieved Lydia would surely be to have the weight of the farm taken off her shoulders and what a pleasure it would be for her to have Willis's company about the place, all three of them became virtually euphoric. The bottle of claret was soon drained and, when they moved to the lounge for their coffee, it was – all three – as the best of friends. None of them imagined that Lydia would need any persuading as to the course of action they had decided should be pursued. In fact Julia could hardly wait to rush over and tell Lydia about it and, as far as Willis was concerned, Edward said that there was nothing to stop him coming up to Knockfane later in the summer.

When Julia went over to Knockfane the following afternoon she found Lydia in Crotty's Meadow – 'single in the field' like the solitary highland lass – as she later told Fergal. Expecting her sister to be thrilled, she gushed out the plan that had been decided, enthused as to how all Lydia's problems would be solved, and she waited for Lydia's reaction. She was staggered when Lydia seemed unmoved.

As they walked back to the house, Julia recounted details of the meeting in the Gresham, how Edward had changed entirely, how he had only Lydia's good at heart and was quite happy for her to stay on in Knockfane. How fine and sensible Willis was growing up to be and how marvellous it was that there would again be a young Willis Esdaile as Master of Knockfane.

'You all met up, behind my back as it were, and talked about me?' was Lydia's response.

'Nonsense, Lydia,' said Julia, 'we didn't talk about you at all. It was just about the future of Knockfane.'

'Pappy decided the future of Knockfane,' said Lydia.

'Well really, Lydia,' said Julia. 'Edward and I, even Marion if the truth be known, try to help you and, instead of being grateful, you choose to put your own ridiculous slant on things. You can be the very limit at times. We all want the best for you. So make your mind up now and have Willis come and live with you, and sooner rather than later.'

'I'll consider it,' said Lydia, 'but I am not making any decisions just yet.'

'But it has already been decided,' said Julia.

Willis did not come to live at Knockfane that summer although his father continued to advance his cause. In doing so, Edward deemed himself to be reasonable. But that was not how his sister, Lydia, perceived it and, as Edward persisted, she became all the more determined. Nor was she shaken in her determination by Julia's constant urgings about the absurdity of the situation. But Fergal, in whom Lydia confided over many issues, counselled her to take her time.

'You seem very happy the way you are,' he would say to her, 'why change things?'

And Lydia agreed with him entirely.

23

Young Willis

WHEN LYDIA CONSIDERED the plans which Edward and Marion, Julia and dear Fergal too, had made for her future and the future of Knockfane she did not care for them any more than when Julia first proposed them. In fact, the thought of having her existence impinged upon by another person in the house – however delightful young Willis might prove to be – filled her with dread. She avoided, as much as possible, further discussion of the matter with her sister and nor did she give in. It was out of the question as far as she was concerned for Willis to come and live with her and, as to any more long-term arrangements over the future of Knockfane, they were out of the question too.

She did, however, ask Willis to come and help her one summer when the harvest was very behind on account of appalling weather throughout the month of June. She had become fussed at the prospect that the wheat would never be saved so that when Julia suggested – as she did continually – that it would be a load off Lydia's mind if Willis came, Lydia agreed. He put things in order straight away so that all was done in a matter of a week or so. Lydia was relieved when she saw the grain safely up in the loft and the straw stored in the barn.

When Willis went home to Derrymahon again, Lydia found that she missed him. She had got used to him coming in at midday for his dinner and she enjoyed chatting to him in the evenings. He was interested in hearing about his grandfather and asked her about Knockfane in the old days. When, therefore, some other crises arose on the farm in the autumn, Lydia thought nothing of asking him to come and help again and the same happened in the spring. It was then that Lydia thought that she would like him to stay on and she had a proper discussion with him and arranged to pay him a wage. In that way, when he was almost twenty-one, Willis moved to Knockfane at Lydia's behest and without the interference of Julia, Edward or Marion.

It was from that moment that things changed.

Willis had been raised in the belief, quite erroneous as it happened but nevertheless inculcated in him by his parents from an early age, that he would one day 'come into' Knockfane and so his move to live with his aunt seemed to him to be merely a step in that direction. But Lydia, although cognisant that Edward and Marion wanted Knockfane for Willis, did not at all see the arrangement in the same way. She needed help with the farm, Willis was willing and amenable, and – as she found him pleasant company – she was happy to employ him. As to the longer term, it had on occasion vaguely strayed into her mind – but soon strayed out again – that she might one day bequeath Knockfane to Willis but in the meantime she had her life to lead and leading her life meant being Mistress of Knockfane. And that was not a role that she envisaged sharing with anyone, least of all her 20-year-old nephew.

She liked him and she had on his earlier stays at Knockfane spotted that there was in his manner much of her father about him. He had none of the edge of Edward and, as to Marion, it came as a relief to Lydia to discover that the boy seemed to have escaped the influence of his mother's character entirely. She conceded to herself – and occasionally voiced the same to Julia – that, be it due to his father or his mother, Willis had been very well brought up. He was polite and personable, considerate and kind, and she was happy to welcome him to Knockfane. But she did so in the belief that he was there to do her bidding.

When it came to work, Willis – as Lydia was to discover – was not shy. Nor was he incompetent. On the contrary, he was both extremely industrious and entirely practical. In normal circumstances he would have been an asset to any enterprise but it was his misfortune that Knockfane, as far as he was concerned, was not a normal enterprise. Had he been content to merely work for Lydia along the lines she had envisaged, all would have been well. But – and this must come as no surprise – he was not content with that, partly – it has to be said – because he did not fully understand the lines which Lydia, in her mind, had drawn. He was young, he was energetic, and he was able and, while he may have lacked experience, he had grown up with farming in his blood. Coming to Knockfane, he could not help but see the need for what he deemed improvements and he was oblivious to the fact that his aunt did not want improvements at all: in actual fact she dreaded them. She had her ways of doing things on the farm and, while she needed Willis's help, the help she needed was in carrying on as she had always done. She did not want to modernise: Willis wanted nothing else.

The farm machinery was all hopelessly old and out of date and Willis soon said that 'they' would need to replace most of it. Lydia was horrified by this and while she knew that the old Allis Chalmers tractor was always giving trouble, and indeed seemed to be out of commission more often than in actual working order, she felt the investment required in buying a new Fordson would be enormous and she suggested to Willis that he look around for a model that was second-hand. She urged similar compromises in respect of the other machines as well for, although she knew that she was very well off – Pappy's residue had amounted to a considerable sum – she had never spent lavishly in all her life and she saw no reason to start now. Willis, on the other hand, thought there was nothing lavish in what he proposed. Every expenditure, therefore, required negotiation, with Lydia trying to rein in Willis's extravagance, as she saw it, and Willis attempting to modify what he regarded as his aunt's inherent miserliness.

The same applied to other aspects of the farm as well. Since the time of the Land Reclamation Scheme in the 1950s, when her father had seen to it that several of the low-lying fields were drained, very little had been done to improve the land at Knockfane. Willis wanted to make up for lost time. He proposed going into silage and reducing the amount of meadow for hay and he wanted to construct a silage pit: to Lydia there was nothing wrong with hay and she had no wish to make the change. He suggested ploughing the River Field and sowing it in wheat: Lydia was aghast. 'Except for the time of the Compulsory Tillage during the Emergency, it had always been in pasture.' Willis saw the wood on the other side of the Liscarrig road as a wasted investment and suggested felling the trees and selling the timber. Lydia just said no. He was keen on fertiliser and said the whole farm needed potash but to Lydia crop rotation and farmyard manure had always been fertiliser enough and why go to the expense of buying artificial? Willis thought they should have many more sheep, Lydia viewed that as mistaken. He wanted to start a dairy herd: Lydia put her foot down. The back avenue needed to be resurfaced according to Willis: 'couldn't the potholes just be filled in?' Lydia asked.

Things between aunt and nephew gradually became more fraught so that, instead of the agreeable chats about the old times which Lydia had so much enjoyed when Willis had first come to Knockfane, she began to dread mealtimes and the long evenings once tea was finished. She had never taken to television but she found that, rather than having a discussion which might lead to discord, she was glad to watch anything and, once the evening news was over, she would go to bed.

Julia was impressed by Willis and thought him a charming young man and it is true that Willis, as a general rule, went out of his way to please. That is how Lydia, initially, saw him too. But, before a year of his residence at Knockfane was up, Lydia had changed her mind and had formed the opinion that Willis was a 'proper young pup'. This was not like Lydia who, in the normal course of events, saw the best in everyone. But it was symptomatic of the strain under which she was now existing.

It was inevitable that things would, sooner or later, come to a head and, as it happened, it was sooner.

The incident, in itself, was relatively minor. Willis, in the spirit of tidying things up, decided that what remained of the old slates on the roof of the loose boxes should be replaced by a new roof. Thinking that this would please his aunt, he went ahead and ordered sheets of corrugated asbestos roofing. But when Lydia saw the old broken slates partly removed, she was incensed.

'Those slates had been there for more than a century,' she said to Willis. 'It doesn't matter in the least if one or two of them is damaged.'

She was exceedingly angry and, in that moment, she said to herself that Willis must go.

'I spoke very harshly to him,' was what she said when questioned by Julia about the episode.

'How?' said Julia.

'I told him he must leave and that he must never ever darken the door of Knockfane again, so long as I live,' said Lydia.

'Is that all?' said Julia. 'I'd hardly call that harsh.'

24

Rumours

AFTER THE DEBACLE with Willis, and when things at Knockfane had fully calmed down, Lydia seemed to gain a greater confidence. The change was noticeable, particularly to Julia. Lydia was approaching forty but that landmark – although a chill wind for many – did not seem to cause her any particular despair or discomfort. On the contrary, as with a skiff setting out in a squall, the stiff breeze of advancing age seemed to fill Lydia's sails, propelling her cheerfully across the shallow estuary that was daily life at Knockfane. Julia observed the development in her sister and was pleased that Lydia was becoming very much her own person; but when Lydia's progress in this respect indicated that she might be becoming too much her own person, Julia's indulgence began to crumble. The change applied to Lydia's appearance as well. She had never troubled with her clothes and for years Julia had been telling her that she should smarten up.

Lydia knew that she had a good figure and, unlike Julia, she was not susceptible to putting on weight. Julia had to be very careful in that respect – and she was. Lydia did not have Julia's long limbs but she was far from being dumpy and, to

Julia's persistent irritation, Lydia always looked younger than her years. Her dimples stayed as dimples well into adulthood whereas Julia's finest feature – her striking profile – had to be rigorously maintained if it was to be preserved.

At first Julia did not comment to Lydia on her improved look except perhaps to say that she thought a dress, which was obviously new, suited her. But when one new dress was soon followed by another, and another, and Lydia's stock of shoes and handbags and hats and gloves – even nylons – seemed also to have been greatly augmented, Julia felt it incumbent upon herself to bring the subject up.

'You looked very well at the harvest festival last Sunday,' she said to Lydia. 'Was that a new frock you were wearing? I don't think I've seen it before.'

Lydia had been wearing a bottle-green georgette dress with a cowl neckline and a belt which accentuated the line.

'You didn't get that in Nora's in Athcloon,' Julia continued.

'No,' said Lydia, 'I saw it in Slyne's on Grafton Street. They often have nice styles there, suitable more for our age than for younger women.'

'Slyne's,' thought Julia, 'not cheap.'

With time, Julia became obsessed with the turn her sister had taken; and from being so critical of Lydia's dowdiness in the past, she progressed to complaining, mainly to Fergal, about how extravagant Lydia had now become.

'What is the point of it all anyhow?' she would say, 'stuck there in Knockfane all the time with no one for company.'

Lydia's brightening up, as it were, was reflected in other aspects of her life as well. She started going about more and often drove up to Dublin for the day. She revived the friendship with her old school friends, Heather and Joan – both of whom were married with children – and she met up with them on a regular basis. On Sundays, taking someone with her, she would go on visits, to gardens or houses open to the public, and when the parish ladies committee organised a weekend trip to Iona, she went along. She talked of going to the Holy Land when she heard of a group being arranged by the bishop and it was only at the last moment that she decided against.

Next, Lydia established her picnics. Remembering the picnic she had organised down by the river when she had first come home after leaving school, she decided to revive the event. The first year was a warm sunny day and she had about forty guests. The workmen from the farm came in their Sunday best and helped out and Lydia made a point of inviting their wives and children too. Mrs Rooney, Rose's mother, came with two of her other daughters who were home from England on holidays so Lydia had lots of helpers. Most of the guests brought some food, cakes and sandwiches and the like and Lydia served her homemade lemonade as well as tea freshly brewed on an open fire.

Apart from the swarms of midges which proved to be a torture on account of the proximity of the river, the picnic was a great success, although many of the elderly guests found sitting on the grass an agony. But people talked about how delightful the afternoon had been and how unusual, and Lydia was pressed to make it an annual occasion. She was easily persuaded but the next year it was a cold day with a wind off the river from the east and the picnic was much less agreeable, and the requests for the outing to be made an annual event were significantly fewer. Nevertheless Lydia's enthusiasm remained undimmed and, from year to year, she continued. It never crossed her mind that some of her guests came to dread the annual affair and she was always surprised when someone could not come: 'They must know that I am always the last Saturday in June, so how could they be away,' she would grumble.

Observing these developments, Julia chose to indulge Lydia and not make any comment or criticisms. It was Lydia 'making the most of things' and Julia was prepared to humour her. She adopted the same attitude in respect of many – although not all – of Lydia's other doings as well. But when a rumour reached her that Lydia had been seen having her dinner one day in the Country Shop Restaurant on St Stephen's Green in Dublin, and that she had been in the company of a clergyman, Julia's benevolence quickly turned to alarm.

It was only a rumour and it was by no means clear who had actually seen Lydia there, but the very idea of it, and the implication, was enough to set Julia at full tilt. She assumed what was, to her mind, 'the worst'.

'It's that Mrs Beatty,' she said to Fergal, 'I know it.'

She was referring to the dean's wife.

'Everyone knows she is always matchmaking: finding wives for widowed and lonely old clergymen. That's how Canon Hipwell came upon the new wife a few years ago after Mrs Hipwell died. The Beatty woman even boasted about how she had found the bride – as she insisted on calling her – down in Roscommon.'

'I'm sure Lydia wouldn't succumb to anything so foolish,' said Fergal.

Then he became quite tickled by the idea of Lydia's romance in the Country Shop.

'But maybe such a thing wouldn't be so out of the question,' he said.

But Julia was incandescent.

'Mrs Beatty would have a way of convincing Lydia to think of marrying,' said Julia. 'It's disgusting, that's what it is, and to some dilapidated old archdeacon or the like as well ...'

Fergal realised that, as far as his wife was concerned, it was not the moment for levity.

'I'm sure there is nothing in it,' he said. 'It's just gossip and rumour. No one ever knows how these things start. Why don't you just ask Lydia?'

But Julia could not bring herself to enquire of Lydia as to the identity of her clerical friend: she was too embarrassed and, more to the point, she was too furious. But she kept her ear to the ground for further evidence.

When none was forthcoming over the months that followed, and no new sightings were reported, she found that she was quite disappointed.

25

News from New Zealand

LYDIA, THE FARMER and Mistress of Knockfane, had her routines. 'Keeping one's nose to the grindstone' was how she often saw her life, but as the grindstone in question was Knockfane, she did not find that keeping her nose to it was any particular chore. She loved the place as she had always done and she loved her life as a farmer.

Mornings, she would get up before Rose came down and make herself a cup of tea. This she would drink standing at the Aga while the dogs outside the window, knowing that she was about to come out, jumped and yelped and whined. She would do the rounds of the yard with Daly and discuss with him what needed to be done that day: she seemed to seek his advice but Daly knew from years of experience that that was merely a ruse and that the Mistress always knew precisely what she required doing, and by whom and when. She would get back into the house by nine. Rose would be up, porridge would have been made, breakfast would have been set in the breakfast room, and a fire also lit there. She always sat in the same chair, to the left of where her father used to sit: the carpet under his seat was fully threadbare but at Lydia's feet it was merely worn. When the post arrived, together with *The Irish Times*, Rose would bring the newspaper in: the letters were saved for later and remained on the hall table.

It was on one such morning, the year was 1977, that a letter arrived in the post for Lydia that was out of the ordinary; but in spite of Rose's best efforts – and her curiosity – its arrival did nothing to interrupt Lydia's routine.

'Brown was here with the post earlier than usual,' Rose remarked when she brought in *The Irish Times*.

'Thank you, Rose,' Lydia said as she took the newspaper.

'That fellow has become desperate cheeky,' said Rose.

Even though she knew that her Mistress did not care for conversation at this hour of the day, she remained at the breakfast room door.

'He would nearly ask you what you had for your breakfast. I could hardly get rid of him at all today.'

'I'll look at the letters later,' said Lydia.

'Maybe I'll be getting them for you now?' said Rose.

Lydia opened the newspaper and started to read.

'I think I saw a foreign-looking one among them,' said Rose. 'In fact, that Brown had the neck to hand it to me separately. It's from New Zealand. I just happened to notice the stamps, all over the envelope they are.'

'New Zealand?' said Lydia.

She put down *The Irish Times*.

'Must be something to do with Uncle Todd,' she said. 'It's years since we have heard anything from them.'

'Will I be getting the letter for you now, Miss Lydia,' said Rose.

'I'll look at it later,' said Lydia.

She poured the milk on her porridge and reached for the sugar.

'That'll do for the moment, thanks Rose.'

When Lydia had finished her breakfast, she looked at the letters in the hall and, seeing that most of them were bills and statements, left them there. She examined the stamps on the New Zealand letter. Taking it into the morning room, she sat down and opened the envelope and then, turning to the last of its several pages, looked at the signature. 'Todd' it read in a busy hand and, above it, 'Your affectionate (and long-lost!) cousin'.

'Todd,' Lydia reflected, 'I never knew Uncle Todd had called one of his sons by the same name. You'd think that, after the way Granny treated him, the last thing he would have wanted would be to call a child after her.'

And then she recalled that it was always said that, had she herself been a boy, she would have been called Todd, her Granny's maiden name.

Seated on the sofa, she read the letter. It was – as she had suspected – from one of Uncle Todd's children. He wanted to come to Ireland and see 'the old homestead' as he put it. 'What would be the best time of year?' and 'Maybe he would stay for three or four months and get to know all the family. He could give some help around the place.' The letter gave no indication as to what age he might be but Lydia worked it out that he must be in his late twenties. He talked of other brothers and sisters; both his father and mother – Auntie Grace to Lydia – had died several years ago. The family were all still living in the Canterbury region near Christchurch. His eldest brother lived in the home place but farming had become very difficult as wool only fetched a fraction of the price it did a few years previously. He himself had a job – although he did not say as what – in Christchurch.

Lydia did not think too much about the letter after she had read it. But Rose's curiosity was not to be easily assuaged and later that morning, for the sake of some peace, Lydia shared with her the gist of what the letter from New Zealand said.

'Come here, to Knockfane? All the way from New Zealand? Is that what he intends, Miss Lydia?' said Rose. 'Lord God! That would be a desperate journey.'

'Young people nowadays think nothing of travelling the world,' said Lydia.

'I'd just hope, if I were you, that he'll want to go home again,' said Rose. 'Sounds to me like he's thinking of making a proper stay of it.'

'There would be nothing to keep a young fellow like that around here,' said Lydia. 'It would be all so different to what he's used to. He'll find that out for himself once he's here.'

'Do you mean to say you're going to let him come?' said Rose. 'Mrs Sale will have something to say about it, that's for certain.'

'Nothing may come of it,' said Lydia. 'It's probably just a notion the fellow got into his head and we won't hear anything more.'

26

A Minor Confusion

LYDIA DID NOT feel that Todd's letter required an immediate reply – any more than an immediate invitation needed to be issued either – and nor did she feel that it was pressing to relay its contents to Julia. And so it was not until Julia came over to Knockfane a week or two later that Lydia showed it to her.

'It's a bit gushing,' was Julia's response when she read it. 'If he really is, as you think, in his late twenties, it all sounds a bit juvenile to me. I mean this nonsense about wanting to get in touch with the spirit of his ancestors and learn about the family history. And he seems to have no clue as to what Ireland is actually like. What are you going to do about it? Are you going to let him come?'

'I wouldn't be very keen,' said Lydia. 'It would be an upset having someone here all the time. And what if people talked?'

'Do you mean about your having a man staying in the house? Now, that's ridiculous Lydia. He is our cousin, after all, and as far as we know, maybe half your age. So that's not an excuse. Besides, it would do you good to have some company instead of always being stuck here all alone.'

As being alone in her beloved Knockfane, and being free to do as she pleased, was a source of great satisfaction to Lydia, she was not immediately accepting of Julia's point of view; and the thought that her serenity might now be interrupted by the arrival of a young New Zealander endowed, as Julia surmised, with a juvenile outlook was not a prospect she could anticipate with any great enthusiasm. Nevertheless, after being coaxed by Julia, she did agree to reply to the letter and try to find out more.

Agreeing to reply to the letter and actually doing so was not the same thing to Lydia and, in the event, several weeks went by and she had not replied. Julia would ask her from time to time if she had heard anything further and Lydia, without revealing her own recalcitrance, would state, quite truthfully, 'no'. In time, this lack of development began to irritate Julia. The more she thought of Todd coming to stay with Lydia and 'bringing some life to the place', as she put it, the more she thought how splendid it would be, so that when there was no progress, she became dispirited.

After some weeks had elapsed, Todd wrote to Lydia a second time. He was still intent on coming over – in fact it looked as though he now wanted to come with some urgency – and he had gone so far as to book his passage. He would be arriving in London in six weeks' time: how would he make his way to Liscarrig from there?

Lydia was not someone who ever panicked and she did not panic when she read Todd's second letter. But she was, however, bothered. Six weeks hence would be one of her busiest times on the farm and the thought of having a guest in the house was horrific. There were practical matters to be considered. Where would he sleep? The spare room had not been used for ages and would need a proper spring clean. And the bathroom? There was always a shortage of water in the house during the summer months and, from what she had read, foreigners – accustomed to a hot climate – always insisted on having a bath every day. It would just not be possible. She wished she could air these anxieties with Julia but she knew from experience not to do so: it would just lead to a lecture. And so she did as she always did. She made the best of the situation and convinced herself that Todd's arrival would be no trouble at all and, in that frame of mind, she told Julia that he was coming and gave her the date. Julia was thrilled by the news but, after digesting the arrangements, made it clear that her enthusiasm was entirely for Lydia's sake.

'It'll bring some life about the place,' she said for the umpteenth time.

Lydia had Rose clean the spare room but when she had done so it still looked very dowdy. There was a bad stain on the ceiling from where the roof had leaked a few years previously and the old distemper on the walls was peeling off in places. Lydia thought of having the room redecorated and then she thought, 'Why should she?' She just had Corrigan from the yard touch up the ceiling. When all was finished, Lydia thought the room looked quite respectable: all that was needed was to make up the bed and, when that was done, Lydia replaced the old knitted counterpane with a pink candlewick that had been in her Pappy's room.

Todd was to arrive in London on the fifth of the month and, saying that he wanted to take a ship to Ireland, 'to make it seem more like coming home', Lydia had explained to him that he would need to get into London and then by train to Holyhead and the Mail Boat across to Ireland. From Dublin, he could get a bus to Liscarrig: there was a good service with a morning and an evening bus every day. Lydia would meet him if he could manage to telephone from Dublin to say what time he would be arriving.

Driving into Liscarrig on the morning in question – someone had telephoned from Dublin on Todd's behalf with the time of his arrival – Lydia was confident that she would have little difficulty recognising her visitor. He would certainly be the only stranger on the bus. She parked the Austin near the bus stop and, knowing that the bus would be late, she waited. Eventually it drew in and quite a number of people got off: what they had all been doing in Dublin, and why they would be returning so early in the day, Lydia could not imagine. Then she became puzzled: there was no sign of Todd. She could not have missed him as she had been standing on the pavement all the time.

'A mystery,' she said to herself.

She shrugged and started to make her way back to the car. Then she heard a voice call after her and the accent was unmistakeable:

'Cousin Lydia, it's me, Todd.'

She turned around and there before her, in front of Cooney's shop, was a juvenile replica of Granny Esdaile. It was as though the girl had stepped from the photograph frame that had always been in the drawing room. Lydia was flabbergasted.

'I just knew it had to be you,' said Todd. 'You are exactly as I had imagined.'

She put down her suitcase on the pavement and stood back, her hands by her sides, and looked straight at Lydia.

'Am I how you imagined me?' she asked.

27

Cousins

AS THE BUS pulled away from the kerb and the other passengers dispersed, Lydia was left alone on the footpath with her cousin. Ordinary civility demanded that she should say something and, in addition, Todd had asked her a question. But with confusion welling up inside her and anger, almost, that she had allowed herself to be so misled, Lydia could think of nothing to say.

She was not accustomed to being tongue-tied.

As a child, she had been quiet but that was because Julia always had so much to say that, before Lydia had advanced very far through life, she had come to the conclusion that it was easier to allow her big sister to say it. Whenever circumstances demanded it, however, and all the more so after she had gone away to school and out from under Julia's shadow, Lydia could be quite loquacious. Given to understatement, she was also witty. But as she stood on the street in Liscarrig on this warm June morning, loquaciousness and wit both deserted her.

She realised that Todd had never actually said in any of his letters – her letters – that she was a girl and that it had been entirely Lydia's own assumption – although Julia was also to blame; and she could see that it would perhaps be odd to spell out one's gender in a correspondence. But that did not alleviate the fact that – through her own fault, she knew – she had been led astray.

She had heard Todd's question, 'Am I how you imagined me?' and she knew she had to respond.

'Well, not exactly ...' she heard herself say.

Todd beamed at her.

'... but there's a strong family likeness, I would have to say that,' Lydia added for good measure.

Todd cut a robust figure, in manner as well as physique. She had what might be called 'an outdoor build' and she had an outdoor voice and attitude as well. Lydia attributed all of this to the fact that she had been brought up in New Zealand where everyone, she supposed, had to face the hardships of life in the outback. Or was that Australia? Lydia was not sure. She was certainly nearer in age to thirty than twenty and everything about her was blatantly casual: from her untidy hair to her lack of make-up, from the clumsiness of the way she was dressed to the tiny suitcase with which she had set out to travel the globe. She had blonde frizzy hair, a more golden blonde than one would normally see in Ireland: Lydia assumed it was because of all the sun. And if she had ever been possessed of a hairbrush, it was evident from her appearance that she must have left it behind in Canterbury. Her face, flat as a dinner plate with a very strong chin that jutted forward, was far from being pretty; but, nevertheless, it had something, although what that something was, it was difficult to decide. It was almost as though she was on her way to being, one day, quite handsome although it was equally evident that she still had some way to go in that direction. But it was Todd's voice that made the most immediate impression. It was inordinately rich and deep, so much so that Lydia found herself reasoning to herself, 'No wonder I thought she was a man.' But then she remembered that she had, at that stage, only Todd's handwriting as evidence.

The guest from New Zealand treated Lydia from the moment they met as though they had known each other from the cradle and, as they drove home to Knockfane and Todd chatted away in the car beside her, Lydia realised that she need not have been too concerned about making the spare room comfortable: Todd would have bedded down in the hay shed without a moment's demur. Nor would the bathroom be a problem: if the water ran short, Todd would be more than likely to go down and bathe herself in the river.

That afternoon Lydia went into the drawing room and picked up the framed photograph of Granny Esdaile from where it had stood for years on the mantelpiece. It was taken at the time of her marriage in 1888 when she was only twenty-three but her clothes, in the fashion of the time, made her look more mature. As it was an engagement photograph, Lafayette the photographer had made an effort to make the picture look romantic and that was how Lydia had always viewed it. But as she held the frame in her hands, and having met Todd, Lydia saw for the first time that there was more to it than that. It was as though the copy, Todd, being more like the original – Granny Esdaile – than the original itself, brought out the truth in the prototype. Miss Rebecca Todd, who was about to become Mrs Willis Esdaile, might look demure but Lydia could now see that there was also determination in the face. And, as this was the girl who became a woman who did not love her husband and later banished her son, Lydia could recognise heartlessness in her eyes. Here was the flat face and the jutting chin that her granddaughter from the other side of the globe, whom she would never know or see, would inherit. It was uncanny,

Lydia thought. She put the photograph down and took a moment to look around the room: as it was rarely used there was, even in summer, a mustiness about the place and a dampness in the air. Lydia came out and closed the door behind her.

Julia did not care for Todd from the start. Nor did Rose. In the case of the latter, it was easy to understand. She was used to being at Knockfane with Lydia, alone, and she did not welcome any intruder and, all the more so, a female intruder who was on an equal footing to her Mistress. She resented having to attend on Todd and she made it clear that she did not think Todd was worthy of being attended upon, much less by her. She would 'forget' to make Todd's bed, omit to lay her place correctly at table, and make a show of tidying up if Todd left any of her belongings around the house. She complained to Lydia about Todd all the time, albeit in an oblique way, and so much so that, within a few weeks, Lydia had become very, very exhausted.

Julia's reaction was different. Todd was just too direct and offhand for her taste and she loathed the fact that Todd – in her words – 'made so very few concessions to being a woman'.

'I don't know who you could introduce her to,' Julia said. 'No one around here would understand her, and that's a fact.'

'She's from New Zealand,' Lydia would say, 'she's bound to be different.'

'All the women in New Zealand can't be ...' Julia searched for the word, '... masculine ... like that,' she said. 'If they were, there would be no future for the place.'

Lydia, who by this stage had grown accustomed to Todd and did not see her as all that manly, tried to make excuses for her to Julia.

'Well, I just don't like her, and that's the end of it,' Julia would say. 'There's something about her. And I don't think you should encourage her to stay too long.'

Lydia did nothing to encourage Todd one way or another. They chatted, as much about life in New Zealand as of the old days at Knockfane, and Lydia learned something of how difficult life had been for her Uncle Todd when he first went out. She had known something of this from her father who had gathered as much from his brother's letters in the early years, although Lydia had never had occasion to give it much thought. Todd said that it was only rarely that her father shared any of his bitterness about being banished from Knockfane: whenever he talked about Ireland, it had always been with longing and affection. Some of Todd's brothers and sisters – her older brother Kim in particular – on hearing about the grandeur of the home place in Ireland, resented the way their father had been treated and the fact that he had been, to all intents and purposes, disinherited. They thought it was unjust and Lydia could see their point; but Todd did not seem to share their indignation.

At least, Lydia did not think so.

28

A Fateful Move

LYDIA'S GUEST FROM New Zealand did not take long to settle in. In fact, within about an hour of arriving at Knockfane, she was behaving and conducting herself as though she had lived there all her life. Not understanding fully the implications of Rose being Lydia's maid, Todd accompanied her into the scullery when that first dinner was over and announced that 'she would wash, if Rose would dry'. Lydia was startled by this but she could not think what to say. No such uncertainty clouded Rose's mind and she was ungracious enough to tell Todd to 'git out from under me feet, will ye, and laive me git on with me chores'. The incident was but a tiny spark but one that soon flared into a conflagration and within a short time Rose was consumed by hostility, jealousy and resentment in respect of everything to do with Todd.

Julia's distaste soon developed into an acute dislike and she talked of little else except how Todd might be ejected. Forgetting entirely how she had insisted that Todd should be invited and that it would do Lydia good to have 'some life about the place', she now declared that the experiment had proceeded far enough and she carped on and on at Lydia to put an end to Todd's stay without any more ado.

Julia had an ally in Rose even though it would have been out of the question for Julia to acknowledge as much to Rose herself. In spite of this constriction, she did contrive to indicate that she had an open and receptive ear and, should Rose wish to inform her of Todd's misdemeanours, it was within the bounds of possibility that she would listen. As it happened, Rose had a copious and incontrovertible supply of information in respect of Todd's nefariousness and she was more than willing to share this with anyone, and that included Mrs Sale. In this way, Julia was able to muster her arsenal for when she discussed Todd's expulsion with Lydia and demand explanations of her sister for the unnaturalness, and even the deceitfulness, of much of Todd's daily routines and behaviour.

Lydia found it as difficult to respond to Julia's concerns as she did also to Rose's insinuations. It was, after all, she who had closest contact with Todd and, while she would acknowledge that her cousin was an independent spirit and had some unusual habits and enthusiasms, Lydia could not see that the young woman was actually evil or that she had something to hide which is what Julia had taken to suggesting.

Lydia, in fact, had grown quite fond of Todd. She liked hearing her unrestrained views on any number of subjects. She came to admire her disdain for the conventions and even wished that she herself might on occasion be able to emulate her, even moderately, in that respect. And she was intrigued by the freedom with which Todd lived her life. More and more she saw in Todd everything that she herself was not and she came to envy this in her cousin. She reflected on how, as a young girl, she had never been able to get away from Knockfane, not even to a secretarial course in Dublin and she remembered how she had viewed Julia's suggestion of Paris as preposterous. Yet here was Todd who had travelled halfway round the globe without the slightest compunction. Nor did Todd have the weight of an inheritance on her shoulders and she was not bound, as Lydia was bound, to a way of life and to a legacy – Knockfane – that spanned the generations. Uncle Todd, Lydia began to see, had been released from the obligations of being an Esdaile when his mother sent him into exile; and while he – and his children – might never have seen that as a stroke of good fortune, as they eked out their existence in New Zealand, it crossed Lydia's mind, as she chatted to Todd, that that is what it might have been.

While Julia saw in Todd a large canvas, a dark picture of a treacherous sea, Rose perceived her as a series of sketches, preliminary studies as it were, for the finished work. To these two connoisseurs, the seascape that was Todd had choppy waves in the foreground, a ship run aground in the middle distance, and some threatening squalls on the horizon; and in the opinion of both of them neither the painting nor its sketches was suitable for hanging in the picture gallery that was Knockfane. Everything about Todd was unacceptable to Julia but Rose was able to detail the parts which constituted the whole and she did so by means of a catalogue of Todd's transgressions and iniquities.

Some of these were minor but others, in Rose's view, were momentous and one of the most momentous of all was Todd's move from the spare room into the spaciousness and graciousness of the late Master's bedroom.

After she had been at Knockfane for a month or so, Todd casually said to Lydia one day that this bedroom was everything she had always imagined Knockfane would be. Her father had often talked about the house and had described it to them when they were children: room by room, corner by corner, and even the sounds, the smells and the draughts. His description, Todd said, of the master bedroom was so vivid that, when she first walked into the room, she felt she had been there before. Lydia was charmed when she said this and she did not stop to think that the room Uncle Todd would have described would have been the room as occupied by Granny Esdaile. It did not cross her mind that her mother, Annette, had subsequently so altered it and so cheered it up that it would have been quite impossible for Todd, based on her father's description, to feel that she had ever been there in the past. It was only later that she realised that Todd had to be mistaken.

Todd took to referring to the room quite frequently and then one day quite unexpectedly – at least unexpectedly as far as Lydia was concerned – she said:

'Cousin Lydia, could I sleep in there one night? It would mean so much to me. It would make me feel that I really had come home.'

Taken aback by the proposal, Lydia could not on the spur of the moment see any reasonable objection and to her astonishment she heard herself say:

'You can sleep there every night, if you wish. Why not?'

Rose made no attempt to conceal her shock when Lydia asked her to tidy the room and make up the bed.

'Is it the Masther's bedroom that you are meaning?' she said.

She was in the pantry skimming the cream from the crock of milk.

'No one sleeps there, Miss Lydia. It just wouldn't be daycent to let … her ladyship … in there. Not daycent at all.'

She settled the ladle in the milk and covered the crock with muslin.

'What's wrong with her own room, can I ask? If you are asking me opinion, I think you should talk to Mrs Sale before doin' anything like that.'

Lydia did not at all see why she should have to discuss the plan with Julia and her irritation at Rose's impertinence – and her reference to Todd as 'her ladyship' – served only to quash any reservations that she might have had in permitting Todd to move to the bedroom of the Master of Knockfane.

Without any further discussion, Todd installed herself there later that week.

29

Gathering the Evidence

WHILE THE MOVE to the master bedroom might be said to have taken up an entire chapter in what amounted to Rose's 'Book of Evidence', there was an ever-growing number of clauses, paragraphs, sections and sub-sections in other parts of the book which constituted her irrefutable case against Todd.

It was Lydia who did the cooking at Knockfane, as she had done for years. She kept most of the ingredients for her cooking – flour, sugar and butter – as well as tea, cocoa, cakes, even nutmeg, under lock and key. This was because Rose regarded it as her absolute prerogative – loyal and devoted to Lydia though she was – to help herself as generously as she deemed fit before setting off home to her family on Sunday afternoons. Rose was quite brazen in her stealing and Lydia would excuse her – but rarely reprimand her – by telling herself that 'the poor thing' didn't know any better and that the Rooneys, after all, had always been thieves.

But if Rose considered it her privilege to help herself to food as liberally as she pleased, this was not a privilege which she was prepared to extend to anyone else and least of all to someone who already constituted a threat to her position on other fronts as well. Todd might well have moved into the Master's bedroom but, when Rose discovered evidence that she had also been in the pantry, something had to be done.

'I'm certain there was more than half that "caramel custard" left after the dinner yesterday and that I had put it on the shelf in the pantry,' she would complain to Lydia. 'But when I went in this morning, it was all gone.'

It was not just caramel custard which disappeared. According to Rose, all sorts of things like whipped cream and cheese and scones and cake and chocolate krispies also went. Even tapioca pudding with sultanas – especially tapioca pudding with sultanas – was not safe.

Lydia did not put too much store on all of this. If Todd was peckish at different times of day – even during the night – it was hardly thieving to help herself when there was all the food in the world available. She conceded that it might be more thoughtful if she would mention her snacking to Rose and seek her approval but it hardly constituted a major transgression and was certainly not sufficient cause to despatch her cousin back to New Zealand.

Then one morning when Lydia was in the yard, Rose stomped out to find her. Lydia knew by the way Rose was walking that she was excited and agitated and, if that was not evidence enough, the young woman's face – flushed purple – confirmed the impression.

'Have you been at your papers in the black desk in the morning room, Miss Lydia?' Rose demanded.

She did not wait for an answer.

'Someone has been at the drawers, I know it, and it's not been me,' she said.

Lydia started to speak but Rose did not mean to be pacified.

'No one is supposed to touch that desk except yourself, Miss Lydia. It was the same in the Masther's day, although he always kept it under lock and key. That's the way it should be now too. But Miss Butter-wouldn't-melt-in-her-Mouth has been at it and God forgive me for sayin' so.'

'I'm sure Miss Todd wouldn't dream of doing such a thing,' said Lydia.

'There's strange goings-on, Miss Lydia, I'll tell you that,' said Rose, 'as certain as Our Lady herself is Queen in Heaven.'

She marched back into the house.

That afternoon, when things were quiet, Lydia examined the desk. She could not be sure if the papers under the lid had been disturbed. Everything – bills, letters to be answered, bank books and statements, reports – got thrown in there when they arrived in the post and Lydia would sort them out once a month or so. More important documents – deeds, conveyances, farm maps, schedules, inventories, family records – were crammed into the drawers below. Some of these were tied with coloured tape, others were stuffed into worn envelopes. Lydia rarely opened any of them and, when she did, it was only ever to look for something that, invariably, she could not find; and then the papers would get piled back in again. There was no order to them and, when Lydia opened the drawers to see if they had been tampered with, she really could not tell. Lydia did not bring up the subject of the desk, disturbed or undisturbed, with Rose again and nor did she deem it worthy of mention to 'Miss Butter-wouldn't-melt-in-her Mouth' either.

She giggled to herself when she thought of the expression but it did not, as far as she was concerned, describe the Todd she thought she knew.

If Lydia did not notice when Todd was overcome by the cravings of a healthy appetite, or if she was not convinced that her cousin's exploration of Knockfane had extended to the recesses of her private desk, she did begin to observe that Todd had become more lax and lethargic than was the case when she first arrived. Similarly, she would occasionally be given to bouts of great activity and Lydia might return from an outing to discover that some enormous chore had been accomplished such as the nettles by the ash pit being mown down or the logs in the fuel shed being stacked. Generally, however, Todd spent more time in her room, rarely went into Liscarrig, took even less care over her appearance, and gave up on her efforts to make herself pleasant to Rose. Towards Lydia she was still the same but, nevertheless, there had been a change although it was not sufficient for Lydia to have any great concern and she still did not mind Todd's staying on at Knockfane.

This amiable atmosphere prevailed for several weeks following Todd's supposed meddling in the morning room but it was shattered one day by a further intelligence from Rose: the lock on the gun press in the boot room had been tampered with. Lydia could see this for herself when she examined the bolt. It was padlocked and the padlock was old so that the recent scratches were very obvious. Only Lydia had a key to the gun press and it was only Lydia who ever opened it. Her father's shotgun, together with a supply of cartridges, was kept there. Lydia became alarmed when she saw that someone had tried to open the press and she knew that she had no option but to ask Todd if it had been her.

She reflected for a few days on what she would say and how she would bring up the subject but, for the life of her, she could not come up with a strategy which would make her enquiries seem casual.

'Why on earth would Todd want to go near the gun?' she asked herself.

She had no doubt but that Todd, having been brought up on a farm, would know how to handle a shotgun and she appreciated that she was probably a very good shot as well. Lydia felt frightened.

But, before she had a chance to feel even more frightened, things came to a head and the tampered-with gun press faded into insignificance.

30

The Unexpected

ONE OF LYDIA'S regular activities was to go into Liscarrig every Friday to get the week's messages, change her library books, meet old Mrs Tyrrell for dinner in the Mulhussey Arms, and have her hair washed and set by Doreen. She would always leave Knockfane about half-past-ten and get home shortly before six. Every Friday, she did the same and, every Friday, she followed the same order of things.

First to Rafter's for the groceries where she would leave in a list, coming back to pick up the box at the end of the day; then to Hart's for rashers and perhaps a bacon joint as well. Depending on the week ahead, she might go to Skelly's for a roast or some chops. At Rowe's she collected *The Farmer's Journal*, *Woman's Weekly* and *The Leader* and then she headed to the hotel. Mrs Tyrrell, who was a vague family connection – Lydia had forgotten exactly how – was well into her seventies and lived alone in the town and it was Lydia's weekly act of charity to meet her for dinner and listen to her talk of times gone by. After dinner, Lydia went to the library where Miss Quinn, like Mrs Tyrrell, always expected a chat although her conversation – unlike Mrs Tyrrell's – generally focussed on the literary. Miss Quinn, unusually for a librarian, liked reading. Then it was on to Doreen. While Mrs Tyrrell looked forward to reminiscing and Miss Quinn expected a critique of the books Lydia was returning, Doreen required no such exertions. She demanded only an ear, receptive or not, into which she might discharge the weekly gossip of the town. Lydia dreaded this, and she certainly never gave Doreen any encouragement but, as she was the only hairdresser in the town, she had no alternative. With her hair newly done, Lydia would pick up a loaf at Langley's and call back to Rafter's. When she got home, Rose always had the tea ready.

It was on a Friday such as this in the November following Todd's arrival at Knockfane that Lydia's routine was brusquely interrupted.

When she stepped into the salon of Miss Doreen McEvoy, coiffeuse and beautician of Liscarrig, she had to apologise for being late. She had been detained at the library – although she did not think it proper to mention that as an excuse to Doreen; but Miss Quinn had insisted on a debate about *Middlemarch*, the book Lydia was returning.

'I could never have any patience with Dorothea Brooke,' Miss Quinn said, 'she wasted her life on that Casaubon fellow without ever seeing that he was a pompous fraud of a man.'

'Do you think so?' Lydia had asked. 'I read it that she felt it was her absolute duty to believe in him and support him.'

'But she was so obstinate, Miss Esdaile, and secretive. And tell me, is there anything more tiresome than an obstinate and secretive woman?'

Miss Quinn had the answer to her question, and to many other questions about the book as well, and the result was that Lydia was very late in leaving the library.

'Thanks be to God you're here at last, Miss Esdaile,' Doreen exclaimed when Lydia came through the door. 'I thought you would never come.'

She turned up the heat on a dryer under which peered the flushed countenance of Mrs Skelly, the butcher's wife, and she dashed over to Lydia.

'There's desperate trouble at home, it seems. An accident or the like. Rose Rooney telephoned. You're to get home right away and have Dr Bell come with you.'

Lydia looked startled.

'But my appointment,' she said. 'You don't think I'll have time to have a set?'

'I think you'd better head off straight away, Miss Esdaile,' said Doreen.

Mrs Skelly manoeuvred the dryer so as to permit a more ready access to her little pink ears.

'It sounded very serious,' said Doreen, 'very, very serious.'

Lydia rushed to find her car and drove out as fast as she could to Dr Bell.

'I'll go ahead of you,' he said when she told him what had happened. 'I'm sure it's nothing to worry about. All those Rooneys are very excitable so it's probably just Rose making a fuss.'

When Lydia got home and drove into the yard, Rose came running out the back door. Her apron and stockings were all spattered in blood.

'Oh! Merciful Mother of Jesus, Miss Lydia ... thank God you're here. Dr Bell is above with her now.'

She fell to her knees, moaning and wringing her hands. They too were covered in blood.

'Pull yourself together and whisht for goodness sake, and do stop that wailing,' said Lydia. 'And tell me what happened.'

'Sacred Heart of Jesus,' said Rose. 'Don't go in, don't go in … you'll be desthroyed by the disgrace of it. Desthroyed. Just thank the Lord the poor Masther is no longer with us, God rest his soul. It would have killed him. Don't go up anywhere near her, Miss Lydia.'

Lydia hurried into the house and headed for the boot room. The gun press was still locked, she saw that, and there was no sign, either there or in the kitchen that there had been an intruder or a struggle or an attack of any kind: no furniture overturned, nothing. Rose was now collapsed at the kitchen table, even more incoherent than she had been outside. Thinking of a cup of tea, Lydia went to put on the kettle but it was not where it usually stood at the side of the Aga. At that moment, she heard Dr Bell coming down the stairs. She went out to the hall. There was no sign of any disturbance there either: no blood on the carpet or on the bannisters. She wondered if someone had got in upstairs and attacked Todd in her room.

'Oh! Dr Bell,' she said.

He descended the last few steps and Lydia was surprised to see that he was smiling.

'What on earth …?' said Lydia. 'Tell me, I'm prepared for the worst.'

'I think you'd better sit yourself down, Miss Esdaile,' said the doctor. 'The news is not all bad, but you may be in for a shock.'

Lydia went over to one of the chairs that flanked the big hall table and sat down.

'What?' she said. 'An accident …?'

Dr Bell removed the stethoscope from round his neck.

'A fine baby boy, Miss Esdaile,' he said, 'and a happy and healthy mother too.'

'Gracious me,' said Lydia. 'Goodness, gracious me. I had no idea, no idea at all. Not an iota.'

'It's sometimes that way, you don't notice,' said Dr Bell, 'and he is over a month premature. Evidently she was in labour for not much more than an hour.'

'The same when Flossie, Jock's mother, had the pups last time,' said Lydia. 'Just sprang them on me, out of the blue.'

'Rose had the presence of mind to send Daly up to fetch her mammy. There's nothing about babies Mrs Rooney doesn't know.'

Rose had now come out to the hall.

'Isn't that right, Rose?' said Dr Bell.

'Thank God she came down as quick as she did,' said Rose. 'I don't know what I would have done. And the screaming from Miss Todd! It beats me that you didn't hear it in Liscarrig, Miss Lydia.'

'You did very well, Rose,' said Dr Bell. 'The little fellow wouldn't have survived without you.'

'Don't put that curse on me, doctor,' said Rose. 'The Holy Virgin herself will never forgive me.'

'Go and clean yourself up, Rose,' said Lydia.

She turned to Dr Bell.

'You've been very kind,' she said. 'Thank you. Perhaps we shouldn't mention in the neighbourhood what has happened, just yet. I think you'll understand, doctor.'

'Of course,' said Dr Bell.

'Now, I'll have Rose bring us tea. You probably feel like a cup, Doctor.'

'Well, it wouldn't go amiss,' he said.

31

Willis Again

LYDIA DID NOT go up and see Todd immediately. Shocked, it took time for her to appreciate that a baby had appeared, quite unannounced at Knockfane and that it had not been invited or anticipated. She was not without charity, and nor was she lacking in consideration for others, but an unexpected baby even in the best of families, was an unwanted baby and all the more so if it presented itself to the world without the customary accessory of a father. It was an awkward state of affairs, but it was by no means an exceptional one, Lydia reasoned; and the means of resolving it, as far as she was concerned, was quite easy to determine.

'I'll call Mr Holt tomorrow,' she thought, 'he dealt with the adoption when the Stuart girl got herself into trouble a few years ago and no one was any the wiser. It's not like in the old days when it would have to be sent to an orphanage. It'll be a godsend to someone. Protestant babies always are.'

Suddenly, Lydia felt much better.

She did not know what she was going to say to Todd. She was not sure that she even wanted to see the baby. She felt that Todd had betrayed her: 'Why didn't she confide in me?' she wondered. 'She must have known that I wouldn't have thrown her out.' She pondered as to whether Todd's family in New Zealand knew about the pregnancy or did Todd even know about it herself when she decided to come to Ireland? The birth was premature: Todd should have had another month to make plans. What had she intended?

'The things that happen!' Lydia reflected. Her thoughts turned to Knockfane. She remembered Julia's drama so many years ago. That was all about a baby too. She smiled to herself when she mulled it over. It dawned on her suddenly that she was the last baby to be born at Knockfane and that she had been born in the same room: forty-one years ago. And then the tragedy when her mother died a few days later. What must it have been like for her father with a baby only a few days old, without a mother, and his wife dead? These were darker questions and, from the shadows which they cast, Lydia found herself thinking, 'What if Todd were to …?'

She shuddered. It was though the blood was draining from her veins.

It was about nine o'clock when she went upstairs. Mrs Rooney was in the room and stood up when Lydia came in.

'She's dozing now,' she whispered.

And then, flushed with pride as though she was the mother herself, she gestured for Lydia to look at the baby. Lydia saw that Rose had made a makeshift cot out of the straw hamper that had been used in the past for sending out the laundry. It was stamped on the outside, in large black letters, 'Esdaile, Knockfane'. Lydia peered in. The baby, still very red looking, was quiet. It had no hair and had been wrapped in an old linen towel.

'Funny little chap,' Lydia thought. 'What a way to come into the world!'

The room was warm with a good fire flickering in the grate. The curtains had been drawn and, in order to reduce the glare from the light, the bedside lamp had been placed on the floor and the ceiling fixture turned off. It was all very cosy. Lydia was taken by the atmosphere in the room, it made a change from the Knockfane she was used to, but she could not think exactly how. Mrs Rooney bustling about, and the smells of the turf mingling with the carbolic and Dettol that had been used in cleaning up, and Todd comfortable in the bed: she looked soft and, Lydia thought, feminine for the first time ever.

Todd opened her eyes.

'I'm sorry, Cousin Lydia,' she murmured. 'I'm very, very sorry.'

Mrs Rooney tiptoed out of the room.

'I wanted so much to tell you,' said Todd, 'and I tried to, but I just couldn't.'

'Don't exert yourself with any worry now,' Lydia said, 'just rest.'

'I didn't know what to do,' said Todd. 'I thought ... I prayed in fact ... that I might lose it. When I did things like cleaning the windows and the strenuous work outside, I hoped that that might end it all. I even thought of shooting myself.'

'Don't,' said Lydia. 'Don't talk like that. You've brought a life into the world and that's a wonderful thing to do.'

Todd raised herself a little in the bed. She was very pale: washed out in fact. Lydia wondered if Dr Bell had left any instructions, or any medicine, because Todd certainly looked as though she needed something. It was obvious she had lost a lot of blood.

'Cousin Lydia,' she croaked.

'Yes ...?' said Lydia.

'I am going to call him Willis ... after your Pappy ... after all the Esdailes.'

'There's no need to think about things like that at the moment,' said Lydia.

She was standing on the hearthrug at the fire. A framed photograph on the mantelpiece of herself and Julia as children with their father had caught her attention. She was trying to remember when it was taken.

'No, I've decided,' said Todd.

Lydia felt for Todd at that moment. She saw how exhausted she was and she wanted to be kind.

'It's always the parents, Todd, who have the baby christened, after the adoption, and they choose the name. So you don't have to even think about that,' she said.

She moved over and sat on the end of the bed.

'How are you feeling now?' she said

'I'm not giving him away,' said Todd.

'And do what?' said Lydia.

'I'm keeping him.'

She smiled at Lydia and then she closed her eyes.

32

Legally Bound

IT WAS THE following evening before Lydia felt strong enough to report on events to Julia. She telephoned Coolowen and, in suggesting to Julia that she might like to pop over, tried to sound casual. But Julia was not fooled and nor was she in any mood to be casual.

'What's the matter, Lydia?' she said. 'Something's happened, I know it. It's her again. It has to be. What is it this time?'

Lydia's nerve failed her: and not just her nerve, but words as well. She did not know what she could say or how she might say it and, in her resulting quandary, she said nothing.

'Lydia, what?' said Julia into the phone. 'What have you found out? More of her stealing food, I suppose?'

Julia was referring to Rose's catalogue of delicacies which were in the habit of disappearing from the pantry.

'Is it the chutney again,' said Julia, insistent.

'No, it's not chutney, Julia ...' said Lydia.

'Well, what is it?' said Julia down the line. Her voice was becoming strident. 'What, Lydia?'

Lydia hesitated. She thought she heard little cries from her father's bedroom and, foolishly imagining that Julia might be able to hear them too, she blurted it out:

'... it's a baby, Julia. She's had a baby.'

There was silence from the other end.

'Julia?' said Lydia. 'Are you there?'

In the short twenty-four hours since Todd's unexpected confinement, Lydia had moved on from her initial shock; and the infant, who initially had been merely a commodity to be dealt with, had become, in her considerations, flesh and blood. Lydia had held him in her arms, had watched Todd – guided by Mrs Rooney – feeding him, and she had found herself cooing over him as any woman confronted by a newborn would be tempted to do. The words, 'the baby', had become familiar to her and so, when she said them to Julia, they sounded almost matter of fact. But Julia, lacking Lydia's knowledge of what had taken place, was stunned.

'Do you mean a miscarriage?' she demanded. 'Where?'

And before Lydia had a chance to reply she added, 'Is she alright?'

It was not said in any tone of solicitude but rather in one of hope.

'She's very, very weak,' said Lydia, 'but the baby is fine. He's very tiny but Dr Bell says he'll survive.'

By the time Julia came over with Fergal an hour or so later, she had had time to adjust her mind to the unexpected turn of events and she was extremely cross. She was cross with herself that she had not insisted more firmly that Todd's stay should be terminated; she was cross with Lydia for, among other things, not noticing that the girl was pregnant; and she was very cross indeed with Todd for bringing the unfortunate and indelicate situation upon them. She had no wish to see the baby and she did not want to confront Todd either. Uppermost in her mind was a desire to have the matter settled as quickly as possible and that meant having Todd and her offspring removed, either together or separately, from Knockfane and without a whimper of delay. She voiced the view to Fergal, who was at the wheel, that Todd had greatly abused their kindness and hospitality and that, in having a baby without any thought of being married much less providing any evidence of a father, she was nothing more than a common tramp. She had brought disgrace on the family which would take years for Lydia and herself to live down and that was not to mention all the worry and trouble she had caused which she, Julia, could very well do without. Just as Lydia, in her initial ruminations, had felt straight away that Mr Holt should be asked to arrange the adoption, so too did Julia and, on her arrival at Knockfane, she announced to Lydia that they would go and see the solicitor the very next day.

'He'll be able to get in touch with the adoption agency and prepare all the papers for Madam to sign,' said Julia. 'That way it could be out of here in a week' or so and no one is likely to know anything. Then she can then get herself back to New Zealand where she belongs.'

'It's all quite straightforward,' Mr Holt assured them when they went to see him the following morning. 'Normally it's all done before the birth but, as that's not been possible, I'll get in touch with the adoption agency straight away. There won't be any delay.'

'She hasn't mentioned anything about a father,' said Lydia. 'Does that make any difference? Would he have to sign something?'

'Technically, yes,' said Mr Holt. 'But the situation often arises, as you can imagine, that the father is ... how shall I put it? ... not forthcoming. His signature is not essential.'

Julia and Lydia looked relieved. They knew that they could rely on Mr Holt and it was a load off their minds that he would be able to settle things for them immediately. He had shared their astonishment – and their concern – when they first told him what had happened and he had understood completely that they would want to have the baby adopted. He liked being asked to take charge and to be of service again to the Esdailes. They were, after all, his most eminent clients. Julia and Lydia put on their gloves and, picking up their handbags from the floor, prepared to leave.

'There is just one small point,' said Mr Holt. 'It may not become relevant but I do have to mention it.'

Julia and Lydia settled back again.

'Yes?' said Julia.

'It's more a matter for Miss Esdaile than yourself, Mrs Sale,' said Mr Holt. 'It concerns your father's will. Your father could never have envisaged a situation such as this arising and it certainly wasn't his intention when making his will. He wanted to protect Miss Esdaile at all costs, as you will recall … but legally …'

Mr Holt looked directly at Lydia.

'… if you'll forgive the formality, Miss Esdaile …'

Julia noticed that Mr Holt, unusually, seemed to be uncomfortable.

'But legally … Knockfane now actually belongs to this little chap. Your own rights to the place for life have automatically been terminated by the fact of his birth.'

Lydia went blank. She felt dizzy and thought she was going to faint. Julia looked at her and then she looked at Mr Holt.

'I'm not sure I understand,' she said. 'What are you suggesting?'

'The clause in the will,' said Mr Holt. 'Your father was very conscious of the fact that your dear mother died in giving birth and he feared for the same happening again,' said Mr Holt.

'And ...?' said Julia.

'Well, you'll remember that, as a result, he stipulated that Knockfane would automatically descend – on birth – to any Esdaile child who was born there. He envisaged a situation whereby your sister might have married and then possibly died in childbirth. He inserted the clause to prevent her husband – who would not have been an Esdaile – inheriting.'

'But that is not what has happened,' said Julia, 'this is different.'

'It may be different,' said Mr Holt, 'but it is also the same.'

Julia was now very flushed. She had been sitting with her ankles crossed throughout the conversation but she now put both feet firmly on the floor. Her costume had a tight skirt and she tugged it down deftly over her knees. She stared at Mr Holt and then she looked across at Lydia and then back again at Mr Holt.

'It's time we called a shovel a shovel, Mr Holt,' she said. 'Are you saying that this ... this ... foundling, who is nothing whatever to either my sister or myself, and whose mother has ... has ... just ... blown in and only been a great nuisance to us both, are you saying that Knockfane is now his?'

'That's it,' said Mr Holt, 'in a nutshell. It's an extraordinary state of affairs but unfortunately, very unfortunately, it is the case.'

'I don't see why we need to tell her anything about it,' said Julia.

She sat back in her chair.

'About Pappy's will and its ridiculous stipulations, that is. She's likely to be none the wiser.'

'I'm afraid we have to,' said Mr Holt. 'We are your father's executors and we are legally bound.'

33

Further Arrivals

WHILE JULIA HAD become flushed, vocal and very, very flustered at Mr Holt's exposition of the delicate situation that had arisen, the information which he had imparted had the opposite effect on Lydia. She had become very pale and, for a while, she said nothing. Eventually, as Julia protested further to Mr Holt, Lydia intervened.

'I think, Julia, we should talk things over with Fergal,' she said, 'before deciding anything. In the meantime, Mr Holt, perhaps you would just look into the procedures for an adoption. It may be that you should come and speak to Miss Todd: about the adoption that is, nothing about the will for the moment.'

'Edward will have to be consulted,' said Julia.

Julia and Lydia went back to Coolowen. Fergal was there and they told him all that had happened at the meeting. He was as shocked as they were and equally at a loss as to what they should do. All three recognised that they should tell Edward but decided not to do so for the moment: it would only mean Marion trying to take charge and bulldozing her way.

Over the next few days, Lydia had time to think. Julia was constantly on the phone, asking this, wanting that, and suggesting one course of action or another, most of which appeared to Lydia to be quite impractical and impossible. Lydia, meanwhile, spent some time every day with Todd, chatting with her as she was accustomed to do. They talked about the baby, skirting the subject of adoption, and one day Lydia was able to ask Todd who the father was. 'No one important,' was all that Todd would volunteer. She was not pregnant when she first had the idea of coming to Ireland and only became so later. She had not told her family before leaving New Zealand but she had written and informed them since. They were not in the least put out as it was not an unusual occurrence among their friends and they felt that, in having the baby at Knockfane, Todd was 'among family' as they said. Lydia was startled that, from Todd's perspective, everything was so normal and there was no sense of crisis whereas Julia and herself were at their wits' end with worry and concern.

Rose, having survived her sudden and dramatic introduction to midwifery, was entranced by Willis and, at the same time, completely changed in her attitude towards Todd. Saying that Todd was 'a wonder the way she done it all on her own' and that Willis 'was the grandest little gintleman I ever seen', she took to spending more and more time upstairs while neglecting her other duties. Soon Lydia began to find that her breakfast was not always ready when she came in from the yard. The fire in the morning room was often not fully stoked. The rashers which came from Hart's were all gone by Wednesday as Todd was having them for breakfast every day. And then Lydia found six bottles of Guinness stout in the press in the pantry.

'Have you taken to the drink, Rose?' she asked.

'It's for His Lordship,' said Rose. 'The Mammy always took a glass of porter every day when she was feeding us, said it made all the difference. Her Ladyship didn't like it at first but she's got used to it now. And it's doing His Nibs a power of good.'

Lydia said nothing. She was not sure she cared for the turn which things had taken between Rose and Todd and, all the more so, as she had so recently had to listen to so many allegations and complaints. Although less than two weeks old, the baby had already altered Knockfane's domestic routines and it seemed to Lydia that she was no longer in charge and she did not know if she was pleased or annoyed. She was interrupted in her thoughts by a further observation from Rose.

'She's gone off the tapioca pudding, though,' she said. 'Says she could never look it in the face again.'

At that Rose cackled and hurried back upstairs.

Lydia knew in her heart that the situation could not continue and Julia knew it as well. There was a baby, and a secret baby at that, in the house and the baby's mother too. Their existence could not remain concealed for long and, as the possibility that the baby could be adopted and quickly removed from Knockfane receded behind the reality of Willis Esdaile's will, Julia and Lydia became all the more confused. It was only when Fergal became firm that the sisters were able to concede, however little they liked it, that Todd had some rights and, more to the point, so did the baby Willis.

'And sooner or later,' said Fergal, 'we are going to have to take the bull by the horns and inform Todd about the clause in the will. But before doing that Edward will have to be told about what has happened. It means, if nothing else, that his own Willis is now out of the picture as far as Knockfane is concerned and that is not likely to go down well, you may be sure.'

There the matter rested. It was time to stop making a secret of things: there was nothing to be secretive about. Their cousin had come from New Zealand in order to have her baby in the old family home; her husband had been unavoidably detained. The baby would be christened in Liscarrig church in a few months' time. After that, mother and infant would return to New Zealand.

But although this plan took care of their immediate quandary, it was only in the vaguest way that it addressed arrangements in the longer term; and that was for the very good reason that there was no longer term as far as Julia – and Fergal to an extent – was concerned. Todd would stay on until Willis was old enough to travel all the way back to New Zealand in about six or nine months. After that, contact with the New Zealand family would be maintained, much more so than had been the case in the past, and then, when the baby came of age in twenty-one years, he would inherit Knockfane and decide for himself whether he wanted to come and live in Ireland. Lydia would then be at a stage in her life when she would probably be more than happy, as the Sale sisters had been when Fergal first came to Coolowen, to have Willis's help and company about the place.

It was only Lydia who wondered to herself if this was really how events would transpire and, as she lay awake at night, the thought crossed her mind that Todd might want to stay on for longer than nine months. It was obvious that she had settled into the routines of motherhood with the same casualness and easy-going innocence that governed her entire existence.

One afternoon, when Todd returned from a stroll down the avenue while Rose nursed Willis upstairs, she joined Lydia in the morning room.

'I'll go and make a cup of tea for us,' she said. 'Would you like a biscuit with it?'

It struck Lydia that everything at Knockfane had descended into a muddle. Her maid was upstairs minding a baby, while her guest – which is what Todd was – was offering her tea. It should have been the other way around and it was Lydia's prerogative to ask for a biscuit rather than been offered one as though it were a favour. The fire in the room had burned down so that it was scarcely more than embers in the grate and Rose had not stocked up the turf basket. Lydia, resisting the urge to go and get some turf herself, decided that the time had come for her to get firm with Rose. As to Todd, she did not know, any more than she had ever known, how to deal with her as firmness was something to which her cousin was completely immune.

Todd came in with the tea. She had not set it on a tray, she had not used the tea cosy, and she had not brought the afternoon cups: the biscuits, she had left in the packet rather than putting them on a plate. She poured out two cups and, handing one to Lydia, asked her how much milk. This was a further affront: Lydia liked to put her milk in first. Taking her own tea, Todd huddled up to the fire.

'Kim is coming over,' she said. 'With Lauren. They're bringing the four children with them.'

It was as though she was announcing that the postman was about to arrive.

Lydia thought she had not heard correctly or, at least, that she had heard but that she had misunderstood. She took a sip of her tea but it tasted like washing-up water: obviously Todd had not heated the pot.

'Kim?' she asked eventually. She tried to sound as casual as Todd.

'My big brother,' she said. 'They want to see Willis and they want to see Knockfane. They want to see me too, I hope! The kids are very excited at the thought of it. But so are Kim and Lauren.'

'This is a bit of a surprise, Todd,' said Lydia. 'Don't you think you should have asked me?'

'It was they who decided,' said Todd.

From the morning when Todd's first letter arrived at Knockfane she had, as Lydia now reflected, been a continuous source of the unexpected. First of all she turned out to be a girl and not a man, and then there were all her other antics as well. Next there was the baby: that was hardly anticipated and now, it seemed, Lydia was to have all Todd's relations – a family of six – on her doorstep as well. Not that they would be just on her doorstep for that matter. She would have to have them to stay and, after coming all the way from New Zealand, it would most probably be for at least a month.

'When?' said Lydia, 'and for how long?'

'Oh! they're coming for good,' said Todd. 'In about six weeks. When they heard about the will, it decided them.'

'I don't understand, Todd,' said Lydia, 'What will?'

She found that she was becoming cross and, in her exasperation, she had not fully taken in the full significance of Todd's allusion.

'Your Pappy's will,' said Todd. 'I came across it in the drawer there.'

She nodded towards the desk in the corner.

'Todd, you had no business ever going near my desk,' said Lydia.

But she might have well said 'you had no business getting up in the morning' for all that Todd seemed to care.

'Isn't it well I did?' said Todd. 'Otherwise how would

I have ever known to stay on and have Willis here, and in the master bedroom too. I wasn't sure what exactly it meant when I read it first but then I sort of worked it out. I copied it out and sent it to Kim and he was able to get it confirmed that, if I had my baby here in Knockfane, the place would automatically be ours.'

'Ours?' said Lydia.

'Mine, and Kim's,' said Todd, 'until Willis comes of age. We'll hold it in trust. That's what Kim found out.'

34

The End

ROSE'S DESCRIPTION OF Todd as 'Miss Butter-wouldn't-melt-in-her-Mouth' came back to haunt Lydia. But, while she had smiled to herself at the epithet in the past, she did not smile at it now. She was completely puzzled. 'Gall' is the word that came to her. 'She has the gall to tell me that she has rifled my private desk,' she thought; 'and the gall to announce that, behind my back, she and her brother have sought formal advice on rights they never knew they had.' Lydia reflected on the sheer impudence of it all, including the plan for Kim and his tribe to come over with the intention, apparently, of settling at Knockfane. 'Where will I go?' she wondered. It would be a nightmare having the place – her home – taken over. It would be the end.

She thought of her father and his inexorable and unexplained opposition to Edward which was the root of her current predicament. Had Pappy bequeathed Knockfane to Edward, which would have been the normal thing to do, and made some other provision for her, this absurd state of affairs would never have arisen. Instead of that, Pappy – thinking only of the past and what had happened with Annette – had made this ridiculous stipulation in order to protect her, supposedly, from the designs of a fortune-seeking husband that she was never likely to find. Her anger mounted as she went over it all and she found – to her discomfort – that her rage was directed, not at Todd, but towards her father. He had brought all this upon her.

The temptation was to see Todd as completely evil. Deceitful, treacherous, unkind, disloyal, amoral were all words that might reasonably be used to describe her. It was unnecessary to give her the benefit of any doubt. But yet Lydia still held back. She could not fully believe that the girl was like that. It was Todd's open attitude to everything, her apparent simple-mindedness, her disposition to think that nothing mattered which governed her actions and however self-centred that might be – and it was utterly self-centred – it was not deliberately wicked. And so Lydia, although very much put out by Todd's conduct, did give her the benefit of the doubt and tried to make allowances for her. This was not easy, but it was possible and it was all the more possible when Lydia thought of baby Willis.

Lydia no longer considered him as a commodity, and a commodity that needed to be banished as quickly as possible at that. She had even taken to referring to him as Willis. She had thought about it. Her grandparents, who had once occupied the room which Todd – and Willis – now occupied, were Todd's grandparents too. The photograph in the drawing room of Miss Rebecca Todd – her grandmother – came to mind. Had fate dealt a different hand, it could have been Todd's father who inherited Knockfane and it could have been Lydia's father who was ostracised to New Zealand. By the same token, it could be Lydia – returned from New Zealand – who now occupied the ancestral bed. Instead it was Todd. Lydia, in her fairness, saw that Todd had as much right to be there as she had; and if the son, which her father had hoped she, Lydia, would produce, had in fact been born to Todd, what was the difference? He was as much entitled to Knockfane as her own son – had she ever provided one – would have been.

Lydia was weighted down by all these considerations and all the more so as she still had to inform Julia of the latest developments. The news that the family circle was to be greatly extended by the arrival of a platoon of six Esdailes from New Zealand would be a further blow. Her sister was agitating for Mr Holt to come and tell Todd about the will and 'get it over and done with'. It would be a severe shock for Julia to discover that Mr Holt's legal expertise would no longer be required because his role had been usurped by some New Zealand solicitor who had already advised Todd – and her brother – very succinctly.

In the event, when Lydia told Julia that Todd knew all about the will and that Kim was coming over, Julia came straight to the point; and it was not a point that Lydia had considered at all.

'They can't just descend here like that,' Julia said. 'Can they Fergal? It would surely be trespass if nothing else. We'll obtain an injunction to restrain them. And get an eviction order for Miss Todd at the same time.'

Then she turned her attention directly to Lydia.

'I cannot understand how you were ever persuaded to let Todd come here in the first instance,' she said.

Lydia, although agitated and upset and fully cognisant of the horror of her situation, was tempted to respond, but she did not.

Whatever else might be said about Todd, and by this stage quite a lot had been said although there still remained a sufficiency that had not been discussed, Lydia and Rose could only report that, as a mother to her son, she was without compare. She had an instinctive tenderness and warmth that was completely at odds with her personality and she was punctilious to a fault in attending to the baby's every requirement. Admittedly, she only paid heed to those requirements which she deemed to be reasonable and at times when Willis was, in her view, excessively demanding, she ignored him. She fed him promptly at certain hours and, no matter how much he cried, would make no exceptions. Fearing any form of skin rash, she did not approve of giving him too many baths but when changing his nappy – which she did according to a diligent timetable – she would sponge him vigorously and then dry him by the heat of the fire. TCP, which she demanded in quantities, seemed to play a signal role in his care, although neither Lydia nor Rose could discover the exact purpose to which it was applied. 'The Gripe', it became apparent, terrified Todd and, at the slightest grimace from the laundry basket, she would pounce on the bottle of gripe water and administer it copiously. But one day, when Willis was almost four weeks old, the gripe water did not work and he continued his agony. Mrs Rooney was called and pronounced that it was only 'a touch of colic' and that it would pass. But Todd was worried and she demanded of Lydia to take her and Willis to the hospital in Athcloon. There they stayed overnight. Three days later, back at Knockfane, the baby was reluctant to feed and the following morning seemed unable to swallow. Dr Bell was called.

'Not good,' he said when he had made his examination. 'It's diphtheria, I'm afraid. There have been two deaths in the hospital already and another child is critical.'

Lydia looked at Todd when he said it and Todd looked down at Willis. Rose, who was already on her knees black-leading the grate, prostrated herself even further. 'Jesus, Mary and Joseph,' she wailed, 'we're all scutthered.'

Two days later, Willis was dead.

35

Departures

TODD'S EXACT REACTION to the tragedy was difficult to fathom. She said nothing, although Lydia could see that she had wept a great deal. Rose had also wept a great deal, so much so that Lydia became very, very exasperated. Knockfane's domestic routine was in tatters. Meals were late, beds unmade, ashes left in the hearth. The staircase had not been dusted in weeks, the brasses in the hall not polished, the furniture in the dining room not waxed. No baking had been done, the firewood not brought in, the vases of cut flowers throughout the house not refreshed. There was a clinker in the Aga and a baby, albeit a dead one, in the laundry basket. Even the dogs had not been properly fed. Lydia was exhausted by it all.

Julia was very little help although it was she who suggested that Canon Mayhew, who was the rector of Athcloon should be asked to come and talk to Todd and that is what took place.

Willis, he comforted the grieving mother, would go to heaven: indeed, he might already be there.

'He is, to quote the scriptures, "without fault before the throne of God".'

Todd stared at him.

'That's because he was a Protestant,' said the Canon. 'Now, had he been a Roman Catholic ...'

But before Canon Mayhew had a chance to delve into his mind and recall to the best of his ability the Catholic concept of Limbo, Todd interrupted him.

'I don't believe in religion,' she said.

The rector pressed on.

It would have been Todd's intention – he was confident of that – to have had Willis baptised, he stated, and on that account the infant could be accorded a Christian burial.

Canon Mayhew, aware that 'a Christian burial' would mean 'an Esdaile burial' and the use of the family plot, had checked his 'theology' with Lydia before talking to Todd.

The funeral took place two days later. There was no church service, just the 'Order for the Burial of Children' said in the family graveyard at Knockfane. Only Todd, Lydia and Fergal were there. Julia would not go and Rose said that she couldn't be sure if Father Reilly would approve of her attending and so she stayed away.

'"Man that is born of a woman hath but a short time to live ..."' intoned Canon Mayhew.

Todd seemed not to be listening and she certainly showed no sign of emotion.

'"He cometh up, and is cut down, like a flower ..."'

Lydia was reminded that she must get around to staking the chrysanthemums or the wind would finish them off altogether. The ceremony was over very quickly and the little party went back to the house. Todd did not linger for a cup of tea but went straight up to her room.

It was just a week later when she announced that she was going back to New Zealand and that she would be leaving the following Monday. It seemed very sudden to

Lydia but she said nothing to make Todd change her mind. On the Monday morning, she drove her into Liscarrig and, as Todd was about to step into the bus, she handed Lydia a little brooch.

'It's just a cheap thing,' she said, 'but it was all they had in Rowe's and I wanted to give you something so that you would remember me.'

'I will always remember you,' said Lydia. 'Always. There's no doubt about that.'

Todd got into the bus and took a seat. She waved as it pulled away.

Lydia heard nothing from her after her departure. It turned out she had gone to relatives of her mother's in Scotland and had spent Christmas and much of the month of January with them. Lydia only heard this afterwards when she had a letter from Mrs McConnachie saying that Todd had been there and asking if Lydia knew where she was now. Apparently, in Mrs McConnachie's words, 'she had left some trouble behind her that they were anxious to resolve' but the letter did not specify what the trouble was and Lydia did not enquire when she replied to say that Todd had never been in touch since the day she left Knockfane. It was almost sixteen years before Lydia had any news. When Todd's letter did come, all those years later, it was as though she had been in communication all along. She was married and living near her brother in the outskirts of Christchurch, her husband was a metal worker and they had five children. She remembered the lovely time she had had at Knockfane and hoped that she had been a help to Lydia. There was nothing in the letter about what had happened and no mention of the baby, Willis. She hoped Lydia was well, and Julia and Fergal too, and maybe she would see them all in New Zealand one day. Lydia meant to write back but somehow she never did.

Her own life had moved on in those years and the episode with Todd had appeared more and more unreal as time went by. For a long time, she and Julia did not talk about it. They could not, and both of them wanted to forget the horror of what might have happened had Willis not died and how things at Knockfane would have been changed. With the passing of the years, the memory became less threatening and eventually the sisters were able to reminisce about the dreadfulness of Todd's visit and even laugh as they recalled some of the direst details. These conversations always ended with them both shaking their heads and remarking how incredible the whole thing had been.

'Even to this day,' Julia would remark, 'I often wake up in the night and think it can never have happened and that it was just a dream.'

'Me too,' Lydia would add. 'And I see Knockfane gone to rack and ruin and myself living in a room on the street in Liscarrig like old Mrs Tyrrell.'

But Lydia was not reduced to living in a room on the street in Liscarrig: she was living in Knockfane where she belonged.

36

Julia's Suspicions

WITH ALL THAT had been happening in her own life and at Knockfane, Lydia had not noticed that Julia was 'not well'. She could be forgiven for this as Julia had not noticed it either and it was only Fergal who had observed the change in his wife. There was nothing the matter with her physically: it was her state of mind that became a cause for concern.

On the surface, she was just the same old Julia. Bossy, interfering, dictatorial, and always confident that she was right. But Julia had always had a fun side too and, when she was not bossing and interfering, she was good company. Her determination and self-assurance had always been a source of awe in others, and not least in her younger sister, but it was also a source of amusement. Fergal, more than anyone, had always been amused by it and from the day when, as an 11-year-old, she had told him that the vine at Coolowen was 'the True Vine' and that it was 'hundreds or thousands of years old', he had admired her self-confidence and assurance. He had loved her for it. He still loved her but he was unsettled by how she had changed. She had lost her verve.

'She is often quite hysterical,' Fergal confided in Lydia. 'The slightest upset such as the rabbits getting in and eating the cabbage plants or, as happened the other day, Mrs Lyster calling up to the house unexpectedly, sends her off. She went into a proper tail spin over that, saying that she was ashamed that the house was so untidy when, as anyone can see, there is never so much as a pin out of place.'

'Maybe you should take her away on a holiday,' Lydia said. 'Portugal is supposed to be very nice. Or take the car and make a tour in France. She would like that and it would take her mind off herself.'

'I suggested that,' said Fergal, 'and she almost bit my head off. Asked how I could even think of such a thing when there was always so much to be done about the place.'

'Oh! dear,' said Lydia. 'I don't know what to suggest.'

She looked at Fergal. She hated to see him so worried and she felt cross with Julia that she would treat him so badly. His hair was fully grey now but, in other respects, he had weathered the years well and he was still a very handsome man. The gentleness that had endeared him to people when he was young became him all the more as he had got older. Lydia remembered how much her father had always liked him and how much he used to enjoy their chats. Julia was the only one who never seemed to fall for him fully. That was what had made him all the more keen, Lydia supposed. She thought of the callous way Julia had married him in order to suit her own selfish purposes but now, it seemed, she had forgotten just how much she owed to him and how grateful she should be. Instead of that she had become a burden to him, and a torment.

Lydia had always loved Fergal but she loved him like a brother: she had never wanted him for herself. But seeing him so distressed she did reflect on how different things would have been, for Fergal and for her, if it had been she whom he had married. She was sure that Fergal must sometimes think the same. Down through the years he had always confided in her and, without ever stressing the fact, he had always been a support to her. There was a very deep love and friendship between them.

'It's as though she has become a different person,' Fergal said another day.

He had taken to coming over to Knockfane more and more often and, although he attempted to give the impression of being his usual self, the conversation with Lydia soon turned to his problems with Julia. Lydia never offered any advice as she knew not to interfere; but, if Fergal wanted to get things off his chest, she realised it helped him if she listened.

'She has everything,' he would say, 'everything she could possibly want, and yet she's not satisfied. And nothing I do can make her more so. I might as well not be there.'

'I could try and talk to her,' Lydia said, 'but I'm not sure it would be any help. Have you thought of suggesting to her that she might see a doctor?'

'Do you mean a psychiatrist?' said Fergal.

'Heavens no!' said Lydia.

She was alarmed at the thought that Julia was on the verge of going mad. But when she considered it afterwards she realised that that was no longer what psychiatry meant and that perhaps Julia should indeed see someone like that. When she had suggested a doctor she had been thinking of Dr Bell and the possibility that there might be something physically wrong with her sister. She could just be run-down and in need of a tonic.

If Lydia did not deem it wise to offer Fergal any opinions or indeed any positive advice about Julia, neither did she see fit to address the matter, except in the most indirect way, with her sister. All her life, Lydia had been subjected to Julia telling her what she should or should not do and it would have required a considerable adjustment for her to adopt a similar role. She could not even bring the subject up with Julia, much less offer her any counsel. When Julia came over to Knockfane or Lydia went up to Coolowen, Julia was always very brisk, 'getting on with things as best she could' as she put it but Lydia could see what Fergal meant and that Julia was abnormally active and restless. On other days she would be feeling sorry for herself and seeming listless and then she would confide in Lydia that everything had really become quite impossible. When pressed by Lydia as to what precisely had become impossible, Julia was always at a loss to provide the full catalogue which Lydia demanded and, in her desperation, was only able to state a single source for her discontent.

'It's Fergal really,' she would say. 'That's the nub of it. He has become so distant. Sometimes I feel he might leave me. I don't think he has anyone else but I wouldn't be surprised.'

'Really, Julia,' Lydia said, 'don't talk nonsense. Fergal has always adored you. He does everything possible for you.'

'Not any more,' said Julia. 'He's there, of course. He's always there and we are together all the time but I know from him that his mind is somewhere else. In fact the more I think about it, the more I feel that some tramp or other has got her claws into him.'

'It wouldn't be possible, Julia,' said Lydia, 'it just wouldn't be possible. Such a thing would be remarked upon and gossip would spread like wildfire. Poor Fergal, how can you dream of saying such a thing.'

'He's often absent during the day,' said Julia.

'He very often comes over here,' said Lydia, 'he has always done that. He likes a chat.'

'There's that Mrs Pococke,' Julia said, 'the husband died not all that long ago. She was years younger than him. Everyone knows she is now on the prowl. She would quite likely make a pitch for Fergal.'

'Julia!' said Lydia, 'has Fergal ever mentioned Gertie Pococke? Has he ever even so much as passed the time of day with her? I can assure you that he would no more look at someone like that than he would walk to Timbuktu. Besides Mrs Pococke is not like that. It's just that she likes to dress nice.'

'Nice!' said Julia, 'did you see the cut of her in church the other Sunday, with a skirt up to her bum? I wouldn't call that nice.'

Lydia had become angry with her sister and in her anger she said what she had decided she could never say.

'You are not well, Julia,' she said. 'That's the fact of the matter. You are having delusions. Thinking these wicked things – because they are wicked things – about dear, dear Fergal is insane. I am going to take you to see Dr Bell and, if you won't come, I'll go and see him myself and tell him that I fear for your mind.'

'You must do no such thing,' said Julia. 'My mind is perfectly sound, I can assure you.'

'It may be, Julia, but at the same time you are not well,' said Lydia, 'and if you won't agree to see Dr Bell, I am going to find a specialist in Dublin. You need to talk to someone before you get any worse.'

Lydia told Fergal that she had spoken to Julia about her state of mind but she did not tell him that his wife was imagining that he was involved in an entanglement. It seemed so preposterous. Lydia laughed to herself when she thought of it. Such things did not happen in Liscarrig: at least, they had not happened for a very long time. In spite of her certainty, however, Lydia found that she became embarrassed whenever she ran into Mrs Pococke and, in her confusion, cut short any conversation. On the one occasion when Fergal mentioned the woman, apropos very little, she reacted the same way. Afterwards, she became ashamed when she found herself wondering if in fact there could be any truth in Julia's suspicions. Fergal, she thought, would be quite justified in seeking solace with someone but it would be so out of character for him to do so. As to Julia, Lydia found that having mentioned going to see Dr Bell on the one occasion it was easier to bring up the subject again but Julia always just brushed her suggestion aside. Then, one day, matters came to a head.

Mrs Pococke telephoned Coolowen and spoke to Julia as Fergal was out and about. Her bees were swarming, she told Julia, and the swarm would have to be removed. Her usual man was nowhere to be found so could Fergal oblige her by coming over as soon as possible.

'The absolute cheek of her,' Julia said to Lydia when she hurtled over to Knockfane. 'How brazen can someone be? I was so dumbfounded I just put down the phone.'

'Julia,' said Lydia, 'how could you? It was a genuine plea for help. Why wouldn't she turn to Fergal when everyone knows he is such an expert with your own hives? In point of fact, if there were anything between them, he would have been the last person she would have telephoned. Don't you see that?'

But Julia was incapable of seeing anything and just broke down in cascades of tears. Lydia called Dr Bell on the spot and asked him to come out to Knockfane.

And that was the start of Julia being on a regime of pills for a number of years to come, the end of Fergal's supposed romance with the tempting Gertie Pococke – who shortly thereafter married the vet in Athcloon – and Lydia's relief that she was free to get on with her life in the certain knowledge that Julia, notwithstanding her diet of daily medication, would be sure to find some cause to censure her.

37

Knockfane's Attractions

FINDING CAUSE TO censure her sister did not take Julia long and was prompted by Lydia's decision to take paying guests at Knockfane.

'They'll come for the fishing,' Lydia explained to Julia. 'Bed and breakfast. It's time the house was properly used.'

'I see,' said Julia. 'You are going to have total strangers staying in your house. You're likely to be robbed of everything you've got. You wouldn't know who would take advantage of an opportunity like that.'

'The new Tourist Office in Athcloon will send the people,' said Lydia. 'They'll know them.'

'How could they know them?' said Julia. 'I think you are being very, very foolish and I wish you wouldn't get involved in this. It's an invitation to disaster.'

'I'll be able to get a grant to install extra bathrooms,' said Lydia, 'that alone will make it worth my while.'

The tiny River Scarva which drained the lands of Knockfane had the reputation, perhaps exaggerated, of having 'the finest fishing in the whole of Ireland'. Etching its course through the limestone pastures of the county, it was rich in everything that the Irish brown trout most loved to grub upon, from the summer sedges at the water's edge to the blue-winged olive flies which shimmered across the surface on late warm evenings. Although Lydia had never fished, she was familiar with the Scarva's renown and it struck her that it would be a simple matter to 'spread the word'. So, in spite of her experience of house guests – the memory of the visits of her nephew Willis and, later, her cousin Todd remained fresh in her mind – she decided that it was almost her duty to have paying guests come to Knockfane.

Without too much ado, she prepared for her first season but then was somewhat disappointed when her only guests in the first month was a gruff couple from Germany who spoke not a word of English but yet managed to convey that they found everything about Ireland an abomination. They only stayed one night, ignored the appeal of the Scarva, saw nothing to admire about Knockfane, and refused at breakfast to eat rashers. Instead, they asked for cheese and then made known their disgust that the processed and tasteless Golden Vale which Rose produced was, in their view, not cheese at all.

Lydia was somewhat disheartened by this debut and wondered if she should say to the Tourist Office that she did not want any Germans in the future but, before she had a chance to do so, a French mother and daughter arrived in a battered pale blue Renault 4 and stayed five nights. Unlike the Germans, they were enchanted by everything they found. When speaking to Lydia, they made do with a broken English for their ordinary needs but when reaching for a superlative, as they did quite often, they reverted to French. Knockfane was described as a 'petit château' and 'vraiement impressionant', the farmyard as 'très mignon'; the garden was 'adorable' and the ensemble of the avenue and the lawn, 'un parc magnifique'. Rose was 'une domestique très correcte'.

They loved their bacon and sausages but Lydia was mildly put out at their insistence that 'les cochons irlandais' were so very famous. Although they were not interested in fishing, they spent time down by the river and wandered through the fields collecting wildflowers. Lydia was delighted by their visit and, when they waved goodbye on the last morning, it was with the promise to return again the following year.

The summer continued with other guests staying – but none so delightful as Madame and Mademoiselle – and not as many either as Lydia had hoped to receive. But she was cheered in August to receive a call from the Tourist Office enquiring if she would have two rooms available in early September for a week as a pair of Englishmen would like to come for the fishing. The trouble was that they wanted full board. Lydia saw this as no problem at all.

'It stands to reason that they would want to eat all the fish they catch,' she said to Rose, 'and as they will be out on the river in the evenings, they can have their main meal in the middle of the day.'

The booking was confirmed and Lydia was surprised to receive a cheque in the post in full payment for the week. It amounted to £190.

'That's nearly enough to pay all my expenses for the entire season,' she said to Julia when she showed her the cheque. 'Everything else will be profit.'

'You would need a good profit,' said Julia, 'being stuck with a pair of old duffers like that in your house for a whole week. I don't know how you can contemplate it.'

38

Fishing

THE 'TWO OLD duffers' who arrived at Knockfane that September were Dr Switzer and Mr Stokes. Dr Switzer was a general medical practitioner in Worthing and his fishing accomplice, Mr Stokes, was his brother-in-law. They had never been to Ireland before. It was almost nine o'clock the night they arrived but, in spite of the lateness of the hour, and saying that they had eaten something on the way, they insisted on getting in some fishing before going to bed.

'The evening rise is always much the best,' Dr Switzer said.

Lydia nodded.

'At least, in Scotland it is. But these Irish fellas might be a bit contrary. We'll see.'

He smiled when he said it. There was a playful wickedness in the smile and Lydia appreciated that his allusion to the 'contrary Irish', even though he was talking about the fish, was not intended to be critical or patronising.

The air was still warm that evening with almost a full moon promised for later on. When darkness came after ten o'clock, it rose – flushed orange in the eastern sky – and illuminated the silhouettes of the two fishermen, like a pair of poachers, on the river bank. It was after eleven when they came in. Lydia offered them Ovaltine and, when she suggested that they might care for a ham sandwich, they jumped at the proposition. Rose served it to them on a tray in the drawing room.

'I'll bring yis yer breakfast in the dining room, across the hall there,' she said to them. 'What time would ye be wantin' it?'

'Seven?' they enquired.

'And ye'll be havin' the lot,' she stated.

The two men murmured their assent. They could understand very little of what Rose said and, even if they had understood more, they would not have appreciated the Irish convention of making a statement as a means of asking a question.

Lydia had never thought of a man as being elegant but that was the only word she could think of to describe Dr Switzer. He was not so in any affected way and nor did he contrive to be dapper: he was much too tall for that and his dress, although carefully planned, was not in any way effete. If he was proud of his hair, and the manner in which it was brushed and oiled gave every indication that he might well be, he was quite justified in being so. There was not a hint of baldness and its former colour – for Dr Switzer was completely grey – was revealed by the woolly black of his eyebrows and the straggly hairs on his fingers. He had a slim figure and held himself very well and, of his many fine features, it was perhaps his hands that were the most refined. They seemed to Lydia to be wasted entirely on an ordinary family doctor and more appropriate, in the delicacy of the fingers, to a Harley Street surgeon. If one was to search in history for an artist capable of conveying on canvas Dr Switzer's masculine comeliness, one would look no further than John Singer Sargent.

The doctor spoke in an accent that was not oppressively British and he conveyed the impression, by a twinkle in his eye, that his words were never intended to be taken very seriously. Being charm personified, he was immediately sociable. Finding him absolutely delightful in every way, Lydia as well as Rose were very soon captivated. Lydia learned after a day or so that he was a widower – Mr Stokes was his late wife's brother – and that he had a son, Robin, who was 'eating his dinners' as a prelude to being called to the Bar at the Middle Temple. His daughter, Alice, was married in Canada.

Mr Stokes was by no means a dullard and nor was he entirely without looks or personality; but, in the company of Dr Switzer, he was as an ash tree is to an oak, a custard to a souffle, a melody by Tom Moore to an aria by Rossini. That is not to say that he did not find favour with Lydia. On the contrary, she liked him too and, as it was her habit to always look for the best in people, she managed to find depths to Mr Stokes that the still surface of his character tended to obscure.

Within a day, the two men had settled into a routine. They hastened out to the river after an early breakfast and returned, with or without a catch, sometime before noon. After the first day, they did not take lunch but went off driving and returned to eat in the late afternoon. After that they went back out on the river and there they remained till nightfall and beyond. August had been wet that year but, with the first days of September, the grey and damp disappeared and it was unusually sunny and warm.

For their evening meal, Rose fried the trout they had caught and served them with new potatoes and peas or broad beans from the garden. On account of the hour at which it was consumed, Lydia referred to this meal in the Irish way

as 'a meat-tea'. It did not matter that there was nò meat on
the menu and, after the first evening, nor was there any tea.
Dr Switzer requested wine. This promised to be something
of a dilemma for Lydia. She did not disapprove, but wine
with meals had never been served at Knockfane and nor was
Lydia at all confident as to where she might acquire it. She
supposed that they might have some in the new SuperValu
in Liscarrig but before she had a chance to investigate,
Dr Switzer elaborated that they had not expected it to be
provided and, in consequence, they had brought wine with
them: perhaps they might store it in the cool of the pantry?

Lydia, who did not breakfast with them, joined them
at their meat-tea. She sat at the head of the table and, with
her wine glass before her and Rose in attendance, she felt
for the first time in her life that she was truly chatelaine of
Knockfane. The role enhanced her, as a bishop is enhanced
by the grandeur of his cathedral, and it became clear as the
week progressed that the two men found her every bit as
engaging as she did them.

She asked them about the fishing and she received their
compliments about the Scarva with enthusiasm. They told
her about their days' excursions and the things about Ireland
which they noticed as being very different to England. Dr
Switzer said he liked the general untidiness every place.

'It's like someone who hasn't combed their hair,' he
said. 'It makes a change from the neatness of everything in
England.'

'I'm afraid there's a lot of litter everywhere,' Lydia said,
'people are very heedless.'

But the profusion of litter which Lydia deplored was
neither here nor there to Dr Switzer.

Inevitably the men asked about Knockfane, how Lydia
came to be living there, the nature of the farm, the family

history, the people round about and, one evening towards the end of the week, Dr Switzer questioned Lydia about her parents.

'I never knew Mama,' she said, 'she died when I was born. Pappy never got over it, really, although he lived on for another thirty-five years. He brought up Julia and me on his own.'

'It was just the two of you?' said Dr Switzer.

'Oh! no. We have a brother, Edward. But he was more or less adopted by Grandad, Mama's father, and went to live at Derrymahon – that's in Waterford – when he was still a boy. Eventually, he came into the place.'

'Adopted?' said Dr Switzer.

'Well, not really adopted,' said Lydia, 'I mean, not in any formal sense. It's just that Mama had no brother and so there was no one for Derrymahon. The result was that Grandad made Edward his heir.'

'Even though that meant that there would be no heir for Knockfane?' said Dr Switzer, 'I mean no male heir.'

'Pappy didn't view it that way,' said Lydia. 'You see, he and my brother never fully saw eye to eye.'

'No?' said Dr Switzer.

By now they had finished eating and both Dr Switzer and Mr Stokes were in relaxed mood. The sun had moved round so that it came through the tall windows at an angle, causing a shaft of light that illuminated only the end wall of the room, and throwing into relief the dust on the mahogany plate bucket that nestled under the sideboard. Lydia made a mental note to speak to Rose.

'Oh! dear,' she said, 'I've chatted away far too much. I am sorry if I have bored you. You can't possibly be interested in my family's tittle-tattle. I'm sure you are dying to get back out on the river.'

'On the contrary,' said Dr Switzer, 'it's fascinating the history that is contained within the four walls of a house. And do you and your sister see much of your brother?'

Lydia was taken aback by the directness of the question. It was unlike Dr Switzer to be so personal. She felt quite affronted and reprimanded herself for mentioning anything about her Pappy's attitude towards Edward. However, it was obvious that she had aroused Dr Switzer's curiosity but she had no intention of allowing him to pursue the subject.

'From time to time,' she said, 'but Waterford is quite a long way away.'

And then in order to make it sound as though relations with Edward were perfectly normal, and forgetting entirely the full horror of the episode that took place so many years before, she mentioned that Edward's son, Willis, had once lived at Knockfane for a while.

'Your nephew is called Willis, the family name,' said Dr Switzer, 'but not your brother? So it skipped a generation, as it were.'

'You could say that,' said Lydia.

She stood up.

'Now, to quote our national poet, "the evening is full of the linnet's wings" and there are a lot of very hungry trout down there in the river,' she said, 'just waiting for you. And if you don't hurry up they'll have had a very good dinner of real flies.'

39

A Meat-Tea

DR SWITZER AND Mr Stokes were different to the other guests who had come to Knockfane during the summer although Lydia could not think quite how. They were both very English, Mr Stokes particularly so. Nevertheless, Dr Switzer seemed to have an easy familiarity and friendliness that was, if anything, more Irish. Lydia wondered if she should introduce them to Julia. Dr Switzer had expressed an interest in meeting her. Perhaps she might invite Julia and Fergal round on their last day? Julia was sure to have some insights, however misconceived, about them and it would be interesting to hear what she thought. If nothing else it would make Julia eat her words in referring to them as 'a pair of old duffers'.

Julia was surprised when Lydia telephoned her with the suggestion.

'That's hardly necessary, Lydia,' she said, 'they're just PGs for goodness sake. You don't have to entertain them. It's not as though they are family.'

'I just thought you would enjoy meeting them,' said Lydia. 'It would make for something different, someone new. And Fergal would appreciate some male company for a change, I'm sure.'

Julia and Fergal came over on the Friday. After an initial frostiness on Julia's part, she thawed in response to Dr Switzer's entertaining accounts of his week in Ireland and, by the time the meal was over, she was almost flirting. She was taken aback at the ease, and even graciousness, with which Lydia acted as hostess and, when she first came into the dining room, and her eyes lit upon the wine glasses on the table, she barely disguised her shock.

'It's not quite what I thought having PGs entailed,' she said to Lydia afterwards.

Lydia waited for the barb and the reprimand.

'I mean, I had envisaged something like the guesthouse arrangement we used to have in Tramore or Kilkee. The owners never ate with us and we certainly wouldn't have wanted them to do so either. But you seem to have made the set-up very cosy.'

She blinked quite pronouncedly as she spoke. Lydia had noticed that her sister had taken to blinking like this and she wondered if it was anything to do with the pills she was taking.

'Very cosy indeed,' Julia continued. 'I could see that you have made them feel very much at home.'

'And why shouldn't she?' said Fergal. 'The two men are obviously very happy with everything at Knockfane and if Lydia welcomes them, as she has done, is it not only proper order? It's not supposed to be like staying in a hotel.'

'I'm not sure it is quite correct,' said Julia. 'I mean having two men in the house when you are on your own. People could talk.'

'Really, Julia,' said Fergal.

But he said no more when he saw his wife's frown.

When Mr Stokes and Dr Switzer left on the Saturday morning Lydia felt quite bereft. Rose too found herself at a loose end.

'You couldn't meet a nicer pair of gentlemen if you walked the length and breadth of Ireland,' she said. 'Do you think they'll ever be back, Miss Lydia? Was it all to their liking, like?'

'I'm sure they enjoyed themselves,' said Lydia, 'the weather made a great difference. But they didn't say anything about coming again, so we'll just see.'

Lydia thought about Mr Stokes and Dr Switzer quite often in the days and weeks that followed. She had only one other set of guests before the season came to a close, an elderly couple from Fermanagh with voices that tried her nerves, and then it was October and back to more mundane matters about the farm. Mr Stokes sent her a note to say how much he had appreciated her hospitality and then a parcel came from Dr Switzer. It was a second-hand copy of Izaak Walton's *The Compleat Angler* with beautiful illustrations by Arthur Rackham and he had written the date and a message on the inside cover: 'For Miss Esdaile as a token of appreciation for her conviviality at Knockfane'. Lydia was taken by the word conviviality. It meant more than other words he might have used such as kindness or hospitality or welcome or generosity; it was more personal and implied that it was Lydia's company, as much as the waters of the Scarva, that Dr Switzer had particularly enjoyed during his time in Ireland. She was amused by the book's subtitle, 'the contemplative man's recreation'. She did not think of Dr Switzer as a contemplative man and she had never thought of Knockfane as a recreation; and when she looked through the book, as she did frequently in the weeks after receiving it, it always caused her to smile. She smiled to herself at other things about Dr Switzer and his stay in the house, and when she wrote to him to thank him for the gift, she said how much she had enjoyed his company and how she hoped he and Mr Stokes would come back another time. She felt no shyness in expressing herself so fulsomely because, although greatly taken with the doctor and indeed sensing a warm affection towards him, she knew that what she felt was no more than friendship.

He was not like her father: that was certain. Dr Switzer had treated her as an equal. Nor was he like Edward towards whom she had never felt much affection at any time in their lives. Thinking of other men she had known, she remembered Giles Roleston: it suddenly dawned on her that she had never destroyed the letters she had written to him, twenty-five years or so since, which she had never posted. But she had no urge to write unposted letters to Dr Switzer, she was sure of that. She thought of Mr Benson and how she had felt the day, a few years previously, when she unexpectedly ran into him in 'The Country Shop' when they had joined each other for lunch. They had never seen each other since he had left Liscarrig all those years before but their conversation that day, as they lingered over cottage pie, had brought back many memories and, in Lydia's mind, many yearnings. They had both been reluctant to leave and Lydia was certain, when she thought about it afterwards, that Mr Benson had felt the same as she did.

He had told her about the years of suffering his wife had been through having developed multiple sclerosis when she was still only in her thirties and how bravely she contended with her affliction. He was then an archdeacon but still down south in the Diocese of Ross. His children, a son and a daughter, were at Trinity and were both sporty, like their father. Lydia had so much wanted to see him again after that day but knew that she must not do so; and when she never heard from him afterwards, in spite of their promises to keep in touch when they were parting, she understood that he had also sensed a danger. As a result she had locked away her feelings again in her heart and that was where they had remained; and, in thinking about Dr Switzer, she was confident that he was not, and never could be, the key that would reopen them. She felt a closeness to Dr Switzer, even though she had only known him a week, but there was nothing more to it than that.

Julia, however, saw things very differently. She had been almost hysterical in the car coming home after the trout meat-tea when she had met Dr Switzer and Mr Stokes and in the days that followed she allowed her mind to imagine that her sister had been taken in and that, in falling under the spell of Dr Switzer, she had compromised herself unduly. Dr Switzer was quite sinister in Julia's view and nothing Fergal said would shake her in her belief that he had come to Knockfane for a purpose; and his purpose was far removed, she was certain, from his ostensible aim of discovering the delights of the River Scarva.

'You must be able to see it too,' she instructed Fergal, 'Lydia is a sitting duck to be led up the garden path and someone like Dr Switzer, with all his fancy ways, is the very person to do it. I didn't like him at all.'

'That was not how it seemed,' said Fergal. 'You were chatting away to him. I thought you were delighted by him.'

'I had to be polite,' said Julia. 'And in fact, when I consider it, I don't think I would trust him an inch.'

'Not trust him?' said Fergal, 'what in heavens name do you mean? He has come over to Ireland with his brother-in-law for a week's fishing. There is nothing more to it than that.'

'There could be a great deal more to it than that,' said Julia, 'a great deal more. He's a widower for a start and what could be more interesting to a widower than a wealthy spinster with 600 acres and a beautiful house to her name? Have you not thought of that?'

Fergal saw that there was no point in arguing further and, as Julia had made up her mind that Dr Switzer was wickedness personified, the best he could do would be to try to placate her. He had never before thought of his sister-in-law as a wealthy spinster and he had difficulty in seeing her either as the siren who might lure an opportunistic suitor to the rock that was Knockfane. Lydia, in his view, was far too sensible to be easily misled and furthermore he knew that, unlike his wife, she was content and fulfilled in her life with no overweening desire to complicate her existence by either the pursuit or acquisition of a spouse.

'I'll have a chat with Lydia,' he said to Julia, 'just to put her on her guard. And we'll see. It may turn out that we'll hear nothing more from the said Dr Switzer.'

'Unlikely,' said Julia, 'he'll be back again, just you wait and see. He's not going to let things drop just like that.'

As to the 'things' which Dr Switzer was unlikely to drop, Julia was unclear. Uppermost in her mind was the thought that he would 'take advantage' of Lydia and that expression, she knew from her own experience, could cover a multitude of possibilities. Dr Switzer might prey upon Lydia's affections or, worse still, her money: he might even seek to marry her.

Fergal listened to all these concerns – he had no choice – but as he had seen nothing in Dr Switzer's behaviour that caused him disquiet, listen was all he did. By saying nothing he hoped that, in the absence of any evidence, his wife's obsession would, with time, dissipate. But like a woodpecker at the bark of a fruit tree, Julia would not let the matter rest and she continued her campaign of suspicions over the months that ensued.

'There's something about him,' she insisted, 'I know there is and I am never wrong about these things. I just can't put my finger on what it is. But there is something.'

40

Family Lore

LYDIA'S HOPE – and Julia's fear – that Dr Switzer would remain in touch and perhaps return another time to Knockfane was, in the event, to materialise. He wrote in early March to say that he and Mr Stokes would like to come for the mayfly and might they book for ten days? That visit renewed the friendship that had developed between Lydia and the two men and she got to know them better. Dr Switzer said he would love to bring his son to Knockfane one day but that Robin's making his way at the Bar made it difficult for him to plan and so, when it came to September, the doctor returned again with Mr Stokes.

Thereafter his visits became more frequent. Gradually he became known in Liscarrig and Athcloon – Lydia would have a fork supper when he was staying and in that way he met people – and, more and more, he felt himself at home.

Over his several visits, Lydia had told Dr Switzer much about the Esdailes: forty-thousand-pound Flora, great-aunt Dora in China, Granny banishing Uncle Todd to New Zealand. She did not tell him about her cousin Todd's eventful stay at Knockfane although she did impart something of the convoluted terms of her father's will. When she explained that her Pappy, by his unusual testament, was intent on 'protecting me from fortune hunters', Dr Switzer chuckled.

'Oh! dear,' he said with one of his wicked smiles, 'and I had such hopes.'

They laughed together when he said it.

It was only when he became interested in meeting Edward and Marion that Lydia became mildly agitated. There was very little contact between Derrymahon and Knockfane and for her to make contact with her brother with a view to arranging a meeting with a complete stranger would have seemed peculiar. And so she passed off all mention of Edward so that Dr Switzer soon sensed that he should not pursue his curiosity in that respect.

Although vigilant in observing Dr Switzer's progress, Julia was to be continuously disappointed that he gave no signal as to his true intentions with regard to Lydia or Knockfane. But that did not deter her in her belief that he did have intentions and that those intentions were possibly very sinister. To her dissatisfaction, he made no play for Lydia's hand, was over-generous in paying for his keep, was charming to everyone he met, and treated Rose very well. He struck up quite a friendship with Fergal, got to know Sam, and flattered Julia by asking her about the history of the Sales of Coolowen. He seemed fascinated by how the Sales and the Esdailes had often intermarried over the centuries and that the marriages, as Julia pointed out, were generally on account of some necessity; but, understandably, Julia was not persuaded to divulge the particular necessity which her own marriage to Fergal had entailed.

Dr Switzer was at a loss to understand how Fergal's grandmother, Honor Sale, could have cast out her daughter – Fergal's mother – simply because she had married a Catholic. This aspect of Sale history was made all the more piquant as Sam had recently married a Catholic. 'But nobody minds about mixed marriages anymore,' Julia said, 'not since the Catholic Church abolished their rule that all children must be raised as Catholics. When our son Sam married a Catholic a few years ago, it never occurred to us to raise any objection. Why would we when the girl was so delightful? But, as a sign of the times, that was not how the girl's parents felt about her marrying a Protestant. They only very reluctantly came to the wedding.' Fergal's story – being adopted as their heir by Martha and Eleanor, taking the name Sale, and his marrying Julia – struck Dr Switzer as 'like something out of a book'.

Apart from Dr Switzer and Mr Stokes, Lydia continued to receive other guests and remained on the lists of the Tourist Office in Athcloon; but after a few years, her visitors became fewer and, although she did not voice it, she was not much disappointed. Some people were appreciative and interesting but many were the exact opposite. Rose was getting older and less able for a lot of work and Lydia herself was glad to be without the bother of entertaining strangers. It was different in the case of the few guests who came regularly to fish: she knew them and they too knew Knockfane. They were no trouble.

'My regulars,' Lydia called them.

And if anyone enquired if she meant Dr Switzer when she referred to her regulars, she would reply 'Oh! no, he's more like family.'

41

Dr Switzer's Story

ADAM SWITZER'S PARENTS were both doctors with a family practice in Worthing. After his father died, of a heart attack when he was only forty-eight, his mother continued the surgery on her own until Adam qualified and then he joined her and eventually took things over. His childhood had been very happy: there had been just him and a younger sister and, until he was sent away to Winchester – his father's old school – at the age of twelve, he and his sister had gone to a local church school in Worthing. Frances, his sister, was sent to Cheltenham Ladies College but that had not been a success and Frances had had some sort of breakdown in her third year and was obliged to come home. She never fully recovered and, tragically, took her own life at the age of twenty-two.

'From being a happy-go-lucky, bubbly and adorable little girl, she became introspective, nervy and very sad,' Adam told Lydia when she asked about his family.

She drowned herself from the seafront in Worthing, he said, just near the house. Dr Switzer's mother always maintained that it was his sister's suicide which killed his father and Adam thought she was probably right.

Adam Switzer did not tell Lydia everything about his family. He did not tell her that one day in the summer before he went to Winchester, when he was twelve and Frances was ten, the parents took the two of them to Brighton for the afternoon. They did this from time to time and the children always loved going there: Brighton was bigger than Worthing, there were more people and there was more life, and there were always 'amusements' in the park near the pier. At the end of the afternoon they would have tea in the Old Ship Hotel.

That year, on the day they went to Brighton, the weather was very muddled. One minute the sun was shining and it was warm enough for Mrs Switzer to take off her cardigan; next minute the clouds would come in from the Channel and there would be a whipping wind from the sea. But neither Adam nor Frances minded very much: they were just excited at being there and being with their father and mother.

It was after five o'clock when they got to the Old Ship.

Throughout his life, Adam Switzer had never forgotten that tea for what followed but, in spite of that, he could never recall the details. He remembered his father telling him that he was a big boy now. 'A proper little man' were the words he used and he followed that up with the observation that going away to boarding school was 'a big step on the walk of life'.

'Frances is big now too,' his mother intervened, 'a real little lady and, in only a year's time, she'll be going away to Cheltenham. Won't you Frances?'

When his father next said, 'you know that your mother and I love you both very, very much', Adam became puzzled: Dada had never said such a thing before and it seemed odd for him to say it then. Thereafter, his father's statements became a blur and it was only that night after he had gone to bed that Adam was clear that – as he and Frances were eating the last of the coffee éclairs – their father had told them that they were both adopted. Adam did not fully comprehend what this meant and he was certain that Frances could not have understood it at all; but their father – and mother – had relayed the information to them in a manner that did not open the door for discussion and, in actual fact, throughout the remainder of their childhood and youth the subject was never mentioned by either parent again.

Not at all understanding what it signified, Frances was initially very cheerful about the news and boasted to her little friends at school that 'she was adopted'. Very soon she decided that one of her dolls, and the favoured one at that, had been adopted too; and so was Trigger the family terrier and Sooty the tomcat who lived next door. It was to be several years before Frances was moved to open the catechism that an adopted child is eventually driven to consult: the whys and wherefores of their mother's choice – or lack of choice – in parting with the little baby that they had once been. When Frances did eventually dwell on these questions it marked the beginning of her unhappiness and her failure to find answers which satisfied her were the stepping stones on the track that led to her ultimate disillusionment.

Adam's reaction to his parents' revelation was much more muted and, after his initial surprise, it never seemed to trouble him at all. He wondered, but he never enquired, if Frances was his real sister and if both of them had been adopted from the same parents and at the same time but he never felt the need to pursue this – or any other – line of enquiry. He knew that he loved both his parents and he felt part of them. He wanted to become a doctor because they were doctors and he wanted to be like them in other ways as well. While he did on occasion wonder about the circumstances of his birth and why his parents had decided to give him up, it was not something which preoccupied him unduly; and, while he did tell his wife that he had been adopted – and, at a later stage, also told his children – he never found it necessary to mention it otherwise or even to think about his origins very much at all.

After Winchester, he went up to Cambridge and read medicine and when he took his degree he did his Residency at St Thomas's. Deciding to see something of the world before settling down, he signed on as a ship's doctor and in three years sailed to Africa, the Americas, the Far East and Australia. On his last voyage, with the British India Line and sailing on the *Kampala* from Mombasa to London, he met the girl who would become his wife. She was the daughter of a colonial civil servant, sailing home with her parents who had been posted in Kenya, and she was more than ready to exchange the choppy waters of colonial society in Nairobi for the torpor of being a doctor's wife in a genteel English seaside town. Thereafter Adam's life would mirror that of his parents with the single exception that his children, Robin and Alice, rather than being adopted, were the offspring of his marriage. His wife's death from cancer when she was only in her fifties was a great blow but his mother's death a few years later, at the age of ninety-two, came as a relief rather than a shock. She had lived for years in a flat in one of the large houses in Ambrose Place. And it was in the process of clearing out that flat that Adam came upon an envelope, safely hidden in one of the drawers of her writing desk, marked 'Very Private'. Feeling duty bound to open it, he found therein a birth certificate for a baby boy, born the same day as himself, the birth having taken place in St George's Care Home, Ascot.

The mother was listed on the certificate as 'Annette Odlum, Spinster of County Waterford, Ireland', the father as 'Unknown'.

42

A Quandary

ADAM SWITZER HAD been going to his mother's flat almost every day for weeks in order to clear it out. The process had become a chore to him and he had become more and more dispirited as there always seemed to be further cupboards to investigate and more drawers to be emptied. He wanted to be finished with the ordeal. Having opened the 'Very Private' envelope and glanced at the contents, he put it in his pocket and it was only when he was at home that evening that he took it out and studied the papers it contained.

He was uncertain, taking into account what he knew of the adoption laws of the time, how his parents could have been given such a certificate which he deduced must be his own original birth certificate and different to the one that had always been available to him which listed his Switzer parents. His conclusion was confirmed by other papers in the envelope including an old letter from the Registrar of St George's Home obviously written in reply to to his father which confirmed that the records showed that a baby boy had been born in the home to an Annette Odlum on the very day of his birth. Seeing his mother's name written in the letter brought home to him for the first time in his life the actual reality of his adoption. It made him wonder who this girl from Ireland – his mother – had been, why his father was listed as 'unknown', and what were the circumstances which occasioned 'Annette Odlum' to have her baby in an English home for orphans, and then give the baby up. The documents opened up so many issues for him but, as he sat in his study that evening and sipped on his nightly glass of whiskey, it crossed his mind that he may not have wanted to know the answers.

'I had loving parents and a privileged and happy childhood,' he told himself, 'and a wonderful and contented later family life. Why disturb things now and uncover realities that I may not want to know?'

He decided, therefore, to do nothing and he tried to put the matter out of his mind.

He did not mention his discovery to his son Robin or daughter, Alice, and nor did he tell anyone else. But the questions remained in his head and, like a bee trapped in a web, buzzed in his consciousness. Eventually, he decided that he would act.

He decided to consult his solicitor who was also an old friend. The solicitor made the sensible suggestion that it might be an idea to learn more about Miss Odlum of County Waterford before alerting anyone as to his own – or her – identity; and to that end he recommended getting in touch with a firm of solicitors in Ireland and instructing them to find out what they could. The report, from Moynan, Osborne Purser in Dublin, did not take long to come through and was fully satisfactory. Annette Odlum was the daughter of the late T.E. Odlum of Derrymahon, County Waterford, and she would have been eighteen when Adam was born. She subsequently married a Mr Willis Esdaile of Knockfane and had three children. She had died when she was twenty-nine.

And that was that, as far as Adam was concerned: his mother had died while he was still only a little boy and he would never know who his father was. There was little more to ascertain although the report had indicated that both the Odlums and the Esdailes were old and respected landed Protestant families. It did, of course, cross Adam's mind that, as his mother subsequently had three more children, he must have half-brothers or sisters in Ireland but he was not at all sure that he was very enthusiastic about this connection. He knew nothing about Ireland and it was only by very small steps, one at a time, that he could come to terms with the fact that he himself was at least half Irish.

It was a year or two later that he read an article about the Irish brown trout, and the Irish way of catching them by dapping, in *Trout & Salmon Magazine*. Then he saw a programme on television about salmon fishing on the River Blackwater in County Cork. By coincidence, his brother-in-law, with whom he had always fished in Scotland, mentioned one day that they ought to try Ireland for a change, and so, over the next winter, even though he was only mildly committed to the idea, Adam investigated.

He sent off for information from the Irish Tourist Board in London and waded his way through the packet of brochures and leaflets which they sent him. None of them seemed to tell him all that much and the holiday accommodation listed in the *Places to Stay* booklet seemed to him to be equally unappealing. Then his eyes fell on the name: 'Esdaile', and the place, 'Knockfane'. He was stunned.

There was a description of the house, the number of rooms available, the daily rates, and the attractions of the River Scarva. He read down until he came to the words, 'Proprietor: Miss Lydia Esdaile' and then he could read no more. He shivered and put the book down on his lap.

'This has to be my sister,' he said to himself, 'my half-sister Lydia.'

In the days and weeks that followed, Adam Switzer did not know what he felt. Sometimes, when he was feeling light-hearted, he thought it would be entertaining to go to Ireland, stay as a fishing guest at Knockfane, and surprise his half-sister by telling her who he was. At other times, he saw how reckless such a course of action would be and the trauma it might induce in 'Miss Lydia Esdaile' to discover by such a means that she had a half-brother. Part of him wanted to make the connection and to discover his 'family'; but, unable to decide how such an outcome might be achieved, he would eventually abandon his deliberations and decide that it would all be quite impossible. Meanwhile, Mr Stokes became more and more insistent on the need to make some plans.

'I'm leaving it all to you,' he would say, 'but we do need to book soon. I'm now quite set on the idea of going to Ireland this year and I thought you were too.'

When, at the end of July, and with nothing still arranged, Mr Stokes offered to take over making the plans, Adam found that, within himself, he became quite agitated.

'He wouldn't book Knockfane,' he thought, 'it would mean going someplace else. There would be no point.'

With the realisation that Knockfane, rather than the lure of the Irish brown trout, had now become in his mind 'the point' of his going to Ireland, Adam Switzer conceded that he must do something. He wrote to the Tourist Office in Athcloon that very evening and requested the booking for four weeks hence. He went out and posted the letter before he went to bed.

'I can always cancel if I change my mind,' he assured himself.

But, although tempted to do so in the weeks that followed, he never did cancel and so when he arrived at Knockfane it was, unknown to his brother-in-law and fishing companion, in a state of very considerable apprehension.

43

Being Moved

AS DR SWITZER and Mr Stokes drove in through the gates of
Knockfane, Julia's Angus – that year's heifers – interrupted
their evening grazing to eye the intrusion with curiosity.
Driving up the long avenue, Adam was surprised at the lush
tranquility of the setting and, as the car made its way past
the centuries-old chestnut and beech and the house was still
not in view, he wondered if they had come to the right place.
The grass in the Lawn Field had shot up green again after the
August rain, as if to prove to the visitors that everything that
was said about Ireland was true, and when the car clattered
across the cattle grid which separated the Lawn from the
gravel sweep in front of the house, the dogs – barking a
noisy welcome – appeared from nowhere. The hall door was
open, to catch the warmth of the evening air, and so were
several of the windows.

Stepping out of the car, Adam was suddenly very moved
but he was not at all sure what he felt. The house itself
meant little to him but he was overcome by the sense of
the place. It brought home to him that his mother – the
Annette Odlum listed on his birth certificate – had been a
real person: she had once stood where he was now standing,

she had walked in this place, her voice had been heard in these rooms. Decades had passed but, in spite of that and the fact that he had never known her, Adam could sense her presence. Her other children had been born here and not, like himself, in the anonymity of an English orphanage. He supposed that Annette had died here too.

He looked around him. A giant magnolia, contorted from decades of vigorous pruning and obviously generations old, concealed – almost in its entirety – the end wall of the house. To the other end, a lichen-covered sundial, making a focus on a patch of mown grass, seemed to defy the motto, 'Tempus Fugit', that was carved on its base. In remarking the few late blooms on the Albertine that was attached to the facade of the house, Adam was not to know that it had been planted by his mother her first year at Knockfane. It would, therefore, be almost as old as himself.

No one materialised to welcome them. There was not a soul. Nor could they find a bell or a knocker. The two men looked at the fulsome fanlight above the hall door, without knowing that it was a floral tribute to the ancestor whose money had built the house and were just discussing it when they heard a voice.

'Gentlemin, ye are very welcome. We was expecting ye an hour or so ago. Miss Lydia's above in the garden but if you bring in yer cases, I'll show you to yer rooms.'

They did as they were bidden and, and when Rose had left them, they inspected each other's bedrooms.

'I hope it's not going to be too formal,' said Mr Stokes. 'I mean, I haven't seen a maid in uniform for quite a long time.'

'She didn't seem all that formal, in spite of the black dress and apron,' said Dr Switzer.

The visitors were not to know that it was Rose and not her mistress who insisted that she should dress properly as a maid: she had always done so, she maintained, and there was no need to change.

'I hope this Miss Esdaile doesn't turn out to be a real old dragon,' said Mr Stokes. 'If so, we could be in for a terrible week.'

'I'm sure she won't be,' said Dr Switzer.

But the fact of the matter was that Adam Switzer, suddenly, was not sure at all. It had not occurred to him that his half-sister might be a difficult and charmless old crone. He had been imagining her as someone like his wife had been and that the week at Knockfane was going to be all light-hearted and fun. His brother-in-law's words induced in him a sense of foreboding.

'Oh! dear,' he thought, 'I'm sure I've made an awful mistake in coming. I don't know what could have got into me. But it's too late now.'

When they came downstairs, the door into the drawing room was open and, cautiously, they stepped into the room. Lydia had her back to them, arranging dahlias with branches of copper beach in a vase on a table between the end windows. Glancing up at the convex mirror on the wall above her, she glimpsed the diminished images of the two men as they entered the room. She turned around.

'Well,' she said when she looked at them, 'my "Two Gentlemen of Worthing", arrived at last. I've been very much looking forward to your visit.'

In an instant, Adam Switzer understood that his half-sister was entirely delightful and that he had made the right decision in coming to Knockfane. She was wearing a poppy-red skirt and a striped blue and white shirt. A chain, in antique gold, could just be glimpsed under her collar. She was a very attractive woman, was Adam's first impression: he had earlier worked out that she had to be about ten years younger than himself.

Later that evening, as Adam Switzer stood on the bank of the river in the light of the rising moon, his brother-in-law noticed that he seemed only half-hearted as he went through the motions of casting.

'We're both tired after the journey,' Mr Stokes said to himself.

That was true but, in addition, Adam Switzer's mind was in turmoil. He had, immediately, been greatly taken by Lydia but he could not see how he might break the news to her that he was her half-brother.

As the week progressed and everything at Knockfane proved to be so enjoyable, Adam Switzer put out of his mind tackling things with Lydia. 'It would be better if I just found out more about the family and got to know them more before doing anything,' he reasoned to himself, 'I can hardly just announce it. They could very easily be horrified to discover that their mother, before her marriage and when she was little more than a girl, had made a slip. Perhaps their father never even knew about it. I think I'll need to tread very carefully.'

And tread very carefully is what Dr Switzer did. In fact, he tread so very carefully that he did nothing at all, promising himself that he would return to Knockfane on another occasion when he would be fully prepared and would have worked out beforehand how he might bring up the discussion with Lydia.

But when he next returned to Knockfane, still nothing was said; and then he returned again, and again, and all the time he felt himself becoming ever closer to Lydia – and even to Julia as well – but the closer he became the less he wanted to run the risk of destroying everything by making a declaration. And so matters continued from one year to the next, from one stay at Knockfane to another.

In the end it was Julia who, inadvertently, caused him to act.

44

Reflections

IN SPITE OF the pills which Julia consumed on a daily basis – and she consumed a great many – and the solicitations of Dr Bell, not to mention Fergal's constant care and anxiety, Julia never really recovered her stability and nor did she ever revert to being her bossy and confident self. As for being good fun, as she had been in the past, that too was lost. Instead, she became severe, a constant frown a replacement for her smile, and an attitude which was intended to convey that life was a burden to endure rather than a pleasure to enjoy. She was prone to bouts of extreme activity when all would be well and at such times she would make various plans, for giving parties, going on holidays, redecorating rooms at Coolowen, even meddling on the farm and thereby upsetting her son, Sam. At other periods, she would become extremely dissatisfied: with herself, with Fergal, with Lydia, with Coolowen, and when in that mood she would talk in a fatalistic way – which caused Fergal some concern – to the effect that everything about life had changed so much that it was hardly worth going on. Underlying both extremes was a tendency to become very agitated and angry at the slightest upset and, when that happened, she would lash out at whoever – or whatever – was in the vicinity. Lash out is what she did one day with Adam Switzer and as a result he made the decision there and then that he would have a talk with Fergal and explain to him the reality of the family situation.

Julia came over to Knockfane one morning while Adam was staying there. Thinking that Lydia was at home, she bustled into the morning room to find Adam seated at the little table tying flies. He stood up when she came in but, ignoring this courtesy, Julia bluntly stated that she was looking for Lydia to which Adam replied that Lydia had gone into Liscarrig. Julia took up *The Irish Times* and stood on the hearth rug pretending to read it. Adam sat down again. Then came Julia's outburst.

'I've developed the strongest possible exception to your coming to stay at Knockfane so very often,' she said. 'It seems to me that, since your retirement, you are always here.'

'I believed that I was always welcome,' Adam said.

'Welcome, yes of course,' said Julia, 'but there is such a thing as outstaying one's welcome.'

Adam was silent.

'And it's not just a matter of welcome,' said Julia. 'It's my considered opinion that you are toying with my sister's affections and it is that which I find so very reprehensible. It would be better for all concerned if you desisted from making further visits to Knockfane.'

Part of Adam Switzer wanted to laugh, and all the more so because of the pomposity of Julia's language; but he knew about Julia's condition and he knew that laughter would exacerbate her mood quite dangerously.

'I understand your concern,' he said. 'I've been thoughtless. It's just that I've grown so very fond of all of you over the last few years but I can see that, in coming so often, I have made myself too much at home.'

Julia had marched out of the room before he was finished speaking.

When she got home she was distraught, as she always was after she had made such a scene. She felt such a fool in herself and upset at what she had done. Rushing out to Fergal, she urged him to go over to Knockfane and apologise on her behalf and try and explain away her behaviour. Used to having to make such amends on his wife's behalf, Fergal got into the car straight away. He found Adam Switzer, still in the morning room; Lydia had not yet returned from Liscarrig.

He started to speak but before he had a chance to say very much, Adam stopped him.

'I've been wanting to talk to you, Fergal, for a very long time. Perhaps now is the moment. It concerns a matter of great delicacy.'

At that, he told Fergal everything.

'I've worried and worried for such ages as to how I might bring this up with you all and I've never been able to see a way,' he ended. 'It will probably be a very great blow to your wife and Lydia, but they must be told. I would very much welcome your advice as to how I should deal with it.'

Fergal was silent for a while after Adam had finished speaking. He got up and went over to the window and stood there looking out. The clock on the mantelpiece ticked loudly and then made the gulping sound which indicated that it was about to strike. Adam fiddled with the flies on the table before him. Then Fergal turned round and went across and shook him by the hand.

'This news is both dreadful and wonderful at the same time,' he said. 'It will take time for me to digest it fully and consider all the ramifications. But I am certain of one thing: when Julia and Lydia get over the shock, they will be very,

very pleased to have you as a brother. As, indeed, I already am.'

In the days which followed, Fergal and Adam found the opportunity to have several conversations together. They went over everything again and again and, when they boiled it down, it seemed to them that there were two separate issues involved and that the family, Julia, Lydia and Edward as well, would have to adjust in their own ways to both these factors.

There was the news that their family was to be augmented by the addition of a half-brother. Fergal was sure that both Lydia and Julia would, in time, only be pleased at this but Edward and Marion, not to mention their son Willis, were likely to have an entirely different attitude and Fergal could see trouble coming from that quarter.

Much more complicated for the family than the mere discovery of an extra brother, would be the realisation that their mother had had a secret, and a fairly unpalatable secret at that, and they would wonder, first and foremost, if their father had known. They had been brought up on Willis Esdaile's stories of his great love for their mother and they had witnessed, throughout his entire life, his abiding veneration of her memory. The children knew by heart, as they had heard it so often, the story of his first seeing Annette at the Liscarrig Agricultural Show, his immediately falling in love with her, and the three-year wait – imposed by Grandpa Odlum – before they married.

Adam's appearing out of the woodwork, all these years later, introduced an entirely new chapter to the love story. It revealed that the reason Willis and Annette had not married was because Annette had been committed to another at the time; and, not just committed, but prepared to bear his child as well. The three-year wait to marry had always been portrayed by Willis – and accepted as such by Julia and Lydia – as a test of the love that their father and mother had for each other; but now it would be exposed as no more than a myth.

There were other aspects to the discovery as well. It was likely that Julia and Lydia would wonder, as Adam himself had wondered, who Adam's father was; and what were the circumstances which had led Annette to have this man's son and yet not marry him. She had not even named him on Adam's birth certificate.

All of these considerations were very puzzling and very disturbing and, as it was Julia and Lydia who were likely to be most puzzled and most disturbed by learning of them, Fergal and Adam realised that they had to be very careful as to how they would break the news.

Other thoughts, which he did not share with Adam, also strayed into Fergal's mind. He knew that Julia, but not Lydia, would be exercised as to how people in the neighbourhood would view the development and how the family might present their discovery of a long-lost brother to the world at large. There would be talk, that was certain, and Fergal knew that his wife dreaded 'talk'. In her current fragile state of mind, even a hint of the scandal – because a scandal is certainly how Julia would regard the whole business – was bound to send her into a frenzy and Fergal feared that he himself might be in for a very rough time. Considering this, he wondered momentarily if things should be allowed to continue as they were and Adam persuaded to neither do nor say anything at all.

In thinking about Annette and her choice to give up Adam as a baby for adoption, Fergal's mind turned to Julia and the decision she had made in similar circumstances all those years ago. It did not distress him to recall the events of the time and nor did he feel, much less resent, that Julia had made such use of him. He recalled that her father had put nothing in their way when they said they wanted to go to London for a year: his lack of opposition suddenly made more sense. He thought of Julia's ingenuity and her pluck and he counted himself fortunate that she had turned to him in her crisis. Their marriage had made him a happy man and bringing up Sam as his own son had afforded him only delight. The thought that, as an alternative to marrying him, Julia might have abandoned Sam in an orphanage, as Annette had done with Adam, made him shudder.

None of these reflections were of any help to Fergal, however, in his discussions with Adam and, as the days passed, neither man was any nearer to coming up with a solution as to what might be done. Then, one morning after about a week, Adam said, almost as an aside, 'I suppose there's no point in discussing it with a solicitor.'

Fergal looked at him.

'It's not really a legal problem,' he said. 'I mean there is no property or anything like that involved.'

'Of course not,' said Adam. 'It's just that it may help to talk it over with your Mr Holt here in Liscarrig. After all, he's been familiar with the family's affairs for a long time.'

'We could do,' said Fergal. 'He used to be a bit of an upstart but he's gained some wisdom, not to mention experience, over the years, so he might make a suggestion or two. And, of course, his father was my father-in-law's solicitor all his life.'

'That's settled then,' said Adam, 'we'll try and see him tomorrow.'

45

The Face of the Law

AS HE DEALT with the myriad family, property and financial affairs of town business people and local farmers, Protestants and Catholics, the poor and the well off, and the sundry others whose interlocking lives constituted the community of Liscarrig, Mr Holt had indeed gained much experience over the years. Whether this fund of experience had been augmented in the same period by a corresponding reserve of wisdom was, however, more open to debate. There were some who claimed that he was very sound and others who branded him a fool but, as that was the generally expressed opinion of all solicitors, even those who practiced in Dublin, Mr Holt was far from being exceptional. His age, in the middle fifties, ruled out any possibility that he might be thought an upstart; but the tendency towards pomposity, which had been a characteristic of his youth, had unfortunately become more pronounced. He no longer dreamed of the day when he would make a stir by his brilliance at the High Court in Dublin. Instead he had discovered that the little things of legal life brought truer rewards: a dispute over a parcel of land, occasional cases of cattle rustling, poaching on the Scarva, drinking after hours in Doran's pub, being in charge of an unlighted vehicle, allowing ragwort to grow rampant. These were all matters which regularly required Mr Holt's attendance at the Circuit Court in Athcloon. He enjoyed the tussle involved in pleading the innocence of some out-and-out rogue and having a sentence reduced, even though he was fully cognisant that, if Justice was as blind as she was supposed to be, his client should be put behind bars with a minimum of delay.

He still occupied the same offices, in the old family home as he was given to pointing out, on Castle Street. Miss Jessup had long since retired and her position was now filled by the cheerful young granddaughter of old Mr Skelly the butcher. In contrast to Miss Jessup, whose attitude towards clients had been consistently deferential, Miss Skelly would welcome visitors to the office with an affable informality. She always dressed in the shortest of mini-skirts and, in the summer months, even wore no stockings. Although Mr Holt was frequently urged by his wife to 'speak to that Skelly one about the way she dresses', he never did so. This was partly for the reason that, surreptitiously, Mr Holt derived some small pleasure from Miss Skelly's appearance.

As Mr Holt had already met Adam Switzer a number of times, it was unnecessary for Fergal to perform any introduction when he and Adam came in. The weather was unremarkable that morning but the sky, visible above the rooftops on the opposite side of the street, was sufficiently grey for Mr Holt to feel able to remark that the day might clear up in the afternoon. After this possibility was discussed and enquiries after Mrs Holt and Mrs Sale exchanged, Fergal introduced the subject about which he and Adam had come.

Flattering Mr Holt by saying that the Esdailes had long regarded him as their wisest counsellor and friend, he stated that it was in that spirit that they now wanted to seek his advice.

'Something of an unusual nature has arisen,' he said. 'It concerns Dr Switzer directly but it is a matter for the family as well. It's probably best if I allow Dr Switzer to outline the case to you himself as he is familiar with all the details.'

The use of the word 'case', which Fergal had only employed in the broadest sense, alerted Mr Holt and he extricated a yellow ruled jotter from his drawer and took up his pen.

'I am not sure where to begin,' Adam said, 'but ...'

He spoke for about twenty minutes, without interruption from Fergal, while Mr Holt listened attentively, showing no signs of surprise, dismay, censure or disapproval. Having stated the facts, Adam outlined the ramifications as he and Fergal perceived them: how, in addition to discovering that they had a half-brother, Julia, Edward and Lydia would be faced with the unpleasant disclosure that their mother had had a history and that their father's adoration of her had perhaps been misguided. It had all the potential to be a devastating revelation to them.

As Adam's discourse unfolded, Mr Holt, sitting forward in his chair, had placed his elbows on his desk and had made a cathedral of his hands. He did not take notes but, holding the cathedral to his lips, he had looked directly at Adam throughout in a manner that a perceptive observer might conclude was one of slight suspicion while, at the same time, giving no overt indication as to what was in his mind. There was a silence when Adam finished speaking and then Mr Holt sat back.

'Very interesting,' he said, 'although if you are asking my general opinion, I am not sure how much of a claim you'll be able to make.'

'Claim?' said Adam.

'I think you've misunderstood,' said Fergal. 'There's no question of any claim or some such. Dr Switzer is not thinking of anything like that. In any case there's nothing to claim, except to claim kinship with his Esdaile relations. That's all that Dr Switzer is exercised about. No ulterior motive has ever entered his head and, for the life of me, I can't see what ulterior motive there could be.'

'Knockfane?' said Mr Holt. 'That has not occurred to you?'

Fergal and Adam looked at each other. Both were nonplussed as they separately pondered if they had made a foolish decision in coming to see the solicitor and it crossed Fergal's mind that Mr Holt's years of experience had done nothing to enhance his ordinary common sense. Adam Switzer was very obviously an educated and cultivated man, he was extremely articulate and had outlined the business at hand with great clarity. In spite of that, Mr Holt, in his rush to appear the meticulous lawyer, had completely misunderstood the tenor of Adam's exposition and had failed to see that Adam was far from being a devious and grasping interloper who had descended on Knockfane with cupidity in his mind. Instead, being in a way in awe of Adam, the Englishman, Mr Holt had felt the need to rise to the occasion and demonstrate to the full his superior judicial credentials. But, like a trout that jumps for a mere bubble on the surface of a stream, Mr Holt had risen to an imaginary bait and it was obvious that it would take some effort on the part of Fergal and Adam to persuade him that 'a claim' was the very last thing that Adam intended.

Mr Holt went over all the details and dates with the proverbial fine toothcomb. He stated that he would need to see 'the documents', reiterated how unusual the case was, and underlined his commitment to ensuring that 'the Esdaile name would not be dragged through the mud'. And then, after several hours, by which time Adam Switzer was wishing not only that he had never been adopted but that he had never been born at all, Mr Holt's tone changed. It was though he had satisfied himself as to all his suspicions, and all his imagined points of law, and his adversarial attitude migrated to one of conciliation and pragmatism.

'There is a possibility, albeit remote, that I might have at my disposal the means by which the case could be cleared up to everyone's satisfaction,' Mr Holt said.

Neither Fergal nor Adam were at all sure what this statement meant but both of them, independently, wished that Mr Holt would stop referring to their predicament as 'a case'. They also wished that he would clarify what he had just said and make some positive suggestions or, failing that, allow them to go home.

'You see,' said Mr Holt, 'my late father was the late Mr Esdaile's solicitor and Mr Esdaile had the greatest confidence in my late father, and not only in professional matters ...'

He paused.

'... but in more personal ones as well.'

He pronounced the word 'personal' with a quivering smile and, for a moment, Fergal feared what he was going to hear next.

'Let me give you an example. Among the Esdaile boxes in my strong room there is a sealed envelope. It is addressed to my late father in Mr Esdaile's hand and marked on the outside, "To be opened only when required by circumstances". Quite cryptic really, don't you think? How was my late father, or anyone else for that matter, to know what such circumstances might be? But, you see, Mr Esdaile explained to my late father in person what the required circumstances were. He had such trust in him. That trust has descended to me as my late father's successor and my late father, during his lifetime, explained the meaning to me.'

Adam found himself wondering how on earth someone like this solicitor could ever conclude any business or effect any endeavour and, in an effort to see a funny side, he speculated to himself as to whether Mr Holt spoke to his wife in such conundrums. What turn of phrase would he use, for instance, in asking her to perform such a simple task as turning on the television? His musings were interrupted by Fergal.

'You said, Mr Holt, that you might be able to advise. Perhaps you could tell us what your recommendations would be?'

'Ah! yes,' said Mr Holt, 'let me see now.'

He adjusted his posture as though to indicate that the mantle of his legal responsibilities, although bearable, weighed heavily on his shoulders. He was, however, strong enough to continue.

'The circumstances which Mr Esdaile envisaged as possibly arising concerned his family, his children that is, as much as they concerned Knockfane itself. The impression he gave was that there might appear at some future date an ... unexpected ... member of the family and if that ...'

Mr Holt glanced down at his yellow jotter.

'... circumstance arose,' he continued, 'my late father was to open the envelope in question and follow the directions therein. My late father was always under the impression that Mr Esdaile's anxieties in this respect concerned the New Zealand people, the children of his brother, Mr Todd Esdaile, and that indeed may well be the case. However, if I am to interpret Mr Esdaile's instructions according to the letter of the law, there is no doubt but that Dr Switzer ... manifesting himself as it were ... constitutes a fulfilment of Mr Esdaile's conditions for opening the envelope. I will just reassure myself over the next day or so that that is the correct course of action and we might discuss it further if you come in and see me again. Shall we say Friday afternoon?'

46

The First Letter

WHEN FERGAL AND Adam left Mr Holt's office they were utterly exhausted and nor were they at all confident that the strenuousness of their morning's toil in the vineyard was likely to lead to any vintage harvest. Neither Julia nor Lydia had even been mentioned by Mr Holt, much less any plan suggested for informing them that Adam was their half-brother; and as to this letter – or was it just an envelope? – and the circumstances required for its being opened, they could not see how it would have any bearing on the matter and all the more so as it was intended to refer to the New Zealand cousins. It crossed Fergal's mind that it was very odd that Mr Holt had never mentioned the letter when there had been a real threat – in the form of Todd – from New Zealand; and that he had only brought up its existence now in response to Adam's entirely benign wish to be known to his true family. They went across to the Mulhussey Arms.

'It'll be too late to get any dinner,' Fergal said, 'the most we can hope for is a sandwich.'

'I could do with a gin and tonic,' said Adam.

Although Fergal rarely took a drink, he decided that this was an occasion when he needed one. He ordered half a pint of Guinness.

As they discussed the morning's proceedings and recalled the various nonsenses which Mr Holt had brought up, they became more and more tickled by the experience they had been through and it was almost five o'clock by the time they left the hotel. They had quite forgotten the seriousness of the predicament which had led them to the solicitor's office in the first instance but, when Friday afternoon came and they announced themselves to Miss Skelly, their mood had sobered considerably.

Mr Holt greeted them cheerfully and then, turning to his desk, he picked up a long envelope, faded and crushed at the corners. It was sealed at the back with a dollop of wax made all the more official by having been stamped with an impression of the signet ring which Willis had worn all his life and then left to Julia on his death.

'THE LETTER,' MR Holt said, 'and the instruction I mentioned.'

He pointed to the handwritten words on the envelope: 'To be opened only when required by circumstances.'

Fergal felt an overwhelming urge to grab the packet out of Mr Holt's fat little hands and rush from the room.

'I have reassured myself that it would be appropriate to open it,' said Mr Holt 'and follow Mr Esdaile's directions.'

He took up a long metal paper knife, its handle fashioned from the horn of some beast or other and polished into a decorative whirl. Placing the letter flat on his desk, he inserted the tip of the blade into a corner and, glancing up at Fergal and Adam, slowly and carefully sliced open the envelope. A coroner, making an incision in a corpse, would not have proceeded more cautiously.

Inside the envelope there was, as predicted, another sealed envelope and this was addressed, again in Willis Esdaile's hand, to 'Misses Julia and Lydia Esdaile, Knockfane'.

Accompanying it was a letter which, from what Fergal could see – and much to his relief – was very brief. Mr Holt took it up and read it out loud.

'It is addressed to "Mr Holt, Solicitor, his Successors and Assigns",' he said with some pride, 'I'll read it for you.'

Dear Mr Holt,

My dear daughters, Julia and Lydia Esdaile, and my son, Edward Esdaile, may have occasion to know the contents of the enclosed letter at some future time. Please accept this letter as my instruction to give it to them if you deem the moment appropriate. It concerns their brother, unknown to them or to me in either name or person.

Yours Truly,
Willis Esdaile.

ON HEARING MR Holt read this, Fergal and Adam were stunned. It had nothing to do with Todd's family in New Zealand. Instead, its last sentence made it seem relevant to Adam's predicament and, furthermore, it removed one of their principal concerns: it made clear that Annette must have told Willis that she had had a son before she married him. Julia and Lydia might be assured, therefore, that their father had not held his wife's indiscretion against her and that his devotion to her was as true as he had always projected it to be.

Fergal found that he was touched by the poignancy of the words 'unknown to them or to me' but it was the word 'brother' which held most import for Adam. Seeing written down, in ink on paper, this affirmation that he had a blood family, he felt for the first time in his life as properly belonging: belonging to Julia and to Lydia as their brother. It was as though he had walked out of a door into sunlight.

The fact that Adam could demonstrate that he was Julia's and Lydia's half-brother was sufficient to convince Mr Holt that it would be appropriate for Old Esdaile's letter to be passed to his daughters. Elated that it should fall to him to carry out an instruction which had the gravity of having been issued half a-century previously, he wondered if the momentousness of the task demanded that he should call on Lydia at Knockfane and request Julia to also be there. But Fergal had other ideas. Aware of the effect which the contents of the letter might have on his wife, he immediately thwarted Mr Holt in his plan by saying that it would be more appropriate for him to pass the letter to Lydia so that she might read it first and then, in consultation with him, judge how its substance might be conveyed to Julia. With a degree of reluctance, Mr Holt agreed to this suggestion but he did not disguise his disappointment at seeing the letter, which had been in his strong room for so many decades, guarded and concealed like the relic of a saint in a cathedral treasury, pass out of his hands.

Leaving the office, Fergal and Adam were silent as they walked back to the car. They were as explorers in pursuit of the tomb of a Pharaoh. They had located the burial place and knew that it contained the treasures which they coveted. But they had reached only an outer chamber while the inner sanctum, and the mummy itself, and its accompanying treasures still eluded them.

47

The Second Letter

IT WAS A week or so before Fergal went over to Knockfane,
bringing the letter with him. He and Adam had decided
that it would be better to wait until Adam had returned to
England before learning what Willis Esdaile from beyond
the grave as it were, wished to disclose and the delay gave
Fergal the chance to consider how he might introduce the
subject with Lydia. He did not alert her in any way and on
the May morning in question, he just drove over to see her,
more or less on the spur of the moment.

Knockfane was looking its best in the clear of the late
spring sunshine. The grass, dark green in its lushness, was
newly mown in front of the house, the lime trees on the slope
up to the Faine Field appeared light-headed at coming into
leaf, early roses were in bloom, and Fergal could glimpse,
through the wicket gate, the cohorts of purple irises like
sentries along the wall of the greenhouse. He found Lydia
having her coffee on the seat outside the drawing-room
window. She was opening the morning's letters.

'What a nice surprise,' she said, 'ask Rose to bring you
out a cup. There's more coffee in the pot.'

She moved on the seat to make way for Fergal to sit down.

'I'm sure you miss the company when Adam goes away after he's been here for a week or more,' Fergal said when he had finished his coffee.

'I do and I don't,' said Lydia. 'I've lots of things to be getting on with and it's not always easy when there is someone in the house.'

'I have something to tell you,' Fergal said, 'something that has cropped up.'

He took the letter out of his jacket pocket.

'It may not be all that easy for you ...'

He flattened the envelope on his knees.

'This is for you to read,' he said. 'It's been with Holt all these years, for safekeeping. It's something your father wrote for you and Julia when you were both only little girls. I have an inkling what it is about but I am not sure if I should say what I know before you read it. The best thing may be for you to just open it and see what it says.'

'This is very mysterious, Fergal,' said Lydia. 'Is it very, very nice or very, very horrid, as we used to say as children?'

'Probably a bit of both,' said Fergal.

'Pappy's beautiful handwriting,' Lydia said as she took the envelope, 'it takes me back seeing it suddenly like this after all these years.'

Using her thumb rather than the paperknife that was on the seat beside her, she started to tear open the envelope. Fergal got up from the seat and strolled off across the gravel towards the sundial. He lingered there as Lydia read and after a while, when he saw that she was finished, he came back and sat down again. Neither of them spoke. Eventually, and without looking at Fergal, Lydia said:

'How long have you known? And how much? Does Julia know?'

'I don't know what is in your Pappy's letter, Lydia dear, so I don't know how much I know. But your half-brother ...'

Fergal stopped himself. He suddenly realised that, whatever else the letter might reveal, his father-in-law could not have identified Adam Switzer by name and that Lydia, therefore, would not know that the letter was about him.

'My half-brother?' Lydia asked. She looked at Fergal for the first time. 'But he would be our full brother. Even though he was illegitimate – I hate to use the word – he would still be our brother and, when all is said and done, the eldest of the family.'

Now it was Fergal who was puzzled.

'I'm at a bit of a loss, Lydia,' he said, 'perhaps you should tell me what's in the letter.'

'Here,' she said, 'it's best that you read it for yourself. I'll go and ask Rose to bring out some fresh coffee.'

She went into the house as Fergal took up the letter and started to read.

My dear and beloved daughters,

I write this letter in the knowledge that you may never have occasion to read it. If that is the case, then a sadness and wickedness which has overshadowed my life will never be put right. On the other hand, if you do come to read these words, I know that they will come as a shock to you. In that case, I ask you to forgive me the pain I cause you as well as the secret I have withheld from you for so many years.

Your dear mother and I, as I think you know, loved each other very deeply. We knew, almost from the moment we met, that we wanted to marry each other. But, in the view of your Grandfather Odlum, your mother, being only eighteen at the time, was too young to be so pledged and he insisted that we wait. Subsequently, I acted in a manner that was selfish, unforgivable and irresponsible and the result was that your mother was compromised. Your grandfather was, understandably, outraged. He insisted that your mother and I break off all contact and with great cruelty he sent her to an institution in England where, some months later, our son was born. I was forbidden to see your mother during that time and, even though I very much wanted to marry her and bring up our child, and was in a position to do so, your grandfather would not hear of it. Equally, I was denied any say in respect of our son. Your grandfather decided that he was to be adopted and your mother was obliged to give him up immediately he was born. I never saw him.

After almost two years, your grandfather relented and your mother and I were allowed to marry and, in time, to our great joy you were born. But our heartbreak at losing our son never left us and, even though it had not been our decision, our guilt was never assuaged. It governed our every waking hour and we yearned all the days of our lives for the child we had never known. We felt (wrongly, I suppose) that he had been somehow usurped by Edward and that Edward had taken his rights.

It is difficult to see how the wrong we inflicted on an innocent baby will ever be put right. It is unlikely that he will ever discover who he really is and it is equally unlikely that you will ever find the brother you never knew you had. It is with the knowledge that I am probably writing in vain that I pen this letter to you. But I do so with the prayer that your brother may somehow one day be restored to you and that you will welcome him and accord him his rightful place as heir to the Esdailes and to Knockfane.

Your loving father,
Willis Esdaile

FERGAL DID NOT fully take in the meaning of the letter when he first read it. He had become accustomed to the idea that Adam was Annette's son by a father unknown and so he did not immediately grasp that Willis Esdaile, by his own account, was this father. It was only when he read the words a second time that he properly understood the full extent of what they divulged. He was struck by how calm Lydia's reaction to the revelation had been. She had, he reflected, perhaps read it as a confession on the part of her father and had not understood that it was to lead to her discovering, and sooner rather than later, an unknown brother. The disclosure, he was certain, would be more difficult for her to digest and accommodate when she learned that now, sixty years on, the brother she had never known about had, unknown to her, already become part of her life. She had come to know and feel an affection for Adam Switzer but that was in thinking of him as a stranger. Her feelings might be very different when she discovered he was her brother. As Lydia came back out of the house and joined him, it hit home to Fergal that he had now the very difficult task of putting together for Lydia the two strands of the story: her father's secret and Adam's discovery of who he was. He must explain everything to her in full. He was helped by her asking why Mr Holt had seen fit to produce the letter now. At that, Fergal told her everything. He told her how Adam had discovered who his mother was, how he had investigated and learned about

Knockfane and then, on the pretence of coming to Ireland to fish, how he had discreetly got to know Lydia and his blood family. Thanks to her father's letter of so long ago, Adam now knew at last who his father was, who he himself was and he had found his proper home at Knockfane.

There was a silence when he had finished. The heifers, curious at the presence of the figures on the seat, had ambled up the lawn and positioned themselves along the iron paling that prevented them gaining the gravel sweep in front of the house. Rude in their staring and vulgar in their open-mouthed chewing the cud, they seemed to be waiting for something to happen. A thrush, hoping for a mid-morning snack, angrily attacked the newly mown grass under the weeping ash, showing little concern for the nearby presence of Lydia and Fergal. There was the distant noise of the tractor in the Moate Field where the workmen were spreading manure. Eventually Lydia spoke.

'It's all too extraordinary,' she said, 'a very great wrong was done to Adam the moment he came into the world. It's a wrong that nothing could ever repair. And poor Mama ... only eighteen ... and having to give up a beautiful baby. And for no good reason ... except an old man's anger.'

Lydia's voice trembled. She sort of huddled on the seat and Fergal saw that her eyes glistened wet. He wanted to put his arm around her but hesitated to do so. She would want to cry.

'How could Grandpa Odlum have been so cruel?' she said after a while, 'three lives blighted for ever. And what a terrible secret for Pappy and Mama to live with. It explains so much. I don't mean just the Edward business, although of course Pappy's actions now make sense even though they were not rational. You could, I suppose, say that Edward's life was also soured by the wickedness of Grandpa's decision.'

'In a way,' said Fergal, 'you could.'

He was surprised at Lydia's reaction to the revelations. She was distressed, that was clear, but she was also calm. Then he thought to himself how typical it was of her. She had not considered herself for a moment and her upset was caused entirely by the hurt and injustice which she saw as having been inflicted on her parents and on Adam. Her concern was that nothing could ever make up for the damage that had been caused by Grandpa Odlum's heartlessness.

Fergal had worried a good deal about how Julia would receive the news and he was still not certain as to how he might take it up with her but he felt more comfortable now that Lydia knew. She would be an ally and he felt his apprehensions lift.

'I've not yet told Julia,' he said to Lydia, 'I'll need your help with that.'

For a moment he saw a flash of anger on Lydia's face.

'All of us have forever needed help with Julia,' she said, 'that's why she has always got everything she wanted.'

Fergal was surprised at the vehemence of the statement. Lydia often expressed an exasperation with Julia but she rarely criticised her in any serious way.

'If Mama had been more like Julia, none of this would have ever happened. She would have stood up to Grandpa and seen to it that she got her own way. She would not have given Adam up.'

Fergal had not expected Lydia to be angry but it was clear to him that her anger was not really directed at Julia but more at how much had been lost and the fact that a great injustice had been done. As they chatted things over and she talked about Adam, Fergal could see that she was thinking only of how reparation could be made and Adam made part of the family and of Knockfane.

Driving home to Coolowen, Fergal worried to himself if Adam's being accepted was going to be quite so straightforward. But, before any acceptance could be countenanced, Julia had to be told.

48

Lydia's Secret

'I DON'T KNOW how you can do such a thing to me,' Julia said to Lydia, 'how you can just, out of the blue as it were, come over here and tell me something like this. You know that I'm not all that strong and that there's only so much that I can take and yet you come over here and make an announcement which you must realise is going to greatly upset me.'

'But Julia ...' said Lydia.

'Don't ...' said Julia. 'You've gone quite far enough. My nerves won't stand any more. Dr Bell warned me to be careful, you know that. If you had wanted to tell me this, you could have waited till a more appropriate time.'

'But Julia,' said Lydia, 'the time would never be appropriate for you. You must accept what I'm telling you now.'

'I don't know that I will ever be able to accept it,' said Julia, 'and that's the truth. It's too much of a shock.'

Lydia had come over to Coolowen and, finding Julia alone in the greenhouse dead-heading the geraniums, had told her that she and Richard Benson were going to be married.

When it became known during the holiday month of August that Miss Esdaile was to marry her 'childhood sweetheart', as people took to describing Mr Benson, the news swept through the county like a swarm of bees in search of a summer hive. Disappointed that the announcement of the forthcoming marriage had taken them totally by surprise, thereby denying them the pleasure of weeks of speculative gossip, the people of Liscarrig were simply astounded by such an unexpected turn of events. Such was their amazement, indeed, that whenever they ran into Lydia they did not know if it was appropriate to mention her news at all. As a result, Lydia was at a loss to know if her decision to marry was a cause of universal censure or whether it was regarded with widespread enthusiasm.

But, while embarrassed to say anything to Lydia herself, the same reticence did not prevail as people talked among themselves and, for weeks, Liscarrig and Athcloon talked of very little else.

'I saw the ring when she came in to buy *The Irish Times* this morning,' Bridie Cassidy from Rowe's was able to report, 'not that I liked to stare at it, mind you.'

'They say it's the ring that he gave to the first wife, God rest her soul, and that he didn't see the need for buying a new one,' added a voice with some authority.

'Lord above, even a Protestant – clergyman and all that he is – wouldn't be that mean,' said someone else.

'Do you think they'll ... like, em ... well, you know?'

'Do you mean share the bed? Of course they will, what else? They've waited more than thirty years for it. Nothing is going to hold them back now.'

Unknown to anyone, and most of all unknown to Julia, Lydia had been meeting up with Mr Benson since the time, about two years previously, when she had written to him on the death of his wife. She had seen the notice in the newspaper. On reading it, she was not sure if she should write at all in case her letter would be misconstrued but, after she mulled it over, she came to the conclusion that, as Mr Benson had shared with her the details of his wife's long years of illness on the day they had met in the Country Shop, it was only correct that she should send her sympathy. She was clear in her mind that she had no other motive in writing although the fact that she found it necessary to clear her mind at all did at least raise the possibility that, as she had for long stored in her memory her affection for Richard Benson, she would not be averse to reviving the contact now. Her letter, and his reply, opened the way for their friendship to be renewed and they took to meeting up whenever Mr Benson had occasion to come to Dublin. They would lunch in the Country Shop or, on summer days go out to Dun Laoghaire, walk the pier, and then have a meal in the Royal Marine Hotel. They found lots to talk about and Lydia brought laughter to Mr Benson's life with tales of parish politics in Liscarrig and details of the ups and downs of daily life at Knockfane. The 'church business' which occasioned Mr Benson to visit Dublin all the way from Cork intensified over the two years so that, by the spring of the year in which they were to marry, the spring when Lydia underwent the trauma of discovering that Adam Switzer was her brother, their meetings had become almost weekly engagements. Lydia immediately confided the news about Adam, and the discovery of her parents' awful secret, to Mr Benson. She found it consoling to do so and valued the counsel he was able to provide. Mr Benson was hugely relieved that Adam, whom he had hitherto regarded as a rival for Lydia's affections, was now removed from the field by the inconvenience of consanguinity, leaving the pursuit to him alone. He, in turn, talked about what the loss of his wife meant and how he no longer wanted to stay on in Crosshaven, as the place had too many sad memories for him. But yet, as he was nearing retirement age, it would be a big upset to take on another parish and move to another part of the country and he had tired of the routine of parish life and the petty squabbles and rivalries that it was a rector's lot to mollify.

Lydia had not invited him down to Knockfane. She wanted their friendship to stay private and she feared that Julia might become suspicious and for that reason, although she very much wanted to do so, she had not even confided in Fergal. When Richard proposed, it was not entirely unexpected and, although conscious that it was a lady's prerogative – indeed her absolute duty – to turn down a first proposal, Lydia did not see the necessity of following convention, and so she said 'yes' on the spot.

It was a Sunday and they had gone to matins in Christ Church and then down to lunch at Hunter's Hotel in Wicklow. Afterwards, they set out to climb the Sugarloaf. As they took a rest, seated among the gold of the bogland gorse, Richard Benson told Lydia that he had always loved her and that he wanted her to become his wife. Once she had accepted, Lydia proceeded to lay down conditions.

'I couldn't ever leave Knockfane,' she said, 'you would have to come and live there too.'

'Then it's decided,' said Mr Benson, 'I'll take early retirement, and will be glad to do so, and there's always demand for an available clergyman to take Sunday services. That'll keep me well occupied.'

Lydia told Fergal first and then Julia. In her own happiness, she had not expected Julia's reaction, her sister's failure to appreciate how wonderful the news was, and her censure, almost, that Lydia should find fulfilment. Instead, Julia had only thought of herself.

'I really don't think my constitution can withstand much more of this trauma,' she had said, carelessly snapping off several near-perfect geranium blooms as she did so. 'It's typical of you, Lydia, that you should be so inconsiderate as to impose such a thing on me when you know that I still haven't fully recovered from finding out that Mama and Pappy had an illegitimate child.'

When Fergal came in from the fields that afternoon, he found his wife in very low mood.

'You've heard, I know, about this ridiculous business of Lydia's,' she said. 'As though the family didn't have enough to contend with at the moment without her adding yet another complication.'

Fergal was always patient with his wife and, latterly, in the knowledge that she was no longer quite herself, he excused her a great deal. He saw the selfishness of her response to Lydia's wonderful news and the blindness of her persistence in regarding Adam as illegitimate rather than her own brother, flesh and blood. He was tempted to reprimand her after she had spoken but knew that reasonableness would be a better approach. And so he said to her that he would like her to go over to Knockfane that evening and congratulate Lydia properly, as it was her duty as a sister to do. Furthermore, he added, he wanted her to write to Adam and say how much she welcomed him as her brother. She was to forget about 'illegitimacy' and 'shame' and think of the joy that Adam, as their brother, and Richard Benson, as their brother-in-law, would bring to the family.

Julia was taken aback by the unaccustomed directness of her husband's instructions but that evening, before setting off for Knockfane, she went upstairs to her bedroom, searched out her jewel case from the bottom of the wardrobe, and took out a diamond and seed-pearl brooch.

'Oh! Julia,' Lydia said when Julia gave her the brooch, 'it's lovely.'

'Martha gave it to me when we came home from London with Sam,' Julia said. 'She told me that the crescent moon shape was a symbol of new beginnings and that it would bring me happiness.'

She watched as Lydia pinned on the brooch.

'And it has brought me happiness,' Julia said, 'more or less.'

They hugged each other, standing on the hearthrug in the morning room, and they stayed like that, without speaking, for some time.

'I'm very, very happy for you,' Julia eventually said, 'very, very happy.'

But if Julia found it within her heart to 'forgive' Lydia, as she deemed her act in going over to Knockfane to indicate, complying with Fergal's request to write to Adam was an altogether more arduous assignment. She sat down to write the letter that night but found that she did not know what to say and it was only after several days that she penned a short note saying that the development had been difficult for them all to assimilate, or even to fully comprehend, but that time would inevitably heal the sore that had been opened. In the meantime she was happy to accept Adam as her brother.

She did not show the letter to Fergal. Had she done so, it is fairly certain that he would have been dismayed at her choice of phrasing. And the fact that she now regarded Adam as a 'sore', rather than merely illegitimate, would certainly have occasioned his censure.

49

Questions of Identity

ADAM DID NOT come over to Ireland for several months after the disclosure of his true identity. He was in constant touch with Lydia by letter and in that way he learned of her engagement to marry, but the discovery of his family, and the circumstances of his birth, imposed other obligations upon him. He had to tell his children. Both his son and his daughter were immediately accepting of the news: they were happy for their father, delighted to find family for themselves, and expressed the wish to visit Ireland and Knockfane as soon as the moment was appropriate.

It fell to Fergal to tell Edward and Marion. Taking the bull by the horns, Fergal rang up Derrymahon and spoke to Edward. He told him, in as matter of fact a tone as he could muster, that he had a family issue to discuss and that it would be better to speak of it person to person. If they were agreeable he would come down one day, and sooner rather than later. Edward and Marion were mystified, although they assumed that the issue concerned the age-old and perennial family question, the ultimate disposition of Knockfane. Driving down to County Waterford, Fergal brought Willis Esdaile's letter of half a century since with him and, without many preliminaries, gave it to Edward to read. Nothing was said when he had finished and he passed it to Marion. When she put it down, taking off her glasses, Edward said, 'Why is this being brought up now, after all these years?'

Hearing the coldness of Edward's words and aware that Marion might be inflamed by her father-in-law's half-hearted admission that Edward may have been wronged, Fergal decided that he should be as brief as possible. Without elaborating too much on Adam Switzer, or conveying the fact that he had been coming to Knockfane, incognito as it were, for the past few years, he simply said that Adam had recently made himself known to Lydia and Julia.

'What proof is there that he is who he says he is?' Marion asked, 'I mean he could be God knows who. How are we to know?'

'He has the letter from the `Registrar of the Care Home which states that Annette Odlum of Derrymahon was his mother. It gives his date of birth,' said Fergal.

'That could apply to anyone,' said Marion. 'I mean, Edward's mother might well have had this baby and, if she did, this would be the true record. But how can we be certain that this, whatsisname ... Switzer ... is one and the same? There will have to be some proof. It wouldn't be the first time that someone assumed an identity in order to claim an inheritance.'

Faced with Marion's fire, and her raising of issues which he, Lydia nor Julia – or even Mr Holt – had not thought of, Fergal grasped that his task, and the method he had pursued in accomplishing it, was not to be completed as readily as he had envisaged.

'I'm not sure how to answer that,' he said. 'Julia and Lydia have accepted him. Maybe they have been too trusting but Mr Holt was also satisfied. When you meet him, you'll see that Adam Switzer is a very proper sort of person. Not the type who would engage in "impersonation" as it were. He's a medical doctor.'

'If he's adopted,' said Edward, 'how can he have a birth certificate which gives his real mother's name, Mama's name? It's always the adopting parents' names that are given. I know that for a fact.'

At Edward's words, Fergal immediately saw how, in his anxiety over visiting Derrymahon, he had been temporarily confused. Of course this matter of identity had not been raised before because Adam had his two birth certificates. They were the proof that the baby born to Annette Odlum was one and the same as the baby adopted by Dr and Mrs Switzer. When he pointed this out, Edward and Marion seemed to accept it although the expression in Marion's eyes indicated that she was far from being fully satisfied. Deciding to move the discussion on and direct it away from the tinderbox that was stocked with questions of identity, Fergal said that Adam had expressed an interest in coming to see Derrymahon.

'He thinks of the place as a link in the chain, a missing link,' Fergal said. 'It was, after all, his mother's home, although it's unlikely that he holds T.E. Odlum in any great esteem. He hasn't said anything about him but, after all the upset that T.E. handed down through his callousness, it's unimaginable that Adam would regard him with any affection.'

'T.E. Odlum was a very fine man,' Edward said, 'and a good Christian. He had his faults, no one would deny that, but he was acting within the spirit of the times when illegitimacy was completely taboo. He had no choice but to do what he did.'

Fergal decided not to pursue the discussion of T.E. Odlum's merits, Christian or otherwise. He was hungry. The drive down to Waterford had been long and he hoped that Marion would soon suggest lunch. He could not detect any smells coming from the area of the kitchen. He was relieved when Edward offered him a sherry and Marion left the room.

'Is there a family anywhere in the world,' Edward said, 'that doesn't have fallings-out and disputes? It's always about money and property. Greed, you could call it ...'

He handed the sherry to Fergal.

'... and women,' Edward added, 'it's often they who cause most of the trouble.'

Fergal was taken aback by Edward's sudden attitude of reasonableness. He did not agree with what Edward had said but he was surprised at his conciliatory tone in seeing the troubled legacy of the Esdailes and Knockfane as at one with a universal state of affairs. His wife, Julia, no more than Lydia had, in Fergal's view, never been the cause of any trouble and if Annette's misfortune had been the seed from which the decades of rancour had sprung, it had been well nourished by the actions of the men in the story. Not just T.E. Odlum but Willis Esdaile as well and, if it came to that, Edward himself was hardly without blame.

In wondering how to respond, Fergal had decided not to respond at all. There was a silence. Edward picked up a copy of *The Field* that was on the table behind the sofa and started to leaf through it. Then he threw it back on the table. He looked at Fergal.

'I've always known about this,' he said, 'ever since I was a small boy. Pappy told me. He didn't instruct me to keep it a secret but I've never been able to mention it. He told me as a means of punishing me for something silly that I had done. I didn't understand it at first, I was too young and I couldn't, but I was very upset, very, very upset. I thought it was disgusting and dirty and, for weeks, I had bad dreams about poor Mama, alone in a strange place and having to leave a little baby, the same as we had been, behind her. When I was old enough to make sense of it, I decided it must never be told and that it had been deliberately wicked of Papa to tell a little child such a thing.'

Fergal said nothing. Edward slumped himself down on the sofa.

'Dympna Canty,' he thought to himself, that was her name. He recalled that they had gone swimming in the swamp down in the Bracken Field. It was only February. His father had found them and was livid. It was the next day he told him about Mama and the baby and how they could never think of him, Edward, as their eldest son.

'I have always lived in dread of the day when it would all come out,' said Edward. 'Not just on account of the complications that could arise in respect of Knockfane but because of Julia and Lydia as well. And Marion...'

He got up and fetched the decanter.

'Can I top you up?' he said.

Fergal declined.

'You see, I've never told Marion. I had hoped to avoid it. So, maybe, we won't mention to her now that I have always known, if you don't mind.'

The door opened.

'Lunch!' said Marion.

'It's very simple,' she said when they came into the dining room.

Fergal was alarmed. He had been hoping for a nourishing soup followed by a roast and perhaps a robust rice pudding or treacle tart thereafter.

'We've taken to eating with our health in mind,' said Marion, 'the Continental way. Plenty of fruit and veg, and olive oil. Fish of course, lots of it, and not just on Fridays. Do help yourself.'

She gestured towards the sideboard. Fergal saw the wooden bowl of gleaming oily leaves decorated with nasturtium flowers and a dish of yellow rice topped by three prawns with some lumps of grey fish protruding from underneath.

'Kedgeree,' he said, 'I haven't had it for ages. Julia never makes it now.'

'It's paëlla,' said Marion, 'we have it in Marbella every year. Edward loves it, don't you Edward?'

She did not wait for a reply.

'Difficult to get all the right fish in Waterford, of course. But I find mackerel and a tin of John West salmon make a very good substitute.'

On leaving Derrymahon, Fergal had not travelled ten miles before he stopped at a pub and ordered a plate of cheese sandwiches.

50

An Impediment

WHEN LYDIA WROTE to Edward and Marion to tell them of her impending marriage, she also brought up the subject of Adam. Saying that she knew they would like to meet him, even though she was certain that the opposite was much more likely to be the case, she proposed that, when Adam came over in the weeks before her wedding, she would bring him to Derrymahon. She put the proposal in such a way that it would have appeared churlish for Edward and Marion to refuse but when Marion telephoned and suggested fulsomely that Lydia and Adam might also care to stay the night, Lydia drew the line. She had heard from Fergal about the regime of healthy eating at Derrymahon and she feared that the same pursuit of Continental style might also prevail in respect of accommodation. Lydia liked her own bed and blankets and had only once experimented, unsuccessfully, with a duvet. She knew she could not sleep without taking a hot bath before going to bed and the usefulness and supposed comfort of a shower was something that entirely eluded her. A day visit was, therefore, decided upon and agreed.

In her letter Lydia did not mention one other detail. She did not tell her brother and his wife that, in light of the considerable changes in circumstances that had occurred over the previous months – Adam's being reunited with them and her own impending marriage – she had made a new will. She had wanted to tell them this, but as doing so would have meant also telling them that their son Willis was no longer heir to Knockfane, she decided against. It was not necessary for Derrymahon to be aware of the fact just yet, she reasoned. She was only forty-seven and she intended, and expected to live on at Knockfane for many years to come; the only change was that she would now do so in the company of a husband. Young Willis could never have hoped to inherit the place in the immediate future so the fact that he would now never inherit it at all could hardly cause him any great distress. This is what she told herself and it appeared entirely reasonable.

Having decided that Adam Switzer, and if not him, his son, was the rightful heir to Knockfane, she had discussed her decision to so bequeath the property with Richard Benson. Richard assured her that it was the right decision and that, in marrying her, he had no expectations other than the hope that they would be happy together. Adam and his descendants had an absolute right to the Esdaile legacy, Richard Benson said, and lest there be any doubt, Lydia should refer to her father's letter.

'Your Pappy wrote that you should accord Adam his rightful place as heir to the Esdailes and Knockfane,' he said. 'It's unequivocal.'

She told Adam what she proposed.

'I've decided,' she said, and the manner in which she said it left Adam in no doubt that she meant it and that it would be fruitless to object.

'If it's what you really want to do, and if Julia and Edward are in accord, I would only say that it would be more sensible to leave the place to Robin rather than to me,' he said. 'Robin and his wife have all their lives before them. True, there is no sign of any children yet but I have no doubt but that they will have a family, and sooner rather than later. They could plan and, when we are all dead and gone, they could come and live here and carry on the family connection.'

While Lydia's decision to reassign Knockfane by means of revising her will was simply made and readily agreed to by Julia and Fergal, Adam Switzer and Richard Benson, her attempt to put the plan into effect suffered something of a setback when she called upon Mr Holt to give him instructions. He avowed that it would not be all that simple a matter and that her intended marriage complicated the situation considerably. He spelled out the relevant clauses of the Succession Act, 1965, emphasised the words 'surviving spouse' and 'ordinarily resident', and, to Lydia's alarm, mentioned the phrase 'appropriate the dwelling'. Memories of young Willis's sojourn at Knockfane all those years previously, not to mention the episode of Todd's confinement and subsequent scheming, flooded into her mind: even her father's determined obsession with defeating the designs of the Land Commission came back to her with horror.

It seemed, according to Mr Holt, that in the event of her death prior to that of her husband, her dear Richard would have the right to live on at Knockfane and, if he was of mind to do so, perhaps make a claim to ownership. That, it transpired, was what was meant by 'appropriate the dwelling'. As she sat across the desk from him, Lydia thought of Richard and how warmly she felt about him. She recalled his coming to Knockfane decades since when he was a young curate in Liscarrig, the long chats he pursued with her father which, he now confessed, were merely an excuse to stay longer and see Lydia herself; and how irritated he always was that Willis Esdaile so openly assumed that his visits were occasioned by an urge to pay court to Julia. She reflected on the years and years when she heard nothing of him and how she had always guarded in her affections the memory of him. She thought of her current good fortune that they had found each other again and how they were both looking forward to being man and wife and living together at Knockfane. She knew it would be out of the question for Richard to do any such thing as claim a right to Knockfane and so, with what she hoped was a tone of appropriate indignation, she remonstrated with Mr Holt. But he remained unaffected, brushing aside her objections, and proceeded to paint for her a terrifying picture of the future, after her death, with a dribbling Richard confined to a wheelchair and in an advanced stage of dementia and his grasping children forcing him to sign over to them such rights to Knockfane as they deemed him to possess.

Lydia felt like tears. Richard, although bald, was still a very handsome figure. Tall and erect, and with none of the paunchiness that was normal for a man of his age, he was still athletic-looking in the extreme. The thought of him as a gaga Methuselah made Lydia shudder. She would move out of Knockfane and live somewhere else with him, she thought, if that would mean that her intentions in regard to her will might be put in place. But before she had a moment to develop this idea further in her mind, Mr Holt smiled across at her and, adopting an altogether less doom-laden tone, unfurled a legal scenario by which all his dire projections might be annulled.

Lydia did not understand half of what Mr Holt proposed but it seemed to involve the drafting of ancillary deeds in addition to her projected last will and testament. And when he announced that, once those deeds were executed, her 'nuptials' might go ahead as planned, Lydia felt like leaning across the desk and kissing his piggy little cheeks.

51

Horrid

ADAM CAME OVER to Knockfane in the middle of August and so had several weeks there in the period leading up to Lydia's wedding. She had told him that she would welcome his company and be glad of his help in making last-minute preparations. His daughter, Alice, and her husband were going to come from Canada and Robin and his wife, Jane, were arriving from London. It would be the first time any of them would have met their aunts, Julia and Lydia, and they were looking forward to it and to seeing Ireland and Knockfane.

It was during those weeks of August that Lydia took Adam to Derrymahon. It was she who drove most of the way and when they turned in the gates and approached the house at the end of the long avenue, Adam was visibly affected. Derrymahon was very different to Knockfane. It was a big, square, solid house, its walls punctuated by round-headed plate glass windows: the window frames painted a Burgundy red. The ugliness of the place was accentuated by the fact that, some twenty years previously, the original render had been removed and replaced by pebble-dash. This had become stained and grey in places so that the house, although meticulously maintained, looked neglected. It glowered north, lacked any cheer and, unlike at Knockfane where the lustrous leaves of the magnolia, the grace of the weeping ash, and the blooms of Albertine, made one welcome, overgrown macrocarpa trees, balding at their bases, were the only planting to the front of Derrymahon. The avenue had been surfaced with tarmacadam and the whole was fenced off from the lawn field by a wooden paling. Gloomy is how the place might best have been described and, compared to Knockfane, which was poetry, Derrymahon seemed to Adam to be as prosaic and functional as the pages of a telephone directory.

Edward and Marion proved to be charm itself and Lydia was surprised by the lack of any 'atmosphere'. There was no specific mention of the fact that Adam and Edward were brothers. Nor was there much family chat. Edward talked about their grandparents as though they were his alone and Adam restricted his questions to neutral subjects such as the history of the house, the nature of the farm, and the attractions of the area roundabout. It was all quite strange and Lydia began to feel that it had been a waste of time their coming down.

It was only when they stood up from the table, and Marion suggested to Adam that he might like to see something of the house, that things looked like improving. Lydia and Edward went to the drawing room to take coffee as Marion whisked Adam off. They came, eventually, upon the gallery of family photographs which hung on the upstairs landing and there Marion pointed out who the various people were. Adam had, of course, seen photographs at Knockfane of his mother and so the pictures of her as a child held no surprises for him; but seeing her as perhaps a 6-year-old, being pulled through the snow on a toboggan by a laughing figure who, Marion explained, was Grandpa Odlum, made him gulp. 'How can that man have done what he later did to that little girl?' he thought. Had he not been so obdurate, imposing upon her his cold-blooded and heartless decree, Adam's own photograph as a toddler would also have been part of the gallery alongside the pictures of Edward, Julia and Lydia. Adam wanted to move away. He wanted to get out of this house. He suggested to Marion that she might care to show him the garden.

When they were leaving Edward said to Lydia that he hoped she would not mind if he and Marion did not come to her wedding. He muttered something about family occasions not being their sort of thing but, before he had a chance to add further excuses, Marion intervened.

'"All water under the bridge",' she caroled, 'that's what I say. "Water under the bridge". Isn't that right, Edward?'

She did not elucidate as to which bridge she meant, the volume of the water, or how stagnant and polluted the flow might have been.

'They were very cordial ...' Adam said in the car as they drove away.

Lydia was at the wheel.

'... but, although I don't like to say it, I couldn't care less if I never see either of them ever again.'

Lydia was surprised at the firmness of his tone. He was not normally so very incisive and direct.

'Did you expect otherwise?' she said.

'No, not really,' Adam replied.

It was about half an hour before he spoke again.

'It's a horrid house,' he said, 'so different from Knockfane. Your mother ...'

He grasped the handle and started to roll down the window.

'... our mother ... was lucky to escape from it. No wonder that everything it stands for is so horrid too.'

'It's the past now,' said Lydia, 'but so much has been wasted. You could say that almost a generation was blanked out. Not really, I suppose, in that Knockfane is still there and the Esdailes with it, but you know what I mean I am sure.'

'Yes,' said Adam, 'I know what you mean, dear Lydia.'

52

Another Generation

LYDIA WORE A Sèvres-green silk costume for her wedding. The jacket was tight-fitting but cut away at the skirt, belted round the waist, and with a stiff diamond-pointed collar. She had ordered the silk from London and had had the suit made by a dressmaker. Her hat came from Richard Alan. It was almost a toque but made up of lilac-coloured gossamer petals. Her only jewellery was the gold chain which had belonged to her mother. She did not carry a bouquet. Just a corsage of pink rosebuds from Knockfane lodged among gentians and pinned at her shoulder. Richard Benson wore the clerical frock-coat that is called an apron and the gaiters that his rank as an archdeacon required on a dress occasion. He did not carry a hat.

The ceremony was kept to a minimum, Communion eschewed, and it was only Lydia who received a ring. Richard did not believe in them for men. After the signing of the register, during which Mrs Taylor strenuously pumped some occasionally recognisable hymn tunes out of the harmonium, the guests sang Lord, *dismiss us with Thy blessing, Fill our hearts with joy and peace* and Lydia and Richard came down the aisle as man and wife.

The reception was at Knockfane. It was a buffet of cold meats and salads. Julia had made the wedding cake, all three tiers of it, but it had been decorated professionally by the baker from Tobin's in Athcloon. There were speeches, there were telegrams, there was champagne. It was more like a party than a wedding reception and it was all over by five o'clock when Richard and Lydia departed. They spent the night in Dun Laoghaire and went to Paris the next day. They stayed for ten days and then home to Knockfane.

After the bustle of the weeks prior to the wedding, the house seemed very quiet to Lydia on her return. Adam and his family, who had stayed on at Lydia's insistence 'to get to know Knockfane', had departed a day or so earlier. Rose was there, as always, and had a supper prepared. Julia and Fergal were to come over later. Lydia went into the drawing room while Richard was still upstairs. She found a letter, addressed to Mrs Richard Benson in Adam's hand, propped up on the mantelpiece.

'Dearest Lydia, We did not want to say anything that would have deflected attention from you on your happy day,' it read, 'but Robin and Jane are expecting a first baby, a boy. They can tell these things in advance nowadays. They want your permission to christen him "Willis Esdaile". A bit of a mouthful for the poor child, to be called Willis Esdaile Switzer, but that is what they want.'

Lydia sat down on the sofa. She looked at the letter again.

'Let me see ...' she reflected, 'he'll be Pappy's great-grandson. Yes, his great-grandson. Another generation. Another Willis Esdaile of Knockfane.'